WORDS OF LOVE

THE BLISS COVE SERIES (BOOK 5)

NINA LINDSEY

SNOW QUEEN

PUBLISHING

CONTENTS

Cover designed by Najla Qamber Designs
www.najlaqamberdesigns.com

Published by Snow Queen Publishing

BOOK DESCRIPTION

WORDS OF LOVE
A Bliss Cove Romance

Journalist Brooke Castle is **broke, jobless, and pushing the big 30**. Determined to turn her life around in the new year, she escapes to a remote mountain cabin for a self-improvement retreat. But her plans of quiet solitude are shattered when a booking error forces her to share the cabin with **hot—and grumpy—bookstore owner** Sam Donovan.

Though Brooke has always been rather fascinated by Sam, he's bad-tempered and has a past shrouded in mystery. When a sudden snowstorm prevents them from leaving, they discover **the cabin is much too small for their undeniable attraction**.

Sam has spent the past year fighting his attraction to the

perky, inquisitive Brooke. With his need for privacy, the last thing he wants is a relationship with a reporter. But trapped in the cabin with this romance-loving beauty, he can't resist her warm smile and sunny disposition.

Sam and Brooke spend a **hot, secretive weekend trapped** in the cabin together, but what happens when these snowbound lovers are forced to return to real life?

BLISS COVE SERIES

WE FOUND LOVE

LOVE WALKS IN

AND I LOVE HER

LOVE ME TENDER

WORDS OF LOVE

BOOK OF LOVE

MESSAGE OF LOVE (COMING IN 2022!)

CHAPTER 1

*H*e was late.

Brooke Castle peered into the darkened window of Title Wave Books and tapped impatiently on the glass.

Of *course* he was late. Unless he'd just decided not to show up at all today, even though it was ten o'clock on a Friday morning, and every retail business on the planet was open on Friday—except for Title Wave.

Brooke paced in front of the door and looked at her watch. Most of the residents in the California seaside town of Bliss Cove thought the bookstore's unpredictable hours were a charming little quirk—even if the grumpy proprietor was not.

Brooke had occasionally enjoyed the "quirkiness" of the store hours herself...except for now, when she actually needed to *buy some books*.

Taking out her phone, she scrolled for the Sierra mountains weather forecast. *Snow expected starting mid-afternoon through the evening, possible accumulation of three to four inches.*

It wasn't a dire forecast, but Brooke wasn't accustomed to driving in the snow, and she wanted to reach the Eagle's Nest cabin before the bad weather started. With a four-hour drive ahead of her, that meant she had to leave soon.

"Come on, Sam," she muttered.

She should have known that relying on the bookstore owner to open his business at a reasonable time was a dicey proposition at best, but her best friend Aria had offered her the cabin only a couple of weeks ago, and Brooke had been so busy with job applications that she'd neglected to order the books she wanted online until it was too late for timely delivery.

No problem, she'd thought to herself last night as she was packing for her trip. *I'll swing by Title Wave to stock up before hitting the road tomorrow. I'll be out of here by nine.*

So much for that plan.

This was not the most auspicious start to her New Year's retreat. Neither was her post-Thanksgiving discovery that her grandfather, Charlie Castle, editor-in-chief of *The Bliss Cove Gazette*, couldn't afford to keep her on as a staff reporter any longer...and that he hadn't intended to tell her.

A knot of guilt tightened her throat. She'd been working at the paper since she'd moved back to Bliss Cove two years ago. Though Charlie had given her a job right away, both she and her entire family had assumed her position would be temporary. She'd find a job with another newspaper or a magazine soon enough.

But after she'd crashed and burned so badly at *The New York Times*, she'd found it painfully easy to be back at home working at *The Gazette*, where speeding tickets and jaywalking filled the police blotter and a gingerbread contest scandal had dominated the holiday headlines.

Take that, big scary world with your anxiety crises and disintegrating glaciers. I'm writing an article about the new baby otters at the aquarium.

Brooke hadn't even considered that her staff position might be hurting the paper's already-strained budget...until she'd found out that her grandfather had been paying her salary from his own pocket.

The gesture hadn't angered her—helping each other was what her family did—but her guilt and shame had cut deep. She'd also been forced to admit that she'd stayed at *The Gazette* for so long because it was safe and she was with the people she loved, not because it was helping her move forward in her career or her life.

So in early December, she'd resigned from the paper and begun sending out dozens of applications and freelance article pitches to publications across the country.

Then the rejections had started rolling in, all of which had contributed to her feeling that she was too late. Her time had come and gone. She'd blown her one big chance.

But.

Charlie didn't call her "Sunny Side Up" for no reason. She was known both in her family and around Bliss Cove as being a woman who always looked on the bright side.

Unfortunately, you couldn't be "Sunny Side Up" without also sometimes surrendering to "Sunny Side Down." As her job prospects began dead-ending, she'd had an increasingly hard time being optimistic about her own life.

Seven years after graduating from college, she was still

paying off her significant student loans, and she hadn't taken any steps toward making extra money for IRAs and investment accounts. Not to mention, she was turning thirty this year. It was time to do adult things like get a real job not funded by her grandfather and to seriously plan for her future.

Or, rather...*start* her future.

That feeling has been solidified when Destiny Storm, Bliss Cove's resident fortune teller and purveyor of fate, gave her the Christmas gift of a Tarot card reading that foretold a time of immense *change, decisions, and new beginnings* in the coming year.

Brooke interpreted that as a message that it was time for her to take decisive action. Despite her usually chipper attitude, the universe wouldn't just hand over change and new beginnings. She had to work for them.

Like Gramps always said, a good reporter had to climb the stairs, pound the pavement, and knock on doors.

Speaking of which...

She rapped her knuckles on the bookstore window. Cupping her hand around her eyes, she peered inside again. No sign of life.

Well, she couldn't wait any longer. Maybe she'd find a bookstore on the road when she stopped for gas. Pivoting on her heel, she started walking back to her car when a tall figure rounded the corner at the end of the block.

Her heart thumped against her ribs, as it always did when she first caught sight of the ridiculously sexy...er, *strange* bookstore owner, who'd shown up in Bliss Cove a year ago with no explanation or apparent reason for being here.

A few weeks after arriving, Sam Donovan had taken over

Title Wave, which had been on the verge of shutting down, and quickly roused the ire of the town council with his erratic hours. His tendency to open and close Title Wave whenever he damned well pleased offended Mayor Bowers' belief that all downtown businesses should adhere to a schedule.

In addition to making no effort to please the local officials, Sam had made it clear that he wasn't interested in getting involved in town events. He did attend all the festivals—though based on Brooke's observations, it was mostly for the food.

Despite the mayor's and councilmembers' disapproval, the townspeople were glad to have the bookstore remain open and, by unspoken agreement, they gave Sam both space and privacy.

He approached, an apple in his left hand and a folded newspaper section underneath his arm. He moved with a casual stride that belied the power coiled through his body. A shaft of sunlight broke through the gray clouds and burnished his dark hair with strands of gold.

Brooke suppressed a flicker of awareness. Despite his reclusiveness, a man couldn't *look* like Sam Donovan and not inspire female curiosity.

He was tall, well over six feet, with strong features and thick hair that was perpetually finger-combed. While he often wore faded jeans and old, flannel shirts, the worn clothing seemed to enhance rather than detract from his muscular physique. With his stubbled jaw and messy hair, Sam Donovan was a striking example of scruffy masculine beauty.

Between his looks and his tendency to be a bit scowling

and anti-social, he'd been compared to everyone from Heathcliff to Severus Snape to Mr. Darcy.

According to Bliss Cove's Gossip Train, he didn't appear to have a girlfriend. He'd also declined numerous match-making attempts from both Destiny and other women on the market for themselves or their daughters.

However, Brooke had heard that he'd been spotted having lunch with an attractive woman in Glendale last fall. According to the innkeeper, Mrs. Higgins, they "hadn't just been whistling Dixie, if you know what I mean."

Unfortunately, Brooke did know, and she'd experienced a sharp twinge of irritation at the idea of Sam "not whistling Dixie" with some random woman. Which didn't make a lot of sense, since she had no claim on him.

Given his cranky tendencies, she didn't want to stake one either, thank you. He'd repeatedly declined her requests for stories about the bookstore, he'd ordered her to delete several photos she'd taken of him at town festivals, he'd turned down her offer to help start author events and sign-ings at Title Wave, and he'd refused to participate in the upcoming Bliss Cove Book Fair. Even though he owned the town's only *bookstore*.

In other words, he was like a thundercloud to her rainbow.

"What are you doing here?" His eyebrows snapped together.

"Good morning to you, too." She gave him a bright smile, determined to be Sunny Side Up. "I'm here for the tango lessons."

He frowned and shifted the paper to his other arm.

"I need some books, genius." She indicated the window display. "Title Wave is supposed to open at nine."

"Says who?"

"The world. Including the mayor and the town council."

"Guess they're wrong." He pushed the door open. "We're closed."

"What do you mean, you're closed? You just opened the door."

"I'm not staying." He pushed up his cuff to glance at the old analog watch on his wrist. "I just came to pick something up."

"Well, can you spare ten minutes to actually operate your business?" Brooke lifted her hands in astonishment. "I need to purchase some of your stock. I'm a *customer*."

He expelled a sigh, as if wearied by the very idea of selling books. "Ten minutes. No longer."

"You need to work on your salesmanship, Sam." She brushed past him as he flicked on the interior lights. "You should try aromatherapy, like bergamot essential oil. It's known for boosting your mood and promoting happiness."

Before he could respond, she hurried toward the shelves. She stopped by the Self-Help section and began scanning the titles.

Despite his erratic hours, Sam took excellent care of the store. The shelves were always well stocked with both new titles and backlist, there wasn't a speck of dust anywhere, and the displays were neat and organized.

Brooke loaded half a dozen books into her arms and veered around the corner to the Romance section. Due to the job search, the holidays hadn't given her much time for reading either.

She'd packed some of her personal favorite romance novels to bring to the cabin, but there were at least ten new releases that had been on her radar for weeks. She stacked them on her pile and made her way to the front counter.

Sam was logging in to the computer, both hands on the keyboard, the apple now stuck between his teeth. The newspaper lay on the counter, open to a half-completed crossword puzzle.

Clearing her throat, Brooke dumped the books on the counter. He took hold of the apple and bit into it.

Not once in her life had Brooke thought there was anything remotely sexy about a man eating fruit. But the sight of Sam cupping the apple in his big hand while he tore through the ruby-red peel and crunched into the flesh with his straight white teeth…

Her breath shortened.

Though she wasn't interested in Sam romantically, it wasn't the first time he'd had an electric effect on her body. Whenever she saw him at a town festival, a little zinging sensation went through her like a shock.

Which was all fine and good, but she'd learned the hard way that a *zing* could short circuit in a bad way. Better to avoid them altogether.

"You buying those?" Sam asked around the apple bite.

She tried to muster up some distaste for him talking with his mouth full, but the way he *rolled* the apple over his tongue and bit down again with a—

She had to get out of here.

"I am, indeed." She took her wallet out of her purse.

Sam wedged the apple between his teeth again and wiped his hands on his jeans before he started ringing up the books.

His gaze lingered on the titles—*The No-Brainer's Guide to Self-Enrichment, How To Stop Screwing Up Your Life,* and *I'm Okay, but You're Still Meh.*

Heat rose to her cheeks. She hadn't told anyone about her current existential crisis, and she certainly didn't want Sam speculating about why she needed self-help books.

"I don't need a bag." She pushed her credit card across the counter and tried not to think about how much debt it was already holding.

He stacked the self-help books in front of her, took another bite of the crisp apple, and set the fruit on a paper towel. After wiping his hands on his jeans again, he picked up the romance novels and began scanning them while he chewed.

He was probably rolling the apple over his tongue again. His jaw muscles worked. His throat rippled. The sweet, fruity scent drifted to her nose.

Brooke unzipped her hoodie to let cooler air circulate around her body. Had it always been so warm in here?

Sam glanced at one of the romance covers, *The Pleasures of the Pirate,* which displayed a buxom woman clutching the legs of a shirtless pirate with an impressively unrealistic set of abs.

"For…uh, research," Brooke mumbled, heat crawling up to her ears.

Why hadn't she been organized enough to order her books online? She normally didn't give two hoots what anyone thought of her reading choices, but it wasn't the first time Sam had made her kind of jittery and nervous just by doing…*nothing.*

He was ringing up a copy of *Slave to You,* which bore a

particularly erotic cover of a half-naked man blindfolding a woman clad in lacy lingerie.

"Research for a…um, a Valentine's Day article," Brooke added hastily.

Without a response, he rang up her other romance novels, including *Loving the Billionaire*, *A Knight to Remember*, and *Prince Charmer*.

Still flushing, Brooke turned to examine a display of bracelets. Braided cords held a metal disk, each one engraved with a different word—*Read. Create. Believe.*

She skimmed her fingers over the bracelets and picked one off the rack. A purple cord secured a copper disk bearing the word *Courage*.

"This too, please." She pushed the bracelet across the counter to Sam.

He picked it up, his eyes skimming the word. She'd have sworn she heard his internal scoff.

Her phone buzzed with a call. Since Sam was still at the computer, she excused herself and stepped to a nearby shelf. She pulled her phone from her bag. The name *Michael* popped up on the phone screen.

Her stomach tensed. "Hi, Michael."

"How's it going, B? Any plans for New Year's Eve?"

"Not yet." Catching Sam glancing in her direction, Brooke turned away. "What's going on?"

"So I was reading over your ideas, and they're not going to work."

"I'm sorry to hear that." She tightened her jaw. "Considering you were the one who asked me for them."

"Yeah, bummer." His voice contained a twinge of regret. "I mean, I know you're a great writer and all, but I need something click-baity, you know? A grabby idea people will want to share because it hits them on an emotional level, like the story we did about that kid who was killed at the border. Or stories that resonate with people's lives. We ran a piece last month about finding the perfect pet, and it got the most views that entire week. Can you think outside the box?"

Brooke didn't know. She was good at taking assignments and pitching news stories, but she'd never found her writing "niche," whether that was inside the box or not.

Not that she was about to tell Michael that.

"Of course I can." She hoped she sounded convincing.

"Send me some new ideas by mid-January. That's when we'll choose stories for the February edition. Are you coming to FreeCon later this month?"

"I wasn't planning on it, no." She'd been to the national Freelancer's Convention a couple of times before she'd been hired at *The New York Times*, but she hadn't thought about attending again. "Where is it?"

"Here, in the city. Marriott Marquis. I'm on a magazines and periodicals panel. If you come, we could get together and talk about pitches. I can also introduce you to a bunch of people in the industry. The networking would be great for you."

Brooke knew he was right. She hadn't freelanced in years, and she was out of the loop. Though she still had mixed feelings about the idea of working with Michael, he'd been the only person so far to offer her any opportunity whatsoever.

"I'd love to go to the conference, but I can't come out to New York on such short notice," she finally said.

"I can get you a discounted registration and hotel rate.

I'll also ask around and see if I know anyone looking to share a room. That'll cut your expenses significantly."

She bit her lip. "I'll see what I can do."

"Let me know. I'll check airline rates for you, too."

"Okay. Thanks, Michael." She ended the call and dropped her phone back into her bag.

No question she needed to network more, and the conference would be a perfect place to do that. Especially since she was still struggling to get her foot in the door. The problem was that she couldn't afford any of it—not even at a discounted rate.

Not to mention, seeing Michael in person again would be…weird.

Even now, two years after their breakup when they were on somewhat amicable terms again, talking to her ex-boyfriend knotted her up inside.

They hadn't spoken for months, but he'd emailed her last fall with praise for a story she'd done on Pacific Coast conservation efforts. When she'd eventually told him she was freelancing again, he'd asked her to send him story ideas for his New York-based publication, *Empire Monthly*, which had been funded partly thanks to their breakup.

Or, rather, Michael's mastery of lies and deceit.

Brooke had dismissed the idea outright…until her rejection letters had started piling up like trash in a landfill. Right before Christmas, she'd finally agreed to send Michael a proposal. Despite having to swallow her pride—and face a different kind of rejection from her ex—she didn't regret the effort.

Empire had a wide readership, the pay was good, and it would be an excellent addition to her resume. Since full-time jobs were slipping from her grasp—or weren't even within reach—she'd have to take whatever she could get.

She approached the counter. Sam was watching her, his eyebrows drawn together and frown lines carved on either side of his mouth.

"You done?" he asked gruffly.

She nodded. "Just a business call."

"Then you can pay." He drummed his fingers on the counter. "I need to get going."

"Me too." Giving him a pointed look, she tapped her credit card. "That's why I was here at nine."

After signing the receipt, she grabbed the books and stuffed them into her *Reading Is My Superpower* tote bag. She started toward the door.

"Good luck with your research," he remarked.

She shot him a look over her shoulder. He was watching her leave, still holding the bitten apple. A strange, unexpected heat sparked in her belly.

"Thank you," she replied with as much casualness as she could muster. "Have a lovely day, Sam."

He sank his teeth into the apple again and turned back to the computer. The sound of his juicy crunching lingered in her ears even as she left the store and hurried to her car. She got into the driver's seat.

Her cheeks were still hot. Obviously Sam didn't buy the "research" explanation one bit, and though he hadn't said anything disparaging about romances, his *silence* had been a tad judgmental.

What had he thought? That Brooke devoured romance novels because she was a lonely, almost-broke loser pushing thirty who was scared she'd never get on a stable career path and who spent most of her weekends curled up with obscenely ripped pirates and billionaires because she hadn't had a good date, much less a boyfriend, in almost two years?

Well, that wouldn't be far from the truth.

With a groan, she thunked her head against the steering wheel.

Come on, girl. Focus on the bright side.

She'd have plenty of time in the next ten days to read as much as she wanted. She could finally master the warrior pose without being self-conscious around her fellow yoga enthusiasts. She could dance and sing Beyoncé songs in her pj's without worrying that she was bothering her downstairs neighbor. She could eat ice cream straight from the container (well, she did that all the time anyway). She could practice rune casting. Maybe there would be little woodland creatures in the forest, and she could toss them scraps of food while humming a—

Okay, even Sunny Side Up had her limits.

A knock came at the side window. She lifted her head to find Destiny Storm peering at her from beneath her wild tangle of black curls.

Brooke rolled down the window. "Hi, Destiny."

"Hi, hon." Destiny's smooth forehead crinkled. "What's with the energy of despair?"

"I'm fine. Just…" She twirled her finger beside her ear to indicate that her brain was still in something of a turmoil. "I really need to get away."

"You certainly do." Destiny patted her hand. "With Venus moving through Aquarius, this is a perfect time for you to set positive goals. Have you chosen a word for the new year?"

"A word?"

"I find it very helpful to pick a word, like *love* or *create*, to use as a north star for the course of the year." Destiny flicked a long curl over her shoulder. "It sets your intentions and helps guide your decision-making."

"How do I choose a word?" Brooke glanced at the dashboard clock. Though she always welcomed her friend's mystical advice, she'd intended to leave two hours ago. "Do you need to do an Oracle card reading for me?"

Destiny gave a throaty laugh. "Not for this, sweetie. You just pick your word."

"Randomly?"

"Well, not *randomly*." Destiny's eyes twinkled. "*Upholstery* or *hamburger* might not be the best guiding principles...unless you're a car salesman or a restaurateur, perhaps. Just think about what you want to achieve this year, maybe write down a few words that resonate with you, and then choose one. It's that simple. Well, hello, handsome."

She pushed away from the car window and wiggled her fingers at Sam, who was walking away from Title Wave. He approached the sidewalk in front of the car, giving them both a short nod of acknowledgement.

"Got any special New Year's plans, Sam?" Destiny called.

"No." He stopped to cross the street.

"You should." Setting her hand on her hip, Destiny scanned him from head to toe. "Scorpio, right? Saturn is moving through your third house in January, which will infuse you with passion and ambition. It would be a shame to waste that kind of powerful energy."

"I'm an Aries." Sam met Brooke's gaze for half an

instant. Surely she was imagining the faint amusement in his eyes? Like they were sharing a private joke.

Then he was crossing the street, his long legs carrying him half a block in just a few seconds. He moved with an easy, measured stride that reminded Brooke of a tiger. She could practically feel the flex and pull of his strong muscles under an expanse of warm, taut skin—

"Whew." Destiny fanned herself, her attention also still on Sam. "Sex on a stick right there. But if he's an Aries, I'm Mother Theresa."

With a chuckle, Brooke started the car. "I need to get going, Destiny."

"Have a wonderful retreat, honey. Don't forget to choose your word." With a wave, she stepped away from the car and sauntered down the sidewalk.

As Brooke shifted into gear, she caught sight of her tote bag. She braked again and reached into the bag to remove the bracelet she'd bought on impulse. She rubbed her thumb against the copper disk.

Courage.

Maybe she didn't need to choose a word after all. Maybe the word had chosen her.

She fastened the bracelet around her wrist and shifted into gear again.

Your future starts now.

Drawing in a breath, she eased her car on to the street and started toward the highway.

CHAPTER 2

*B*rooke tightened her grip on the steering wheel and pressed the accelerator harder. Her four-hour drive had been uneventful until she'd started up the narrow road winding into the Sierra mountains. The snowfall was getting thicker the higher she climbed, and the accumulation was heavy and deep. Her car's tires crunched and scraped through the ice.

She shifted into second gear. The little hatchback slipped backward and then sideways. Her heart jammed into her throat. A couple inches of snow was one thing, but this was serious *winter*.

Dragging in a breath, she peered at the curved, one-lane road that she'd been navigating for the past hour. The online pictures of the log cabin had made it look like something out of an Americana painting—smoke curled from the chimney, sunlight glinted off the oval windows, and snow-dusted pines encircled the house like an embrace.

The website had said the cabin was "off the beaten

track," but it hadn't said anything about "so remote you probably won't be able to find it."

The tires skidded again. She gritted her teeth, shoved the car into third, and pushed harder on the accelerator. Her high-school driving instructor hadn't bothered teaching any of them how to drive in the snow—maybe because there never was any in Bliss Cove.

There! Her shoulders sagged in relief as the cabin finally came into view. She urged her car up to the front door and ground it to a halt. She pushed open the door and stepped outside, pulling up her parka hood against the cold, wet wind.

Despite the nasty weather, the tension from the long drive and harrowing climb up the mountain drained away. She'd made it. Now she had ten days alone to regroup and chart her life path, while welcoming the new year in blissful solitude.

She hauled her suitcase and travel bag from the trunk and clomped over the ice-packed pathway to the front door.

Her friend Aria had rented the Eagle's Nest cabin for a getaway with Hunter, her hot significant other, but instead they'd decided to host the first New Year's celebration on the historic Mariposa Street. When Aria had offered Brooke the cabin free of charge for the ten days after Christmas and into January, Brooke had seen it as a sign that a retreat was meant to be.

She'd looked at the online photos of the lovely little cabin and pictured herself curled up beside the fire with her notebook, a quilt wrapped around her legs, and a cup of hot cocoa at her side. She imagined taking morning walks in the peaceful silence, perhaps joined by a chipmunk or squirrel.

She'd watch the sun rise, fill her lungs with cold, clean air, and recharge all her creative energies with ideas that had nothing to do with town council meetings or Artichoke Festivals.

The cabin was owned by Felix Milford, a longtime Bliss Cove resident who'd been working at Metalworks Hardware for thirty years. Since Felix had been away visiting family for the holidays, Brooke had gotten the details from the online website and the rental company.

Per the instructions, she found the key hidden in a fake rock beside the porch steps. Unlocking the door, she stepped inside.

A musty smell filled her nose. She fumbled for a wall switch before remembering she had to crank up the generator first. Luckily, there was still just enough daylight to see.

The cabin consisted of a single room overlooked by a platform loft accessible via a wooden ladder. A narrow sofa and worn armchair sat in front of a stone fireplace, and another door led to a kitchen only big enough for a small refrigerator, a microwave, and a two-burner stove. A square Formica table and two chairs were tucked against one wall next to a bookshelf holding a few paperbacks, board games, and what looked like an ancient CB radio.

It was perfect. Like a woodland cottage in a fairy tale, or a little hobbit hole.

With a laugh, she dumped her belongings on the sofa. A bit of exploring revealed the bathroom and a covered porch in the back stocked with firewood.

She brought in a few logs and found the generator in a little shed near the woodbin. She flipped the Run switch, and the thing spluttered to life with a belch of gassy air.

She hoped that was all she needed to do. She'd have to look for a manual, but first she had to call her mother. She went back inside, turned on the lights and heat, and checked her phone.

Fifty percent power, but no bars in her cell indicator. She frowned. A few walks around the cabin didn't strengthen the signal.

Not so perfect. The website had said the cabin was "cell accessible." Solitude was one thing, but she wasn't stupid enough to want to be off the grid entirely. After setting up her cell booster, she tried again to no avail. She'd promised her mother she'd call when she arrived, so she had to get a signal somehow.

Maybe there was a better chance outside, but it was getting dark and the snow was falling harder. She'd better wait until tomorrow to search for a pocket of cell service somewhere in the woods. Hopefully, her mother would realize that service was spotty in the Sierras.

She made a fire to help heat up the cabin. The ladder leading to the loft was a little rickety, but she'd only need to use it at night. She climbed up carefully, testing each rung before putting her full weight on it.

She pulled herself up to the top. The loft platform contained a huge mattress and two-drawer nightstand with a lamp. There was a little window looking out onto the grove, and a wooden railing separated the bed from the drop to the lower floor.

After climbing back down, Brooke retrieved boxes of food, including a plentiful supply of animal crackers and iced tea, and her bag filled with bedding. She unpacked her groceries and tucked a bottle of champagne into the fridge for the day after tomorrow.

Already the little cabin was toasty warm. She made up the bed and arranged all her fluffy pillows, then changed into her fuzzy pink pajama pants and matching tank top.

She returned to the main room and set her unicorn pillow pet on the sofa along with her purple, faux-fur blanket. She stacked her self-help books and romance novels on the coffee-table. After heating up a package of ramen, she settled on the sofa with her notebook.

Story ideas. Click-baity features. First-person narratives.

An Insider's Guide to Cutthroat Journalism.

Care for your Ageing Skin.

How I Got Knocked Down and...(to be continued)

She tapped her pen on the paper. She'd frequently pitched stories to Charlie, but they were easy to come up with. All she had to do was look around Bliss Cove for ideas. Girl Scout troop events, profiles on interesting high-school students, "behind the scenes" at local businesses, Mariposa Street renovation progress.

Now she needed ideas that went beyond small-town and appealed to a much bigger audience.

Cheerful Tips for Turning Thirty on a Budget.

Ugh. Time for a dance break.

She set her notebook down and reached for her music player. Since the speaker was lousy, she slipped in her ear buds and shuffled to her dance playlist. ABBA's "Dancing Queen" blasted into her ears. She let the vibrant beat start pulsing in her blood, then she got up and began to dance.

Some people took walks or exercised to clear their heads. Brooke danced and sang. She shimmied her hips, grabbed a pen to use as a microphone, and belted out the lyrics. She did the twist and practiced her moonwalk.

By the time Beyoncé's "Single Ladies" came on, she was well into her zone. She threw her hands in the air and executed a few hip wiggles that she'd seen on the video.

Yes! Her blood was pumping, her muscles loosening. Oxygen was flowing to her brain, and soon the ideas would start popping. Put a ring on it, indeed. Seal the deal. With a particularly loud bellow, she spun around and…crashed right into a solid wall.

With a yelp, she started to stumble backward when the wall *reached out and grabbed her shoulders*.

Catching her balance, she tipped forward and came up against a tall, broad figure clad in a freezing cold parka wet with snow.

That's no wall. That's a—

Jerking her head up, she stared into a pair of penetrating dark eyes partly concealed by the shadows of the parka hood.

Oh. My. God.

Panic shot through her.

A big stranger had just broken into her cabin and—

With a shriek, she yanked herself away from him and darted toward the back door, her heart hammering. She was about to bolt outside when she realized she'd be exchanging *death by intruder* for *death by snowstorm*. Her coat and boots were behind him in the foyer. Grabbing the nearest object, she charged toward him in attack.

"Get out!" She began pummeling him, realizing belatedly that her unicorn pillow pet wasn't the most effective weapon. Why hadn't the fireplace poker been closer? "I'm going to—"

"Whoa, wait a second." Surprise colored his deep voice as he held up his arms to block her whacks with the pillow.

"Stay away!" She backed up and held the pillow in front of her like a shield. "I'm a karate black belt who can take you down in less than a second, so you—"

Her voice stopped in her throat as he pushed his hood back and unzipped the parka. Though he was still in the shadows, she was struck with a sudden familiarity. Which made no sense because...

"Brooke?" His voice rolled over her like the start of thunder rumbling.

She tightened her grip on the pillow. *Oh my god, he's a stalker.*

"Wait." He held up his hands and stepped into the light. The overhead beam spilled over his thick dark hair and the strong, masculine lines of his face. "It's Sam."

A gasp caught in her throat. She shook her head, as if he were some sort of mirage. She hadn't expected to see anyone for the next ten days, least of all...*Sam.*

What the heck?

Her gaze collided with his. The earth seemed to vibrate, as if a seismic wave had coursed through the mountain.

"What..." He glanced over the cabin, taking in the fire, her stack of books, the open suitcase on the floor. "What are you doing here?"

"What do you mean, what am I doing here?" She waved her hand up and down to indicate his large figure, her shoulders sagging with relief. "What are *you* doing here? You scared the crap out of me."

She had no idea what was going on, but she'd take Sam over an evil intruder any day.

"I wasn't expecting anyone to be here." With a frown, he kicked the door shut behind him, shrugged out of his coat, and hung it on the rack by the door.

"I wasn't either." She crossed her arms as a shiver rippled through her. "Um, how long were you standing there?"

"Long enough." A touch of amusement threaded his voice, and he shot her a look that she somehow felt clear down to her toes.

Heat rose to her cheeks. "Well, you shouldn't be here. I'm staying in this cabin for the next ten days."

"What are you talking about?" He frowned. "*I* rented this cabin."

"How could you..." She stared at him. "Aria and Hunter paid the deposit in early December. Then they changed their plans, so they offered the cabin to me instead."

"I've rented this cabin from Felix half a dozen times in the past year." He spread his arms out, as if taking up more space would establish his domain. "I paid the full rent before Thanksgiving."

Her heart sank. "Well, clearly there was some sort of booking error."

"Clearly." With a muttered curse, he planted one foot on a bench and began to unlace his left boot.

The movement caused his jeans to stretch over his thighs. Not for the first time—in fact, probably for the thousandth time—Brooke wondered how, exactly, a lackadaisical bookstore owner had crafted such a strikingly perfect male physique. Genetics could only go so far, and he was just so...powerful.

He pulled off his other boot and straightened. She jerked her gaze away. Her breathing was still a little short. Must be the lingering adrenaline rush because, as she'd told herself time and again, Sam Donovan was not her type.

She appreciated the sexy hunk fantasy as much as the next woman, but that was the point. Men who looked like Sam were a *fantasy*, not Brooke's reality. She wasn't interested in men who were unkempt, reticent, and glowered more often than they smiled.

He was glowering right now, his fists planted on his hips and his messy hair falling over his forehead.

"You really shouldn't take your boots off." Since she was still holding the unicorn pillow, she rested her left fist on her hip to match his power stance. "It would be best if you leave before it starts snowing any harder."

"I'm not going anywhere." He stalked into the kitchen and grabbed a glass from the cupboard.

Neither was she. Brooke bit her lip and tossed the pillow back on the sofa. "You can't stay here."

"There was supposed to be a three-inch snow accumulation by tomorrow morning, and there's already at least a foot out there." He twisted the faucet to fill the glass with water. "Even with a four-wheel-drive truck, it took me an hour longer than usual to drive up the mountain. When did you get here?"

"A couple of hours ago."

"In that toy car of yours?" He snapped the faucet shut and opened another cupboard.

"I don't have a four-wheel-drive truck hidden in the loft,

if that's what you're asking." Tension threaded her spine at the way he was marching around like he owned the place. She'd better figure out how to stake her own claim sooner rather than later.

"Look, you can't stay here," she repeated.

Yeah, that would do it.

He lifted the glass to his mouth and drank, his throat muscles rippling. Brooke swallowed hard and curled her fingers into her palms. She had to get him out of here, not get captivated by his hotness.

She hoped he didn't start eating another apple.

"No other cabins in a twenty-mile radius, as far as I know." Lowering the glass, he wiped his mouth with his sleeve, raking his gaze over her.

Goosebumps prickled her skin. She was still only wearing her pajama pants and tank-top printed with the sparkly phrase *The Snuggle is Real*. She brought her arms up over her breasts, sharply aware that her nipples were pebbled against her shirt. Must be from the freezing cold air Sam had let into the cabin upon his unexpected entrance.

Clearing her throat, she turned away and picked up her cell phone. "I'm sure this can all be sorted out with a quick call to the rental office."

"You didn't talk to Felix directly?"

"No, he's visiting his daughter up in Mendocino. Or he was. I think he got back to Bliss Cove today. Anyway, I sent my information to the rental company through the website." She swiped her phone screen. "I'm sure they can find alternative accommodations for you."

"There's no cell service up here."

"The website said it was *cell accessible*."

"It's not." He eyed her multiple cases of lemon-cayenne iced tea and picked up a box of granola bars from the counter. "That's just one reason I come up here."

Brooke punched unsuccessfully at the call button on her screen. "I knew this place was isolated, but I didn't expect it to be completely off the grid."

"It's off the grid." He tore the wrapper off a granola bar and crunched into it.

She frowned slightly. "I'm in favor of sharing, but it's polite to ask if you can have something. Those are mine, you know."

"I know." He worked the bite around in his mouth. "I'd never buy something that tastes like hay."

"One of my new year's resolutions is to eat healthier food."

"Lousy start." He tossed the half-eaten bar onto the counter.

Brooke took a deep, cleansing breath. She was supposed to be sitting in front of the fire with her notebook and novels. She was supposed to be bubbling with story ideas and reading about *love* and the perfect man. Instead she was confronting the utterly imperfect Sam Donovan who ate with uninhibited greed and apparently had zero actual manners or charm.

Shaking the thoughts out of her head, she set her phone down. "What are we going to do about this situation?"

"I don't know about you, but I'm going to get my stuff." He returned to the foyer to shove his feet back into his boots. After pulling on his coat, he strode back outside, letting in another blast of snow and cold air. His boots left a trail of dirty, melting slush on the hardwood floor.

Okay. There was a bright side. He was not a murderous intruder. He probably knew where the generator manual was. He might have brought fruit.

And at most, he'd be here until dawn. Once the snow eased up, he'd drive his big old truck back down the mountain, and she'd be left in the peaceful solitude that was the reason she'd come here in the first place.

Fine. She could handle this.

Grabbing a mop from the utility closet, Brooke cleaned up the slush and stored his granola bar in a Ziploc bag. He made three trips in and out, unloading a backpack and several boxes filled with enough food and drinks to sustain an entire prison population.

"How long were you planning on staying here?" She eyed the boxes as he began unpacking the food—cereal, frozen dinners, instant coffee, boxed mac-and-cheese, peanut butter, bread, bags of chips, and, yes, a box of oranges, apples, and bananas.

"A week." He opened a cabinet, where she'd stored a few dozen snack-sized boxes of Barnum's Animals crackers. After lifting an eyebrow, he closed the door and opened another.

"What about the bookstore?"

"Jake is taking over for a few days."

Jake Ryan, a movie actor who was now involved in behind-the-scenes pursuits, worked part-time at Title Wave and was the only person whom Sam seemed to consider a friend. As far as Brooke knew, the two men weren't *bros* who got together for fishing expeditions and pick-up football games, but they sometimes had a beer at the Mousehole and actually talked. Sam wouldn't turn the bookstore over to anyone but Jake.

He opened the fridge. "I need more room for my food."

"You can't stay here for more than a day, much less a week," Brooke reminded him. "I wouldn't get too comfortable, if I were you."

"Good thing you're not me, then." He tossed her an unexpected smirk. "I always get comfortable."

He *looked* comfortable in the rustic cabin, too. He'd always been disheveled, but here he seemed at home and almost...appealing. Like an unmade bed you could fall right into for a deeply satisfying snuggle.

Except Brooke always made her bed. She enjoyed waking up when the sun rose and starting her day with an accomplished task.

Sam took her jar of peanut butter out of the fridge. "Peanut butter doesn't need refrigeration."

"That kind does. It's all natural without any palm oil."

He set it on the counter and put a carton of orange juice in the fridge. He took out her bottle of champagne and lifted an eyebrow. "You sure you're here alone?"

"Thanks to you, not anymore." She tapped her fingers on the doorjamb. "I brought that for New Year's Eve."

He straightened and set the bottle next to the sink. "You're skipping the big Bliss Cove party?"

"This year, yes." Brooke looked at the floor. Apparently Sam hadn't heard about her resignation. "Gramps assigned another reporter to cover it."

He rearranged her soy milk and eggs to make room for a large container of chocolate pudding. "So what're you doing here?"

"I'm working on a...um, project." At least that was the

truth. She was working on *The Brooke Project*. "Could you please not shove my yogurt to the back like that?"

"I always put eggs on the bottom shelf."

"I appreciate your organizational skills." Reminding herself to be accommodating, she started toward him. "But do you really need that many cans of cinnamon rolls?"

"I like cinnamon rolls."

Of course he did. From what she'd gathered, he liked everything food-related. Despite his lack of involvement in town, he could often be found having dinner and a drink at the Mousehole Tavern or pizza at Nico's. Every time she saw him at a festival, not that she was looking for him, he was munching on a burger or a taco. Or three.

Hardly a wonder. He'd have to eat a lot to fuel that muscular body of his.

"Excuse me." She grabbed the cinnamon rolls from him and bent to peer inside the fridge.

Though she'd intended to assert her dominance, she realized within about a nanosecond that she was at a distinct disadvantage bent over at the waist with Sam standing right behind her.

Literally—*right behind her*. If she backed up one step, her rear end would collide with his hard thighs. Then he'd probably only have to lift his hand a few inches to settle his palm against her ass. Only the thin cotton of her pajama pants would separate his hand from her bare skin.

Her breath shortened.

What was the matter with her? She'd always gotten a little *zingy* around him, but she'd never reacted to him like this before. She'd certainly never imagined him sliding his hand under the waistband of her pants to—

"Got it figured out?" His deep voice rolled over her, eliciting a wave of shivers.

Not wanting him to know he was getting to her, she responded cheerfully, "Almost."

She fumbled to rearrange the food, shoving her yogurt into stacks and fitting his cinnamon rolls into the vegetable drawer. When she finally straightened and turned, he was still standing right behind her, his dark eyes gleaming with either amusement or heat. Or both.

Brooke swallowed and stared at the top button of his shirt. "So that's done."

"Good."

She'd underestimated how small the kitchen would be with the two of them standing in it. Or rather, she hadn't estimated it at all. Sam took up so much space that she was almost wedged between the sink and his body. Her nipples were still hard, too. Damned cold.

"I...uh, I'll just try my cell booster again." She held up her hands and squeezed past him, sharply aware of his gaze. She tried very hard not to notice the breadth and power of his body or to wonder what it would be like to press up against that solid wall of muscle.

God.

She stepped out of the kitchen, trying to control her erratic breathing. She busied herself with her cell phone again, though she already knew it wouldn't work.

Sam made a lot of noise opening and closing drawers and cabinet doors. She deliberately turned her back so she couldn't see him. Snow swarmed against the windowpanes, almost whiting out the glass entirely.

Okay, he really couldn't go anywhere in this weather, which meant she was stuck with him until morning.

She couldn't control the situation, but she *could* control how she responded to it. And she would respond by sitting down and doing exactly what she'd come here to do. She just had to add *ignore Sam Donovan* to the list.

Picking up her notebook, she sat back down on the sofa and concentrated on her list of ideas.

With a snort of amusement, she wrote, *The Eroticism of Fruit.*

Then she found herself idly picturing Sam eating an orange, first peeling the rind with his long fingers, then using his thumbs to cleave apart the wedges before sliding—

"You don't have enough firewood." Sounding annoyed, he stomped out the back door and returned with an armload of logs that would have taken Brooke three or four trips to carry in.

See? He was useful. Another point for the bright side.

After tossing another log onto the fire, he flopped down on the easy chair and crossed his ankle over his thigh. The movement stretched his jeans over his long legs. He looked like a giant sitting on baby bear's chair.

He shifted and pulled a candy bar from his breast pocket. He unwrapped it and took a large bite. The firelight flickered over him, casting his features into planes of shadows and light. A dusting of stubble coated his jaw.

Of course it did. She'd never seen him clean-shaven.

He glanced up and met her gaze. A hot current shimmered through the air.

Probably the heat of the fire.

He held out the candy. "Want some?"

She couldn't tell if he meant it as a peace offering or a tempting lure of the forbidden.

Somewhat to her confusion, she also couldn't decide which one she'd prefer.

"No, but thank you for the offer," she replied politely.

He pushed up from the chair and strode to the window. He peered out at the whitewash of snowflakes, his expression darkening. "Damned weather report. They never get it right."

"I'm sure the weather researchers do their best. Besides, the storm will probably be over quickly." She indicated the back porch. "There's a couple of snow shovels back there, so we can dig ourselves out tomorrow, if need be."

Sam mumbled something under his breath and slouched back to the kitchen. He turned on the sink faucet and began rattling around, taking out pots and opening the fridge.

His noise was not conducive to her productivity. She'd get a good night's sleep and start fresh in the morning, after he was gone.

She set her notebook down and stood. "I think I'll turn in early. It's been an eventful evening."

He made another unintelligible noise. She picked up the bowl of cold ramen and went to the kitchen. She stopped in the doorway, not wanting a repeat of their too-close-for-comfort situation.

Reaching over, she set the bowl by the sink. "Turns out I wasn't hungry, so you're welcome to have this, if you want, or put it in the fridge. I can reheat it tomorrow. Good night."

He stuck a frozen mac-and-cheese dinner in the microwave and hit the start button.

Brooke climbed the ladder to the loft, wondering if she

really could feel him watching her or if her imagination was going into overdrive.

As she fluffed up her pillows, she reminded herself of the reason she was here. She was going to write new story ideas, read her novels, and do all the things she'd intended—yoga, meditation, goal-setting. The grump downstairs wouldn't stop her.

Shoot, she forgot to floss and brush her teeth. She should probably pee before going to sleep, too. She peered over the railing at Sam, who was carrying his dinner to the table in the corner. She'd just hurry past him and take care of her business.

Tucking her toiletries bag under her arm, she gripped the ladder and began the careful descent. The wood creaked. She set her left foot on the next rung. Another creak, and the wooden rung gave way under her weight.

Brooke yelped. The ladder tipped, and she lost her footing. She fumbled to grab hold of the railing and missed. The world reeled around her. In a split-second, she braced herself for a hard impact with the floor.

Instead, she fell right into a pair of strong, male arms.

CHAPTER 3

*B*rooke Castle.

Of all the damned luck.

Sam pulled her tighter against his chest as the ladder crashed to the floor. Her gasp of surprise jolted him with heat.

He caught a whiff of something both spicy and sweet, like cinnamon. His blood grew warm. She gripped a fistful of his shirt and snaked one arm around his shoulders in a move he liked more than he should have.

"Who are you, The Flash?" She stared at him, her brown eyes wide.

"I saw the rung start to give when you put your foot on it." Belatedly, he realized he'd just revealed that he'd been watching her descend the ladder. "I told Felix the last time I was here that he needed to replace that ladder. Obviously he hasn't gotten around to it."

He had a few choice words for the cabin owner, too.

Since Brooke might have been experiencing mild shock, he didn't set her down right away. With her still in his arms, he walked to the sofa. She was as light as a little dandelion puff. He told himself his heartbeat was increasing from exertion rather than close proximity to this woman with her cinnamon scent and soft body. He set her down on the sofa.

When was the last time he'd been this close to a woman, especially one as tempting as Brooke? Much as he'd disliked his self-imposed celibacy over the past year, he'd appreciated the lack of complications in his life. He sure as hell had no intention of changing that now.

Not even with her.

Especially not with her.

"You okay?" he asked gruffly.

"Yeah." She pulled her hands through her hair and took a deep breath, still looking a little rattled. "Thanks for the rescue."

He stepped back, trying not to look at the curves of her cleavage tucked into her snug-fitting tank top. She wasn't wearing a bra—a fact he'd noticed the second he saw her dancing around the cabin—and his body still simmered with heat.

He stalked to the table and picked up his plate. He'd spent the past year trying hard to ignore Brooke every time he passed her on the street or saw her at a town festival. Which was often. She seemed to be everywhere all the time with her camera, notebook, and handheld voice recorder. She was the Lois Lane of Bliss Cove—and that was just one reason he needed to stay away from her.

Unfortunately, her omnipresence made it impossible to ignore or avoid her.

He had, however, managed to notice everything about her, from her shiny brown ponytail to the way her ass rounded out her jeans. She was always either talking to someone, snapping a photo, or scribbling in a notebook. He noticed her serious, interested expression, her habit of unconsciously nibbling on her pen, and the bounce of her camera against her hip.

He noticed what kind of books she liked to read and review for the paper, her routine of walking down Starfish Avenue with a tray of take-out coffees every morning, and the way she bought a bouquet of daisies every Friday afternoon. Her eyes twinkled with curiosity, she flipped her ponytail over her shoulder with her left hand, and her smile generated a full-fledged glow that even penetrated Sam's hard-earned defenses.

But not far enough to soften his resistance to her.

As far as he was concerned, a fortified wall separated him from Brooke. He had no intention of scaling it, no matter how much *noticing* he did.

No matter how good she felt in his arms.

He poured a glass of water and brought it over to her, wishing he'd thought to bring some liquor—more for himself than her.

As soon as she went to bed, he'd get out his laptop and try to get some work done. Maybe he could salvage a few hours out of this night before leaving tomorrow and resolving whatever snafu had led to the double-booking.

"Thanks." She took a few swallows of water.

He picked up the plastic floral bag she'd dropped when she fell and handed it to her.

"I was coming down to brush my teeth, and…" Her voice trailed off as she glanced at the broken ladder, then up at the loft. "Uh oh. How am I going to get back up there?"

"You're not." Sam picked up the ladder and rested it against the wall. He didn't have the tools to fix it, and no way would he let her use the ladder with only a makeshift repair job. "You'll have to sleep down here."

She blinked. "There's no room down here. If I sleep on the sofa, where will you sleep?"

"On the floor."

"That doesn't seem right."

"It's fine." Still, he didn't much like the thought of her on the sofa either, which was okay for sitting, but too small and narrow for sleep.

He studied the loft, then dragged a chair over to where the ladder had been. He climbed onto the chair, braced his foot on a V-shaped support, and hauled himself upward.

"Sam!" Alarm heightened her voice, and she hurried toward him. "What are you doing?"

"I'll toss the mattress and your stuff down." He grasped the railing and pulled himself onto the platform. The bed was piled high with enough blankets and pillows, all shades of purple, pink, and blue, for five beds. He had a sudden, strikingly hot image of Brooke spread out naked over all those pillows, her long hair loose and her—

"Everything okay up there?" she called.

He cleared his throat. "What's with all this crap?"

"What are you talking about?"

"Last time I was here, there were two plain white pillows and a blanket."

"I brought my own bedding." She sounded slightly defensive. "I like nesting."

He had no idea what *nesting* was. "I'll drop all this down."

"I'll catch the pillows."

One by one, he tossed the pillows—many of them in various animal shapes—and blankets over the railing. She caught them and piled them onto the sofa. He dropped her travel bag down to her.

Brooke moved the coffee-table out of the way and backed up as he pushed the mattress over the edge. The queen-sized bed fell with a thud in front of the fireplace.

"Be careful." She hurried over when he started to climb down from the loft, as if she were ready to return the favor by catching him if he fell.

It was kind of a cute instinct. Useless, but cute.

Then again, was there anything about Brooke Castle that wasn't *cute*?

And was there anything about him that didn't respond to her cuteness like a damned compass spinning north?

Which was irritating as all hell because he didn't do *cute*.

He swung himself to the floor, landing heavily on his feet. *Get through the night. Then get out. Away from temptation.*

He set up her mattress next to the sofa—far enough away from the fire to be safe, but close enough to feel the warmth.

"Thanks." She hurried over to spread her multitude of blankets across the bed. "I should apologize for being cranky earlier."

That was her version of cranky?

"I just wasn't expecting you, obviously," she continued, "but I don't know what I'd have done if you weren't here."

He frowned. She'd probably have gotten hurt. And with no cell signal—

Smothering a surge of unease, he retreated to the sofa

and tried not to look at her as she bent over the bed, fluffing pillows and smoothing out the blankets. Too bad the image of her fuzzy pink pajamas stretching over her perfect ass was already etched on his mind with indelible ink.

After Brooke used the bathroom, she came back and tossed the covers aside. With all her pillows and blankets, it took her forever to get settled. The firelight glistened against her smooth, bare shoulders as she jostled around, plumping up animal-shaped pillows, arranging blankets over her legs, and wiggling into the mattress as if she were making a… well, a *nest*.

"Here, you need some pillows, too." She tossed him a couple of large pillows. "Feel free to use that purple blanket. It's really warm."

So was he.

"Good night." Flipping her hair back, she turned and nestled her head against a fluffy blue cushion while hugging a bear-shaped pillow to her chest.

Lucky bear.

Letting his breath out slowly, Sam dragged his gaze from her. He took his laptop out of the case and pushed aside the oversized purple blanket on the sofa. Something lumpy was against his back, and he fumbled behind him to dislodge the glittery unicorn pillow.

He tossed the ridiculous thing aside. While his laptop powered up, he took a sheaf of notes and a printed copy of his work-in-progress from his backpack. After spreading the papers out on the coffee table, he scanned the letter from his editor.

Big problem…negative blight overshadowing your reviews…

getting to the point where it's an inside joke among review-
ers...weak link in the chain...this needs to be fixed in
your WIP.

Irritation clawed up his throat. He tossed the letter aside and pulled up the book on his computer. He scrolled through the manuscript, but with the sounds of Brooke still fidgeting around on the bed right next to him, he couldn't come up with a single sentence.

With a mutter of frustration, he shut down his laptop and set it on the floor.

She was almost completely buried under a mountain of blankets. Her shiny hair, gleaming in the firelight, spread over the pillows.

Sam stretched out on the sofa, which was both too narrow and too short for him to recline with the slightest bit of comfort. After shifting around, he pulled the coffee table closer, stacked his notes to one side, and used the table to prevent himself from falling off the sofa completely.

He tucked a pillow behind his neck and closed his eyes. Slowly, he faded into a hazy slumber filtered with images of a brown-haired beauty with a smile like—

He jerked awake, blinking to clear the cobwebs from his brain. Pain laced his shoulders and neck. He pushed upright, and his spine snapped into place with a hard crack.

Though the cabin was still warm, the fire had died to embers. He peered at the clock. Close to five a.m. Wind lashed against the windows.

A sudden chill raced through him.

Brooke was gone.

CHAPTER 4

*S*am bolted to his feet. "Brooke?"

No answer. The bed was empty, the pillows and blankets scattered haphazardly.

Shit.

He strode to the front door. Her boots and coat were both gone.

His heart thudded hard against his ribs. Shoving his feet into his boots, he yanked open the door. A gust of snow-drenched wind blinded him. He walked onto the porch, squinting through the darkness. No tracks in the snow, not that they'd be visible with this accumulation.

Her car was still parked off to the side, the tires half-buried in the slush and the body obscured by untouched snow.

At least she hadn't been foolish enough to drive, but where the hell was she?

He grabbed a flashlight and crossed the cabin to the back door. Booted footprints, dusted with fresh snow, marked the back porch.

Quickening his pace, he stomped toward the covered woodbin. The bootprints disappeared within a yard of the porch.

"Brooke!" The wind drowned out his shout.

He reached the woodpile and looked out into the trees surrounding the cabin. He'd hiked out here a number of times. The forest went on for miles with no hint of civilization. The closest she'd come to another cabin was a ranger station twenty miles down at the base of the mountain. If she'd gone out there, she was doomed.

"Brooke!" Lifting a hand to block the sting of the wind, he shone the flashlight ahead of him and made his way toward the woods.

Through the swirling snow, caught in the flashlight beam, a blurry figure emerged from behind a grove of trees and started toward the cabin.

Relief hit him so hard his knees almost buckled. Sam plowed through the snow to reach her. She was bundled into her coat, the hood pulled over her forehead. Her cheeks were pink, and snowflakes clung to her eyelashes.

She stopped. "Sam, what's wrong? Why aren't you wearing your coat?"

"What's *wrong*?" He fought to keep his voice even. "I woke up, and you were gone. That's what's wrong. What the hell are you doing out here?"

"Looking for a cell signal." She pulled her gloved hand out of her pocket and waved her cell phone at him.

"Looking for a..." With a curse, he grabbed her arm and hauled her back toward the cabin. "You came out in this mess to use your goddamned phone?"

"Well, I…oof, would you slow down? I'm getting snow in my boots."

He set his jaw and yanked open the back door. "Get your coat and boots off, and go warm up. Now."

"Hey, you don't have to…." Her voice trailed off as she caught sight of his face. She pushed her hood back and lowered her hands to the zipper of her parka.

Sam shoved his boots off and stalked to the fireplace. He stoked the flames, added kindling and another log, then went to the kitchen. As he filled a cup with water and stuck it in the microwave, Brooke appeared in the doorway.

"Were you…worried about me?" she asked tentatively.

His shoulders tensed. "There's a blizzard outside, no other shelter for miles, and you were nowhere around. Was I supposed to *not* be worried?"

"I'm sorry." She rubbed her nose. "I'd promised my mother I'd call her when I arrived yesterday, but with no cell service…I was hoping I could find a signal outside. I didn't intend to go far, and I kept the cabin in sight. I just know she's anxious that she hasn't heard from me, and I don't have any way of contacting her."

A heavy sigh collected in his lungs. He took the cup from the microwave, added instant coffee, and handed it to her. Then he went to the shelf near the back door, where an old radio and mic sat amidst the dusty books.

He flipped a few switches and the dials lit up. "This emergency radio connects to the ranger station. We can contact the rangers and ask them to tell Felix to call your mother for you."

"Really?" Relief brightened her face, and she hurried to his side. "I had no idea."

"I'd have told you last night, if I'd known you needed to contact your mother."

"Can we call the station now?" She peered at the dials. "I don't want her to worry about me any more than she already has. I listed her as an emergency contact when I put my info into the website form, and Felix knows her and my dad anyway. He can easily get in touch with them."

Sam flipped a few more switches and took the microphone from the holder. Crackling static emerged from the speakers. He depressed a button and spoke into the mic. "Station twenty? This is Sam Donovan up at the Eagle's Nest."

A man's gravelly voice emerged. "Read you, Sam."

"I've got Brooke Castle up here too. Can you call the Eagle's Nest owner, Felix Milford, for us? If you can't reach him through the rental company, try Metalworks Hardware in Bliss Cove. Tell him to get in touch with Brooke's mother, Helen Castle. Brooke is fine, but we're dealing with the snowstorm and there's no cell service."

More static, before the man responded with, "Metalworks...Helen Castle. Ten-four. Hunker down, it's getting worse out there. We'll—"

His voice disappeared into a crackle of noise. Sam turned a few more switches and spoke into the mic again, but the static persisted. He flipped off the radio.

"Thank you." Brooke stepped toward him and rested a tentative hand on his arm. "I just knew there had to be a bright side to this whole mix-up, and so far you've rescued me from a fall and helped me call my mom. I really appreciate it."

He nodded shortly. Though her touch was light, he felt

the pressure of her palm clear through his shirtsleeve. Around her slender wrist was the bracelet she'd bought yesterday morning—a braided purple band holding a disk with the word *Courage*.

She was the reason he stocked useless trinkets like that at Title Wave. He'd intended only to sell books at the bookstore. But last spring, Brooke and her mother had come in, yammering about putting together a "book-themed gift basket."

Brooke had been both surprised and disappointed that Sam didn't have a stock of non-book gifts. Next thing he knew, he was placing orders for *Alice in Wonderland* teacups and *Pride and Prejudice* necklaces—and getting irritated with himself for doing so.

"And thanks for worrying about me," Brooke added. "That was really sweet."

He scowled. "I'm not sweet."

"I know *you're* not sweet, but the act of worrying about me was sweet." She skimmed her gaze over his shirt and jeans, which were now damp from melting snow. "You should change and warm up. I'll make you a cup of coffee this time."

Turning away from her earnestness, he grabbed clean clothes from his duffle and stalked to the bathroom. After showering, he pulled on jeans and a T-shirt. His back and shoulder muscles ached from his cramped sleep. If the storm broke soon, he'd get outside and do some kind of workout to loosen up.

When he returned to the living room, the air was filled with weird music—drumming and something that sounded like rain—and a vanilla-orange scent. A cup of fresh coffee rested beside his laptop.

Brooke, dressed in purple sweatpants and a T-shirt displaying a floral peace sign, was seated in front of the fire with her eye closed, her legs crossed, and her hands resting on her knees. A lit candle rested beside her. He suspected it was the source of the fruit-based smell.

"You're welcome to join me," she said without opening her eyes. "I'm working on a new routine that includes half an hour of meditation every morning."

"It's five a.m. It's not *morning*."

"Of course it is. If it weren't snowing, we would be bathed in dawn."

He snorted, even though her remark brought up an image of Brooke *bathing*.

"What's with the music?" he muttered.

"Nature sounds and a tribal drumbeat intended to awaken my subconscious."

Suppressing a groan, Sam sank onto the sofa and picked up his laptop. A week off the grid to work on his book. That was all he'd wanted when he'd booked the cabin. Instead he was contending with a perky, pretty reporter who was apparently here to channel her inner moon child.

He tried to focus on his manuscript, but his gaze kept slipping past his computer screen to Brooke. Her long brown hair glowed in the firelight, and her thick eyelashes created crescent-shaped shadows on her high cheekbones. She had a little mole right at the corner of her left eye, like a tiny punctuation mark.

He jerked his attention back to his computer. He didn't have even thirty seconds to spend ogling Brooke, not if he was going to make his deadline—and he'd be damned if he missed it. Not only had he never missed a deadline, his publisher had already pushed back the publication schedule for his new trilogy. Sam wouldn't be responsible for screwing things up even more.

He scraped his hands through his hair and eyed the stack of romance novels Brooke had left on the table. *For research*, she'd lied.

Sam had never been a genre snob—as a thriller writer who'd incorporated everything from fantasy to time-travel in his books, he had no reason to be. But while he knew romances were a massively successful genre, he'd never actually read one.

He grabbed a well-worn book from the top of the stack and studied the cover, which bore an illustration of a guy with digitally enhanced abs clutching a voluptuous redhead to his bare chest. *Mists of Love.*

He skimmed through the book, pausing when he caught a glimpse of the phrase *"throbbing loins."*

Seriously?

"That's a classic." Brooke had opened her eyes and was watching him.

"With throbbing loins, it had better be."

"Well, it was written back in the day when romance authors used a lot of flowery prose. The story is fantastic, though. It's about a medieval knight who goes on a crusade to win the hand of his lady love."

"Considering she has lush mounds and quivering thighs," he scanned the page, "I can't say I blame him."

She chuckled, and the musical sound lodged somewhere inside him. "Keep in mind that romance novels are one of the reasons you have a bookstore. They're one of the reasons there are publishing houses and readers. Have you ever read one?"

"No." He closed the book and picked up another with a guy in a business suit on the cover. "What's the research?"

Her cheeks grew pink, but she smiled. "Okay, *obviously* I bought the books for myself. I read romance novels all the time. I love them."

"But you know what happens at the end, right?" He rifled through the second book. "With that kind of predictability, what's the appeal?"

"The *journey* to the end." She lifted her arms above her head for a stretch. Her breasts pressed against her shirt. "The messages, too. Love conquers all. Everyone deserves a happy ending. We should all be so lucky to find our One True Love."

"Our what?"

"It's the one person on earth who's perfect for you, and you for them." She pressed her palms together and drew her shoulders back. "It's not necessarily a once-in-a-lifetime thing, but it's when you discover the partner with whom you can be totally yourself without any fear. It's the person you want. The one you choose who chooses you back uncondi-tionally."

"No wonder it's fiction." He tossed the book back onto the table.

"Let me guess." Her voice was dry. "You don't believe One True Loves exist."

"That's the point of fiction. Some of it, at least. To tell stories about implausible events."

"And to tell the truth about life." She pulled one foot up

to rest alongside her inner thigh. "Love is one of the world's greatest truths."

"And the biggest lie. What are you doing?"

"Tree pose. It brings clarity and focus, except when the practitioner is talking to *you* at the same time." She lowered her foot to the floor. "Do you really believe love is a lie?"

Was that *disappointment* in her expression?

Shame flicked through him like the strike of a whip. "Yeah, because when it gets tough, people walk away. That's why the divorce rate is so high and why most marriages are unhappy. People fall in love and get married believing the lie, and then they discover they made a huge mistake. But sometimes they can't walk away…in which case, they just stay miserable."

"Wow." She shook her head slowly, her eyes darkening. "And I thought I had a bad breakup."

If only he could blame "a bad breakup."

"I'm not saying *all* relationships or marriages are unhappy," he amended. "I just don't know of any happy ones."

"Then you haven't been looking." She lowered her hands to the floor, braced her feet, and pushed her rear up into the air.

His blood stirred. Actually, it went into a tornado. His fingers ached to squeeze her soft, round ass. He'd come dangerously close to doing exactly that when she'd been bent over peering into the fridge yesterday.

"I can tell you wonderful love stories about plenty of couples in Bliss Cove alone." Brooke rose to her tiptoes. Her hair fell in a shiny curtain on either side of her face. "My parents, for one. They became high-school sweethearts when my mom asked my dad to the junior prom. Forty years later, they're still together. My grandpa Charlie met my grandma Ruth a month before he went to Vietnam. They were married the day before he left, and they wrote letters every day until they were reunited again. She was the one who encouraged him to become a journalist to tell people's stories. There's no question they had a bond of *true* love."

"Not surprised that you believe in it, then."

"Most people do." She walked her hands backward and straightened. "That's just one of the reasons romance novels are so popular. A lot of women believe in finding the man who is perfect for them, whatever characteristics he might have."

"As long as he's a billionaire who looks like Chris Hemsworth." Sam tossed the novel back onto the table.

"What, you don't imagine Angelina Jolie when you fantasize?" Brooke rested her hands on her hips and tossed her hair back.

Actually, he didn't...but he wasn't about to confess who *had* appeared in his more explicit fantasies.

"Anything goes in a fantasy," he hedged. "So what other qualities does your perfect man have?"

"Well, billionaire Chris Hemsworth is a start." She looked Sam over from head to toe. Amusement gleamed in her brown eyes. "He's lean and...let's see, he has curly blond hair and the features of a nobleman. He shaves every day. He has charm and an outgoing personality."

"Interesting." He narrowed his eyes. Her "perfect man" sounded nothing like him.

"My perfect man knows exactly how to treat a woman, especially me, of course." She lifted a hand and began ticking the points off on her fingers. "He chews food politely and never while talking. He's very social, attends lots of events, and can talk about anything from antiques to the latest sports statistics. He's generous, attentive, and he knows what I want and need without me having to tell him."

"How does he know that?"

"It's instinctive, like a sixth sense." She pursed her lips. "You probably don't believe in that kind of thing. But since my perfect man and I are destined to be soulmates, One True Loves, he would just *know* these things about me."

"What kind of things? Like your favorite food?"

She smirked. "Am I hearing this right? Is Sam Donovan, Bliss Cove's resident curmudgeon, actually teasing me?"

"I'm just wondering how your perfect guy knows *instinctively* that you like fried jumbo shrimp, cosmopolitans, and double-chocolate brownies."

Her eyes widened.

Sam groaned inwardly. *Shit.* Way to speak without thinking first. Brooke was too sharp not to pick up on the subtext of his remark.

"How did you…" Her voice trailed off.

He shrugged, as if it were insignificant. "All girls like those things."

"Not *all*." She crossed her arms. "Rory hates cosmopolitans, and my friend Bee is allergic to shellfish."

"Must've been a lucky guess, then."

She gave him a puzzled stare. She opened and closed her mouth, blinked, then shook her head and went into the kitchen.

Sam turned his attention back to his computer. He was beginning to think he might be in trouble.

CHAPTER 5

*B*rooke reached into the box for an animal cracker and bit the head off a lion. After a breakfast of eggs and Sam's (admittedly delicious) cinnamon rolls, she'd spent the past couple of hours working on her freelance article ideas.

She'd also been trying—and failing—to ignore Sam. He was sprawled on the sofa, one foot on the coffee table and his laptop balanced on his thighs. His messy hair fell over his forehead.

A little flame sparked in her belly. It wasn't that big a deal that he happened to know her favorite foods and drink...except that it kind of was. How did he know, anyway? She'd seen him occasionally at the Mousehole Tavern, but he'd never looked in her direction.

Or so she'd assumed. Had he actually been paying attention to her? Wouldn't she have noticed? And why was it flattering that he knew how much she loved fried shrimp and brownies? *Jumbo* fried shrimp and *double-chocolate* brownies.

As a reporter, she knew well the importance of specifics. If he'd just said, *"drinks and brownies,"* she might've agreed that most women did indeed love those things. Instead, he'd mentioned the exact items she frequently ordered at the Mousehole.

Opening her notebook to a fresh page, she wrote:

1. Inexplicably knows my favorite foods and drink.
2. Came looking for me in the snowstorm. Worriedly.
3. Eats an apple like it's forbidden fruit in the garden of Eden.

(Speaking of which – what would he look like with a fig-leaf loincloth? Never mind, it would probably be too small. Heh.)

4. Arms of steel.
5. Caught me like Superman swooping up to save Lois Lane, a self-sufficient, strong, independent woman who doesn't need a hero but who also wouldn't turn one down.

Brooke reread the list. Whenever she had an issue with someone, she made a point of detailing their more admirable qualities to remind herself to be gracious. Until now, she hadn't actually known many of Sam's true admirable qualities because he kept them locked behind his wall of grumpiness. Though lately, he *had* been acting less grumpy than usual.

She took a sip of her lemon-cayenne iced tea and glanced at him again. The firelight glinted off the dark hair dusting his arms.

For the three minutes that she'd been in his arms after

he'd caught her last night, she'd experienced a shockingly intense surge of both pleasure and safeness. He was incredibly strong and packed with muscle, though she'd suspected as much given the way his T-shirts hugged his broad chest and his jeans fit his powerful legs. She'd had to restrain herself from nestling right up against his chest and reveling in just how *good* he felt.

Not that she had time for reveling. She'd spent two years hiding in the safety of Bliss Cove, and now that she was ready to face the real world again, she really didn't need to be getting all warm and fuzzy about Sam.

No matter how much he'd unwittingly intrigued her over the past year.

He glanced up, catching her gaze. She held up the box of animal crackers. "Want one?"

"You can buy those in large-sized bags."

"Not the same." She jiggled the box by the string. "The classic red Barnum's Animals box is the only way to eat animal crackers. I brought a whole bunch, if you'd like one of your own."

"No."

She ate a monkey cracker and nodded to his laptop. "What, exactly, is it you're doing?"

"Paperwork." He kept his gaze fixed on the screen. "Invoices, payroll, tax prep."

"Why did you come up here to do boring paperwork?"

"So I could be alone." A shutter came down over his face. "You can see how well that worked out."

She smirked. "Yeah, for me, too."

"Why did you want to be alone?"

"I'm on a self-improvement retreat to set goals and intentions for the year." Brooke wrote a numbered list on a fresh page in her notebook. "I'm also looking to do more freelance work, so I'm trying to come up with ideas. Would you read an article about how to make homemade birdseed?"

"No."

She started to cross it off her list, then stopped. "Well, you're not exactly my target demographic."

"Who are you trying to write for?"

"Any publication that's accepting submissions." She rested her chin on her hand. "The editor of *Empire Monthly* in New York asked me to send him a proposal. He rejected my first list of ideas, but asked me to come with more for their February edition. That's one of my projects for my retreat."

"*Empire* is doing pretty well, considering they launched less than two years ago." Sam stretched his arms to the sides and got to his feet.

Brooke was briefly surprised that he knew about *Empire* before remembering that he owned a bookstore. Of course he'd be in the know about magazines and periodicals.

He fiddled with the radio and contacted the ranger station again. Due to the suddenness of the storm and lack of preparation, the ranger announced that they had to wait for the snow to subside before they could get a snowplow up the mountain road. It could still take another two or three days... and that was a guesstimate.

"Looks like we're spending New Year's Eve here." Brooke shook the remaining crackers out of the box and popped them into her mouth. "At the very least, we'll have an interesting story to tell."

"Have you always been a glass half-full kind of person?"

Sounding vaguely annoyed, he switched off the radio and paced to the window.

"I sure have. Gramps calls me Sunny Side Up." She nodded toward the radio. "Did you ask the ranger to contact someone to let them know you're okay?"

He shrugged. "No need."

"You don't have anyone to contact?"

He shook his head and rolled his shoulders back. "I don't have family in the area."

Ah hah. A little piece of the Sam Donovan puzzle. That must mean he had family somewhere else. Well, of course he did. Everyone had family somewhere.

"What about..." A flush heated her cheeks. "A girlfriend?"

He lifted an eyebrow. "No girlfriend."

In addition to being optimistic, Brooke had also always been naturally curious. Which was a great quality for a reporter, but one that had gotten her into trouble more than once.

"Mrs. Higgins said she saw you with a woman a few months ago over in Glendale." She tapped her pen on her notepad, trying not to betray her excessive interest in this topic. "Not whistling Dixie."

He frowned. "Whistling what?"

"I mean, she basically said you were giving off an...um, intimate vibe."

Sam gave a short laugh and picked up a half-folded newspaper from the coffee table. "I'm surprised you didn't write that up as a feature for *The Gazette*."

"Well, it would have been newsworthy." Frustration nudged at her, the feeling she experienced when she sensed that an interviewee or a contact didn't want to give her the information she sought.

She opened her mouth to press for more, when Sam grimaced and rubbed the back of his neck again. Given how uncomfortable he'd looked all contorted on the sofa that morning—actually his big body had been half sprawled on the sofa and half on the coffee-table, with one arm dangling to the floor—it was hardly a wonder he was sore.

Putting aside her curiosity to revisit later, she got to her feet. "Sit down."

Suspicion glinted in his expression. "What for?"

"I won't hurt you." She walked to the sofa and patted the cushion. "Just sit."

Still wary, he sat down. Brooke moved behind him. His delicious scent drifted to her nose—soap, woodsmoke, and some earthy, primal scent that seemed to belong to him alone. Until he'd barged into her cabin, she didn't think she'd ever been close enough to touch him, much less smell him.

Much less experience the brief, strong pleasure of being in his arms.

She settled her hands on his shoulders. He tensed.

"Wow." She prodded at his muscles. "You're all knotted up like a fishing net. Are you always like this or was it the sofa?"

"I have no idea." His voice was slightly strained.

She dug her palms into his shoulders and began massaging. Warmth flowed clear up her arms. He didn't relax easily, not that she was surprised. She rubbed his shoulders, slipped her fingers into the thick hair at his nape, and eased the knots out of his neck.

A groan escaped him, the low, deep sound settling right into her core. Slowly his body began to loosen under her ministrations.

She'd never touched a man like him before, even in a way that was supposed to be clinical and helpful. He was rock-hard, warm, and pliable all at the same time, his muscles flexing and relaxing with every stroke of her hands. Tempted though she was to tell him to take off his shirt, she wasn't about to deliberately face that kind of torture.

Pushing him forward a little, she pressed her thumbs along the ridges of his spine and kneaded the large muscles of his back before moving back up to his shoulders. She could only imagine him lying on his stomach, shirtless, as she straddled his thighs and smoothed her palms over his taut, bare skin before—

Heat coursed through her.

"Okie doke!" Forcing a bright note into her tone, she backed away from him. "That should loosen you up a little."

He grunted, his elbows on his knees and his head lowered. "Where'd you learn how to do that?"

"Oh, I've taken all kind of classes. Reiki, massage, tai chi, aromatherapy." Brooke rounded the coffee table and picked up a few romance novels. "Some of it was for article research, but mostly I've just done it for wellness. I saw that eye-roll."

"I'm not judging."

"You most certainly are." She stacked the books in the crook of her arm.

He straightened and twisted his neck a few times. "If I spent my time judging the things I've seen and heard, I wouldn't have time for anything else."

Brooke's curiosity spiked all over again. "What have you seen?"

He turned to the newspaper crossword puzzle. "I've spent a lot of years traveling. You visit enough places, you see all kinds of things."

"Is that why you took over Title Wave? Because you were tired of traveling and wanted to settle down?"

"No." He crossed his ankle over his thigh and studied the paper. "But not long after I moved to Bliss Cove, I heard Title Wave was going out of business. No one had offered to buy it, so I did. Every town should have a bookstore."

"You kept Title Wave for the town?"

"I wasn't being altruistic." He marked a few squares on the crossword. "I just happened to be there at the right time. I like bookstores."

"And books, I assume. So why won't you staff a booth at the Bliss Cove Book Fair?"

"Because it's a bookstore, not a booth." He wrote another word on the puzzle.

"It wouldn't kill you to get involved in a town event every now and then. And this year, the Book Fair is a fundraiser for The Reading Project. My friend Bee is in charge of it, and she's been trying to raise money for a book-mobile to bring books into different communities. See what a great cause you could be supporting?"

"I see."

"So?"

"No."

"Lord, you're like a wall." Brooke sighed. "Do you *like* owning the bookstore?"

"I don't necessarily like running a business, but Title Wave is easy enough."

Brooke couldn't help grinning. "Except for when you have to go up against Mayor Bowers about your strange hours."

"Well, yeah." A smile tugged at his mouth. "I'm hoping she'll eventually see it as a colorful, small-town quirk."

"I think most people already see *you* that way."

"Glad to do my part."

She couldn't help laughing. For all his scowling reclusiveness, it seemed Sam Donovan was rather...likeable. Sometimes, anyway.

She glanced at the crossword as he wrote in another word. Almost all the squares were filled in. With pen.

She might have been the only woman in the world who thought that was pretty hot.

"You use a pen, huh?" she asked.

"I guess so."

"Gramps always says you can tell a lot about a person who uses a pen for a crossword puzzle." Brooke shifted the books to her other arm. "It says that you're confident and unafraid of making a mistake, but also that you believe there's only one path or direction to take. As far as you're concerned, there's one answer to every problem or question. No possibility of two or more."

"Actually, the pen just happened to be in my pocket."

"Ah. Your instrument of choice was close at hand. As Destiny would say, that was no coincidence." She tilted her chin at the crossword. "Is that *The New York Times*?"

He nodded and tossed the paper onto a side table. "You do crosswords?"

"No, but I recognize *The Times*. Not in the best way, of course."

"Why's that?"

Surprised, she met his gaze. "You don't know about my stint at *The New York Times*?"

"Should I?"

"Everyone else knows. I assumed you'd have heard the gossip at some point or another."

"What gossip?"

Old regret shot through her. If she didn't tell him, he'd find out the truth sooner or later. And for some reason, she didn't want Sam to hear the real story from anyone but her.

"It's embarrassing," she said.

He frowned. "What happened?"

"I was supposed to be Bliss Cove's next award-winning journalist." She blew her breath upward, stirring tendrils of hair at her forehead. "I was always interested in journalism because I had this amazing, award-winning grandfather who was out covering stories on everything from natural disasters to governmental coups. But I don't think I really knew I wanted to be a reporter until Charlie took over *The Gazette*."

"When was that?"

"I was sixteen, so almost fifteen years ago. He'd moved back because my Grandma Ruth had been diagnosed with cancer, and they wanted to be closer to family."

Deflecting a pang of sorrow, she put the romance novels on the table and picked up another box of animal crackers and the bottle of tea. "*The Gazette* was in pretty bad shape back then. Charlie bought it and turned it around. For a while, I worked for him as a go-fer getting coffee and making copies, but he wanted me to write for the high-school paper to get my feet wet before he'd consider hiring me as a reporter. So I became staff reporter for *The Bliss Cove High Tribune*. I covered a lot of stories about athletics, student government, that kind of thing."

She sat on the easy chair and opened the box. "In my junior year, I uncovered a story about ballot-stuffing for the homecoming court. The expose led to an overhaul of the homecoming vote system. The story didn't win me any favors with some of the popular kids, but I got a lot of support from most of my fellow students. And, of course, my grandfather. He was very proud. I worked for *The Gazette* throughout my senior year. Charlie wrote my letter of recommendations for my college applications."

Sam was watching her with a strange intensity, as if he were deciphering emotions she didn't even know she was revealing.

"Where did you go to college?" he asked.

"UW-Madison for my BA in journalism. I wrote for the university paper, freelanced, and continued reporting for *The Gazette* whenever I came back for a visit." She held out the cracker box to him. "For years, people in Bliss Cove had been talking about how I was the next Bob Woodward or Katherine Graham. I worked for a couple of different papers after graduating, but *The New York Times* was the holy grail."

"And you found it." He took a cracker and studied the animal before eating it.

"To my shock." Brooke shook her head, recalling the utter thrill of her accomplishment. "Everyone was so excited when I got the job with *The New York Times*. It was like a hometown girl starring on Broadway or winning an Oscar.

The day before I moved to New York, the entire town threw a party for me. Everyone was there. Eleanor at Sugar Joy baked a gigantic cake decorated like a newspaper. We made newspaper party hats, and Grant from the Mousehole served fish and chips wrapped in newsprint. It was crazy, over-the-top, and wonderful all at the same time. That was my send-off to the big city."

"Sounds like everyone had high expectations."

"Yes." She took a sip of iced tea. "Unfortunately, I didn't meet those expectations. I worked at *The Times* for three years. I loved the big stories, but the pressure was brutal. New York City was also a tough place to live for a girl who'd grown up in Bliss Cove.

"Like so many of the other reporters, I was living on caffeine and adrenaline. To stay competitive, you had to take whatever story they threw at you, so I was constantly driving or flying to different cities to cover a political rally or a congressional hearing. I knew I was doing important work, but I was also meeting some nasty people and fending off bribery attempts, threats, harassment, you name it."

She wiped a drop of tea from her lip, smothering the pain that had once overwhelmed her. "I started getting sick all the time and developed ulcers. I couldn't sleep without a sleeping pill. I was in a relationship, and then the guy turned out to be…well, not the man I thought he was."

She rubbed her chest and stared at the floor. "Not long after we broke up, I was interviewing a senator about a new water bill, and I had a panic attack. I couldn't breathe and ended up passing out. When I woke up in the hospital, I knew I couldn't do it anymore. I turned in my resignation the next day. And the following week, I moved back to Bliss Cove."

Silence fell. Brooke risked a glance at Sam. He was watching her, his eyes dark and his mouth set in a straight, thin line.

"I'm surprised you didn't hear about this," she said.

"Why would I have?"

"Well, it was big news when I moved back." She gave a wry smile. "As you can imagine, after the send-off I had. But of course, everyone in town told me how happy they were I was back, that they'd missed me, and that obviously it was *The Times'* loss. People were super nice and understanding about the whole mess."

"They would be."

A faint warmth seemed to underlie his tone, as if despite his reclusiveness he knew the townspeople would rally around her. Some of the tension eased from around her heart.

"It's been great working at *The Gazette* for the past couple of years." She plucked a hippo cracker from the box. "But I still sometimes feel like I let everyone down, even if they've never made me feel that way. That's just one of the reasons I'm trying to start something new."

"Are you looking for freelance or a full-time job?"

"I've been trying for both." She capped the bottle of tea. "I don't want to work for a national newspaper again, but I really enjoy writing feature stories. So I've applied to a lot of lifestyle publications around the country. To no avail."

"What has your grandfather said?"

"He doesn't know." She let out her breath in a long sigh. "I resigned from *The Gazette* because I found out he was paying my salary out of his own pocket. He knows I'm looking for another job, but he doesn't know about the rejections yet. None of my family does."

Guilt trickled through her. She knew her family would support her even if she collected rejections for the next year, but she didn't want their support for failure again. Especially not after two years of hiding out. This time, she wanted it for her success.

"Why haven't you told them?" Sam asked.

"I want to have something to show or tell them, you know?" She picked at the label on the bottle. "I want to go the distance and to really establish myself. I don't want to quit again."

He studied her, his expression pensive and remote. Curious how easy it was to talk to him so openly when he'd made it clear he didn't want to get close to anyone. What was he like behind that wall? What were his secrets?

"Anyone who rejects you is a fool," he muttered.

Before she could respond, he pushed abruptly up from the sofa and strode to the foyer. Turning his back, he pulled on his boots and parka. The door clicked shut behind him.

CHAPTER 6

*S*am shoveled snow until he was sweaty and his lungs burned. Physical exertion usually worked to loosen him up, but after clearing a path all the way to the main road, his chest was still knotted, his shoulders stiff. Not even the lingering pleasure of Brooke's massage could keep the tension away.

His breath came in gusts of white. Despite his determination not to get close to anyone in Bliss Cove, least of all Brooke, he experienced a painful mix of emotions over her revelation—anger, guilt, admiration, a pride he didn't deserve to feel for her, sadness…and God knew what else.

He didn't know what to do with her openness and honesty in telling him about her past. Not to mention the fact that she was confessing it all to *him*.

He'd spent the past year struggling to keep his distance, not to stare whenever he saw her, to act as if he hadn't noticed everything about her. In return, instead of shutting him down the way he deserved, she opened up like a book and gave him all her stories.

Even more surprising, he understood. He could relate. Though her guilt hadn't come from anyone else, he knew how hard it was to meet other people's expectations and to feel as if you'd disappointed them.

He also knew that Bliss Cove was a place where residents both respected and protected their own. It was just one of the reasons he'd moved there. He'd known instinctively that if he indicated he wanted to be left alone, people would leave him alone. So far, that had proven more or less the case, though the mayor and a few other ladies had gotten overly inquisitive about his marital and dating status.

Telling himself he didn't want a relationship or even to date casually, he'd politely turned down all matchmaking efforts. Only now, in such close proximity to Brooke, was he forced to admit that *she* was the reason for his lack of interest in other women.

He'd been avoiding her so her inquisitive reporter's nose wouldn't sniff out the truth, but he was beginning to realize it was more than that. She could make his heart beat faster, soften his resistance, loosen the persistent tightness in his chest. If he let her, she could ease herself right inside him the way no one had done before.

Maybe she already had.

He stomped back to the house, leaving the shovel on the porch before going inside. He studiously avoided her gaze as he shucked off his coat and boots. He went into the bathroom to clean up before sinking onto the sofa. A hot cup of coffee sat beside his laptop again.

He stared blindly at the document on the computer screen. He'd never be able to work. Under normal circumstances, he'd have seen the appeal in being stuck in a cabin with no Wi-Fi or cell service—if he were alone. If things had gone as he'd planned, he'd have been concentrating on his book with the precision of a laser.

Except things had gone totally wrong, and he was far from alone.

He made a superhuman effort to focus. He eked out a couple of pages of crappy writing. The hours dragged.

By contrast, Brooke's productivity didn't appear to be at all hindered. For the rest of the afternoon, she scribbled out a list of freelance ideas, made lunch, cleaned the kitchen, dusted the bookshelf, worked on a jigsaw puzzle, read one of her romance novels, and performed another seriously distracting yoga session. She went through at least three more boxes of animal crackers and two bottles of her fancy "wellness" iced tea.

As evening approached, she sat at the dining table, shaking up stones in a little pouch and tossing them onto the table.

Sam had been rewriting the same paragraph for hours. It still sucked.

The stones rattled and clanked on the table. He clenched his jaw.

"What are you doing?" He forced his voice to stay even.

"Rune casting." She peered at the stones and opened a little book. "Destiny has been teaching me. It's a method of divination and fortune-telling. I'm just practicing. Want me to do one for you?"

"No." He pushed abruptly to his feet, suppressing a snide comment about the futility of endeavors like fortune-telling.

Brooke put the stones back into the pouch and went to the kitchen. "Soup okay for dinner?"

"Fine."

She opened several cans of soup, poured them into a bowl, and started it heating up in the microwave. Sam shoved his feet into his boots and pulled open the back door. He slogged to the woodbin and brought in more firewood.

"Have a seat." Brooke placed the soup and a basket of bread rolls on the table.

Feeling not unlike a bad-tempered stray dog lured by food, Sam pulled out the chair opposite her and sat with a grudging, "Thanks."

"You're welcome, sunshine." With a smile, she handed him a bowl.

He'd gotten accustomed to his heart doing a crazy spinning thing when he caught sight of her smile from afar, but he had little experience with it up close...and directed *at him*.

After filling their bowls, they began to eat. Sam tried unsuccessfully not to notice the way her lips pursed as she sucked up spoonfuls of soup. Though she'd been needling him with her description of her "perfect man," he couldn't help wondering how much of it was true.

Sure, she'd want a guy like that—someone who was essentially the male version of her—but had she ever come close to finding him? Did her ex have any of those qualities? Had she ever met a guy whom she thought could be her "One True Love"?

Not that he believed in such horseshit. But obviously she did, so no wonder he was curious. Plus, she was all about romance, and he—

"Sam?" She waved her hand in front of his face. "Do you want something to drink?"

"I'll get it." He pushed away from the table and went to get her a bottle of iced tea and himself a soda. When he returned, Brooke was refilling her bowl with more soup.

"When I first moved away from Bliss Cove, the thing I missed the most, aside from my family, of course, was the artichoke soup at the Mousehole." She slurped up another spoonful. "It's funny because I don't actually like artichokes. But when I realized I couldn't have Grant's soup whenever I wanted...I really missed it. The first weekend I was back, my parents took me to dinner at the Mousehole. That first bite of artichoke soup was just about the best thing I ever tasted. I guess it was the taste of home. Did you ever feel like that?"

He shook his head, then surprised himself by admitting, "I never had much of a home."

Her forehead crinkled. "Why not?"

He shrugged. His history was no longer a big deal to him —it was what it was, and being estranged from his brother and father had simplified his life considerably—but Brooke and her family had deep roots in Bliss Cove. She wouldn't understand the idea of never feeling *at home*. Worse, she wouldn't like it.

"I left my parents' house at a young age and never went back." He focused on stirring the soup so he wouldn't have to see the faint distress he knew was rising in her brown eyes. "That was when I started traveling."

"Where did you go?"

"Wherever I could afford to." He took a bite of soup. "Europe, Asia. I spent a year traveling through South America, mostly Brazil and Argentina."

A strange expression flickered in her eyes, like a mixture

of admiration and longing. "That must have been incredible. Did you travel alone?"

"Most of the time."

"Were you scared?"

The question almost startled him. No one had ever asked him that before.

"No." Tearing his gaze from her, he picked up his bowl and walked to the kitchen. "I wasn't scared."

He sensed all the other questions bubbling inside her, felt her push them back down. At one time, he'd have attributed her curiosity to her journalist's instinct. Now, he had the odd feeling it had more to do with *her* and the *Courage* bracelet on her arm.

"You must have some great stories to tell," she finally said.

Yeah, he had stories. Not all of them "great." He turned to put the leftover food in the fridge, signaling that the conversation was at an end.

After doing the dishes, he returned to his laptop. He reread his pages over and over, attempting again to ignore Brooke as she bustled around getting ready for bed. The bathroom door closed, and the shower started.

Sam stifled a groan. Instead of John Kane's next predicament, all he could picture was Brooke in the shower, water spilling through her hair and trailing over her naked body. She'd be rubbing a thick, soapy lather over her—

Stop. It.

He dragged his hands over his face. Three weeks to his deadline wasn't a hell of a lot of time to finish his revisions and fix the subplot. Which he still had no idea how to do.

The bathroom door opened, and Brooke emerged. She

was flushed from the heat of the shower with her wet hair hanging over her shoulders. She wore purple pajama pants and an oversized T-shirt that clung to the damp parts of her body. Her toenails were painted pink.

After folding her clothes neatly and putting them back in her suitcase, she began arranging her mountain of blankets and pillows.

"What's *nesting*?" he asked.

"Oh." She gave a small laugh. "Well, usually it refers to a phase in pregnancy when a woman is getting ready for the baby, but in my case, it just means I like to make little nests, like in my bed or on the sofa, where I can snuggle up and read or whatever."

His mind veered in a dirty direction, imagining her doing "whatever" while spread out over a nest of pillows. With effort, he reined his thoughts back in.

"How did all that bedding fit in your car?" he asked.

"I'm a very efficient packer." She patted an elephant pillow into place. "I've always slept with a ton of blankets... or, even better, in a blanket fort."

"A blanket fort."

"My sister and I used to make them all the time." She crawled to the end of the mattress and smoothed out a pink-and-white striped sheet. "We'd drape all our blankets over chairs and tie them onto the bedposts, then decorate it with fairy lights. We put all of our pillows, stuffed animals, and blankets inside."

"What for?"

She straightened, her eyebrows drawing together in puzzlement. "What do you mean?"

"What was the point of the fort?"

"The *point*?" She lifted her hands. "It was like a little hideaway. We'd turn off all the lights and use flashlights to draw, play games, read books. We ate popcorn and cookies and told secrets. Sometimes we'd sleep there, like we were camping. It was a lot of fun, like creating our own world."

"Huh."

Brooke frowned. "Do you mean to tell me you've never made a blanket fort?"

"I've never made a blanket fort."

That wasn't to say he didn't know what it felt like to sleep in a makeshift shelter, though his experiences hadn't included popcorn and games.

He shifted his gaze back to his notes, feeling Brooke still watching him.

"Come on." She got to her feet and picked up a blue blanket. "Move the coffee table."

"What?"

"We're making a blanket fort."

He expelled a groan. "I don't have time for a blanket fort."

"What, you have somewhere to go?" She tsked and waved her hand at the darkened window. "You need to experience blanket-fort building, Sam."

"No, I don't."

She fisted her hands on her hips. "Give me fifteen minutes, or I'll force you to listen to me doing karaoke with Beyoncé again."

"Great, as long as you do that little dance again too." He eyed her with renewed interest.

She gave an exasperated sigh, even as her cheeks pinkened. "Please? I haven't made a blanket fort in a million years. If you don't have fun, I'll make all our meals and coffee until we're out of here. But I promise, you *will* have fun because fun is embedded in the very essence of blanket-fort construction."

With a sigh, Sam shoved to his feet. This attitude was just one reason Brooke was such a good reporter. No one stood a chance when she unleashed her inner pit-bull.

Or her inner kitten, as the case may be.

"Fifteen minutes," he said.

"Excellent!" Her face lit up and she hurried to the kitchen. "Actually, it might take longer than that, so let's not watch the clock, okay? I saw some rubber bands in a drawer somewhere. After you move the coffee table, get the dining chairs and bring them over near the fire."

Figuring this would go faster if he just did what she ordered, Sam carried the chairs to the main room and moved the coffee table out of the way. He pushed the sofa back and hauled the mattress to the area in front of the fireplace.

Brooke scrutinized the space with the intensity of an architect figuring out exactly how to build the Taj Mahal.

"We'll need some books to weigh the edges down." She arranged the dining chairs around the mattress, then frowned slightly. "Chairs are usually great because they make a nice, high ceiling, but I think these are too low. And the loft supports are too wide to tie the blankets around, so we'll have to figure something else out. Oh, let's turn the sofa around so we can use the back."

Under her instructions, Sam moved furniture, shook out blankets, and untangled rubber bands. Brooke began draping blankets over the chairs, then ducked underneath them with a mutter of frustration. "Just as I thought. These chairs aren't high enough. The blankets are going to droop in the middle."

Sam eyed the wooden supports holding up the loft. He retrieved a tool kit from the utility closet and found a roll of thin wire. After measuring off a length, he clipped it from the roll and tied it around two of the supports, then secured it with duct tape.

"What's that for?" Brooke emerged from underneath a blanket, her hair tousled.

"It's one of the walls." He draped two blankets over the wire, overlapping them to conceal the opening.

After measuring a few more distances, he stretched more wire from the posts to the chair backs. He brought the broken ladder over and set it up alongside the sofa, attaching the last wire to one of the rungs.

"Oh my god, you're brilliant." With a clap of her hands, Brooke hurried to drape blankets over the square of wire supports he'd created around the mattress. He tossed sheets over the top while Brooke ducked inside and organized all the pillows.

By the time they were finished, a ten-foot-square fort made up of colorful blanket walls and a ceiling concealed the mattress.

"Come in!" Brooke's hand appeared behind one of the blankets and waved. "It's perfect! The only thing missing are the fairy lights."

Sam pushed aside one of the blankets and clambered onto the mattress. Brooke had arranged all the pillows in a circular nest, and the firelight shone against the blanket walls, casting everything in a reddish sheen. It was cozy, cute, and...extremely close.

He folded his legs, and his knees bumped against hers. The smell of her fruity soap and shampoo filled his head.

"Hold on, I'll get the supplies." She crawled out of the fort, giving him a tempting display of her ass clad in soft purple pants.

He pulled in a heavy breath. Ten minutes. Fifteen, tops. Then he'd get out of here and focus on his damned book. Even if it killed him.

Which seemed likely.

CHAPTER 7

*S*am adjusted the ridiculous array of animal pillows. Outside the fort, the sounds of Brooke scurrying around filtered through the blanket walls. The microwave whirred, and cabinet doors opened and closed. The cabin lights went off, but the firelight glow seemed to get stronger.

She pushed aside a blanket and handed him a stack of board games, boxes of cookies and animal crackers, a few romance novels, a bowl of popcorn, and a flashlight before wiggling back in.

"See?" She flashed him a smile that hit him somewhere in the middle of his chest. "Isn't this super cool?"

Actually, he thought it was more *super hot*, but he'd better not tell her that.

"Are you sure you've never made a blanket fort before?" Brooke closed the "door" and settled cross-legged on the mattress.

"I'm sure."

Her eyes grazed his briefly, as if she'd sensed a sudden

shift in his mood. She held out a bottle of iced tea. "Want one? They're lemon-cayenne."

Though he wasn't a fan of either iced tea or lemon-cayenne, he took the bottle and popped the lid. As expected, the stuff tasted awful. He took another sip and set the bottle aside.

He gestured to the games. "Which one first?"

"How about Chutes and Ladders?" She opened the game and set up the board.

Despite the close quarters, Sam forced himself to relax. Brooke was so damned adorable with her pillow collection and blanket fort "supplies" that he didn't want to put a dent in her enthusiasm by either leaving or getting turned on. He was a lot closer to the latter than the former.

They chose their markers and started the game. In-between cookies and handfuls of popcorn, they climbed ladders and slid down chutes, with Brooke making it to the top first by about ten squares. Afterward, they played several games of Candy Land, Sorry, and Clue—ending their tournament with seven wins for Brooke and four for Sam.

"My sister Gwen always won more games than me." Brooke put the games in a pile and set them outside the fort. "I'm still convinced she cheated sometimes."

"Is she older or younger?"

"Older by six years. Needless to say, she outgrew blanket forts before I was ready for her to. So I spent a lot of time in forts alone, or with a friend." She opened a box of crackers and held it out to him. "Aria...she's my best friend, the owner of the Meow and Then Cat Café on Mariposa Street. Her mother owns—"

"The Sugar Joy Bakery." Sam bit into a giraffe-shaped cracker and nodded. "I know."

"Oh." She lifted her eyebrows. "Well, Aria and I used to make blanket forts during sleepovers even when we were into our teen years. We'd paint each other's nails and gossip about boys we had a crush on."

An unexpected smile curved his mouth. He could picture that with surprising ease. "Sounds like the ideal life for a couple of teenaged besties."

She grinned. "Who was your *bestie* when you were a teen?"

His chest tightened unexpectedly. Several heartbeats passed before he said, "Didn't have one."

Brooke blinked. "Everyone has a best friend."

"In your world, maybe." He rubbed his breastbone. "I was alone most of the time."

"That's kind of sad." A shadow crossed her features.

He didn't like it. He wasn't used to seeing her look even remotely despondent.

"I was used to it," he said offhandedly. Then, in an attempt to turn her thoughts back to something happier, he asked, "Have you adopted one of Aria's cats yet?"

"Oh, yes." Her eyes brightened. "I was her first cat adoption customer. It was about a week after she'd opened. I was having a coffee in the Cat Lounge, and this beautiful calico named Jojo jumped onto the sofa and curled up right next to me. I guess it's more accurate to say that she adopted me. She's a really sweet cat. Friendly, social, affectionate."

Sounded like a perfect match of cat and owner.

Brooke plumped up the pillows and lay back, gazing up

at the blanket ceiling. A few freckles dusted her nose. The little notch above her upper lip was a perfect curve.

"When I was five or six, my parents gave me this rotating star projector as a birthday present." She made a circular gesture with her hand. "When you turned off the lights, it projected the moon and constellations moving across the ceiling, and it played different songs. My favorite was *When You Wish Upon A Star*. I kept that projector for years, I loved it so much.

"Whenever I built a blanket fort, my dad helped me set the projector up inside. I'd lie there for hours, just thinking about stuff and looking at the stars rolling across the inside of the fort. It was so different from seeing them on my bedroom ceiling. In the fort, they were bigger and brighter and so close I felt like I could just reach up and grab them. I made a lot of wishes on those stars."

The wistful tone in her voice wrapped like a ribbon around his heart. He stretched out beside her, resting his head against the elephant pillow. "Did your wishes come true?"

"Yes, but sometimes in ways I hadn't expected. Or if they didn't, then I needed to figure out the reason why." She stroked her hand unconsciously over her arm, her face still turned upward. "Have you ever had a wish come true?"

"I don't know. I guess I don't believe much in wishes either." He immediately wanted to take the words back, knowing they'd disappoint her. "But it sounds like you had a great childhood."

She murmured a noise of assent. "Because of my parents and my family. I just got really lucky."

He tucked one hand behind his head and tried to picture big, glowing stars gliding over the blanket ceiling.

Brooke shifted, and he felt her gaze. He turned to face her. The muted firelight cast a dim glow over her pale skin and created a gold sheen on her eyelashes. She was the only woman he'd ever known whose eyes were so transparently *open*, like she had no reason to hide anything because she had nothing to hide.

"It's been way longer than fifteen minutes," she murmured. "Did you have fun? Or am I making coffee and meals for the rest of our stay?"

He chuckled. "I had fun, so no need for you to cook. But if you want to dance around and sing Beyoncé, I'd be happy to watch."

She laughed. "You're the only person in the world who would."

"Good. Then it'll be our secret."

"Ah. Blanket fort activity number six." Curiosity lit in her eyes. "Tell me a secret, Sam Donovan."

He'd spent the past year avoiding her in order to protect his secrets. Now, for inexplicable reasons that he suspected had more to do with his attraction to her than his intellect, he was half-tempted to confess.

A *quarter* tempted. But he wasn't that big an idiot.

"I don't like cheesecake," he said.

"Sacrilege!" She clutched her chest and widened her eyes. "Have you *tasted* Eleanor Prescott's chocolate cheesecake?"

"No, because I don't like cheesecake." He shifted to adjust the unicorn and elephant pillows. "Your turn."

"Well, *The New York Times* debacle was my biggest

secret, even though everyone in Bliss Cove knows about it." She looked at the firelight dancing over the blanket ceiling. "I've never told anyone the sordid story of my ex, though."

The muscles at the back of his neck tensed. "Why not?"

"Oh." She expelled her breath in a long sigh, and her eyes fluttered down to conceal her expression. "Talk about humiliating."

He shouldn't ask. Shouldn't dig deeper or breach the wall any more than he already had.

He gazed at the sweep of her lashes and the little mole right at the corner of her eye.

"What happened?" he asked.

She was silent for so long he thought she wasn't going to answer. Then she rolled onto her side and lifted her gaze. Her irises were chocolate-brown, flecked with gold like glitter, and surrounded by a ring of pure black. The kind of eyes a man could lose himself in.

"Have you ever had a fantasy?" Brooke slid her hands between her head and the fuzzy bear pillow. "I don't mean the sexy kind, but a big, epic picture of you living out something you'd always wanted? Like if you were a kid dreaming of becoming an astronaut, and you saw yourself blasting off in the space shuttle and walking on the moon. You could picture all the details. That kind of fantasy."

She waited for his response. He didn't know what to say, so he just nodded.

"I'd always had this grand idea of love, as you can imagine." Her lips curved slightly. "I wanted what the people around me had, and probably what I read in romance novels, too. But because I was surrounded by all these great love stories, I knew it was attainable. When I met Michael, I felt like I'd been hit with a lightning bolt, and in the best possible way. I was convinced he was the other half of my epic romance."

"But you found out differently."

"Yes." Her smile faded. "We met at the Chrysler building. I was late for an interview and running across the lobby to this jam-packed elevator. Michael saw me, and he held the door open until I got there. I was all sweaty and wheezing for breath. He handed me a bottle of vitamin water and asked what floor I wanted. Right when the doors opened again, he pointed to the water bottle and said I owed him a drink. He'd written his cell number on the label."

Slick. Even though Sam had never read a romance novel, he knew enough about life—and women—to see how she would find that appealing.

"Anyway, I texted him a message, he texted back, we met for real drinks…and had this amazing, explosive beginning." A pink flush colored Brooke's cheeks. "I knew early on I wanted to be in it for the long haul, which was my first mistake. I wasn't naive…at least, I didn't think I was, but I was still adjusting to life in New York and trying to prove myself at *The Times.*

"I guess I was trying very hard to see only the things I wanted to see. And Michael was everything I'd wanted. Handsome, confident, charming, you name it. He worked for an advertising company, but he wanted to branch out and start his own company, be his own boss.

"His energy and drive were hard to resist. Not that I wanted to. He was so good at bolstering me up, convincing me that everyone had a rough time at first and my job would get better. He'd do these lovely things to make my life easier

—bring takeout when I had a deadline, which was all the time, show up at my cubicle with my favorite coffee, take me to the airport, send me flowers and care packages. It didn't take long for me to fall head over heels. We were together for almost a year. I thought we were heading toward marriage."

Sam's back teeth snapped together. "What happened?"

"He cheated on me in a big way. I found out when he told me he was going to ask another woman to marry him."

He bolted upright, bracing his hand on a pillow. "He was getting *engaged*? What a fucking asshole."

"Agreed." She twisted her mouth. "He assured me he *wasn't* dating her when we first met, as if that made it better. But then I found out she was from a prominent New York family, and everyone on the reporting staff knew who she was. It was like he thought he was leveling up. I felt like such an idiot."

"You weren't the one who should have felt bad."

"Everything about it was awful." She fiddled with one of the ears on the bear pillow. "Obviously it added to my job stress and…anyway, the whole situation sucked. It also made it harder for me to resign from *The Times* because I didn't want Michael to think he'd hurt me so badly that I needed to flee New York entirely, but then after ending up in the hospital…well, I decided my sanity and well-being were more important than worrying about what he thought. So while I regret trusting him and loving him, I don't regret leaving it all behind."

Keeping his voice carefully controlled, Sam asked, "What was the other woman's name?"

"Oh, it doesn't matter." Brooke rolled onto her back

and blew out her breath. "I don't even know if she knew about me, and if she did...well, it still doesn't matter. I just never wanted my friends and family to know because it was such a humiliating lapse in judgement. And I didn't want them to think I was so weak that I'd let a broken heart ruin my chances for an award-winning journalistic career. Leaving *The Times* was bad enough."

"If you didn't want anyone to know, why did you tell me?"

She turned her head to look at him, and he felt a hot, hard pull deep inside. As if something elemental, beyond a snowstorm and a booking error, had drawn them together.

"Must be the blanket fort," Brooke murmured. "It's a safe place for telling secrets."

He shifted his gaze back to the ceiling. They both watched the firelight shadows dancing over the sheets and blankets.

"Hey." She poked him in the arm. "So far, I've given you my hideous break-up story and my terrible *small-town girl gets chewed up and spit out by the big city* story. So far, you've given me...an antipathy for cheesecake."

A humorless laugh escaped him. That was about all he had to give.

"If confessions were gold, I'd be King Midas." Brooke lifted her hands and mimed a tilting balance. "I know you have this Mr. Rochester/Heathcliff thing going on, but we're trapped in a snowstorm and we built a blanket fort. Tell me a real secret."

"Like what?"

"Like what's your *story*?" Curiosity radiated from her

suddenly. "No one in Bliss Cove knows much about you or your past. Are you secretly an undercover CIA agent?"

He managed to scoff. "No."

"Are you on the run from the law, or are you in witness protection? That's what we were all guessing at first."

"Creative, but no."

"Come on, talk to me." She touched his arm again—this time, more of a stroke than a poke. "You're an international man of mystery, as far as the town gossips are concerned."

"Meaning you?" He slanted her a narrow look. "I thought you were a reporter, not a gossip."

"I am a reporter, which means I hear everything." She arched an eyebrow. "Mrs. Higgins from the Outside Inn thinks you're a gigolo."

He huffed in amusement. "Mrs. Higgins has a vivid imagination."

"Actually, I think she was *hoping* you're a gigolo, but don't tell her I said that." She rearranged the pillows behind her head. "She really buckled down on that speculation when she saw you with Whistling Dixie lady."

Sam scratched his head, both baffled and still amused. "Still not getting the whistling reference."

"Oh." She turned and rested her head on her hand. "So Mrs. Higgins was over in Glendale shopping one day last fall. She went into the Heavenly Café for a chai latte and a lemon pound cake...she loves their pound cake...and she saw you sitting with a woman whom she described as *a brunette knockout with a natural rack*. Her words, not mine, though clearly it was a compliment. Then she said you and the knockout 'weren't just whistling Dixie.' And since no one in Bliss Cove knows anything about your sex...er, I mean your love life, there was all this speculation about your relationship with her."

"For the record, I've never whistled Dixie in my life, with or without a woman."

"Good to know." She raised her eyebrows. "So who was she?"

Though Sam had known a number of knockout brunettes in his lifetime, his agent was the only one who'd fly out from New York to visit him. Not that he could tell Brooke the details of their relationship, though again, part of him wanted to.

"Lynette," he said. "She's just a friend."

"Hmm." Skepticism creased her forehead. "What about the *not whistling Dixie*?"

"No idea. I might have given Lynette a hug and a kiss on the cheek when she arrived. Does that count as not whistling Dixie?"

"I'm not exactly sure." Brooke pursed her lips in thought. "For Mrs. Higgins, probably. I think the rest of us were imagining something a lot more salacious."

"Sorry to disappoint."

"I'm not disappointed." With a little shrug, she reached down and tugged a flowered blanket around her legs before settling back down. "What's Lynette's favorite food?"

"I have no idea."

Their eyes met. A current of heat shot through the air. She was lying with her head on a purple pillow, her long brown hair spread out like silk. He curled his hand into a fist, fighting the urge to run his fingers through all those thick strands.

"You knew my favorite food," she murmured.

"Like I said…lucky guess."

"I'll bet."

A slight smile curved her mouth. The firelight created a reddish glow on her pale skin. Her soft, luscious body made him want to cuddle her, strip her naked, and devour her all at the same time. Before he could give in to one of those urges —or all three—he pushed himself upright. "I'll get out of here so you can sleep."

"You're going to end up in serious pain if you try and sleep on the sofa again." She grabbed one of the pillows. "You can sleep here. There's plenty of room, even with your…er, size."

Of all the bad ideas Sam had heard in his life, this one topped the list. He pushed aside the blankets hanging beside him. "Not necessary, but thanks. Go to sleep."

"I don't think I'll be able to sleep knowing you're so uncomfortable."

"Give it a shot."

"Sam." She clucked her tongue. "I know you're trying to be chivalrous, but I'm not a princess. In fact, I sleep like a hibernating bear. Nothing can wake me up. Plus, this bed is the size of an ocean liner, so I promise there won't be any physical contact. Now lie down and go to sleep."

He groaned inwardly. "If I don't, you're going to threaten karaoke, aren't you?"

"Worse." She narrowed her eyes. "*Opera* karaoke."

"You are ruthless."

"That's why I'm a good reporter."

He studied her for a second, struck by the contrast between her cute, chirpy personality and her dogged journalistic side. Before he could give in to his curiosity with more questions, he lay back down.

"Good night." Brooke wiggled around getting comfortable.

Even with his eyes closed, he was acutely aware of every miniscule movement. He could picture her breasts swaying under her thin shirt. Her thick hair brushed against his arm. Her hip bumped his.

Snapping his eyes open, he grabbed more pillows and jammed them into the space between them.

She twisted to look over her shoulder at him. "What are you doing?"

"Building a wall." He shoved another pillow down by their legs.

"What for?"

"To separate your side from my side." He pushed the last pillow into the space between their heads and stretched out on his back. Now they were totally blocked off. He couldn't even see her.

He could still smell her, though. He didn't eat a lot of sugar, but her sweet scent was making him crave berries and cream. An unbidden image flashed into his head of Brooke slipping a cream-coated strawberry into her mouth, closing her full red lips around the red fruit and—

Blocking the image, he cracked his knuckles and forced his thoughts to the NFL playoffs.

"That's a bad habit." Brooke's face appeared over the pillow wall, a crease marring her smooth forehead. "It can lead to arthritis."

She actually looked concerned about the possibility of him developing arthritis twenty years from now.

He turned away from her. "Good night."

"Night."

The bed jostled.

"Brooke."

"Yes?"

"I don't believe in fate and all that crap." His jaw muscles tightened. "But there's no way that shithead was ever meant to be your epic romance. He didn't come close to deserving you."

She was silent for a long time. Then her hand touched his shoulder. "Thank you."

He heard every single one of her movements as she lay back down and settled into her nest. There was something damned wrong with a guy who'd callously throw away everything Brooke was willing to give. Who'd hurt her to the core.

Some people would turn hard and bitter after that. Not Brooke. She'd just picked up the broken pieces and got on with it.

He almost wished he'd been able to do the same thing.

CHAPTER 8

*a*s Brooke pulled herself from a heavy sleep, she dreamily thought she was in nesting *heaven*. She was surrounded by soft, fluffy pillows and cocooned in blankets, and her body was snuggled right up against an unbearably warm, strong—

Her eyes flew open.

Oh my god.

The pillows between them had gotten totally askew. And despite her assurances last night that she and Sam would have no physical contact whatsoever, she'd scooched across the mattress and was now half—no, *mostly*—sprawled on top of him like a kraken clinging to a Spanish ship.

His T-shirt had ridden up at the waist, exposing the ladder-like muscles of his abdomen. A tempting trail of hair disappeared beneath the waistband of his drawstring pajama pants. Her arms were flung out to the sides and her messy hair was spread over his face.

Worse, one of her legs was wedged between his thighs, and her left hand was smack dab on his—

A gasp caught in her throat. Her fingers twitched.

Was that...was he...

Her heart stopped and started again. If Elvis himself had appeared right in front of her that very instant, she wouldn't have been able to tear her hand away from Sam's groin.

Because...

Wow.

Heat rose to her throat. Her fingers twitched again, a little more inquisitively this time.

Oh, this was so wrong of her. Based on the deep, rhythmic movement of Sam's powerful chest against her breasts, he was still asleep. If she moved slowly, she could disentangle herself from him and move back to her own side of the bed without waking him.

Not that she was in any hurry to leave his incredible warmth.

"Unless you take your hand off me, this is only going to end one way." Sam's deep voice suddenly rumbled through him. "Much as I'd enjoy that, it would complicate things more than we'd like."

With a gasp, Brooke yanked herself away from him and bolted back to the other side of the bed. "I am *so* sorry."

He chuckled, though his expression was strained. "So am I. Don't take it personally."

She blinked. She rather *wanted* to take it personally.

"I mean, I..." Swallowing hard, she tucked a lock of hair behind her ear. "I'm sorry for sprawling over you like that after I was the one who said—"

"Brooke." He held up his hand to stop her. His jaw tightened. "Could you give me a second?"

"A sec...oh!" A blush fired her cheeks, and she practi-

95

cally dove toward the blanket wall. "Of course. I'm so sorry. I'll leave you to your own devices...I mean, to your own... er, I'm just going to make some coffee."

She scrambled out of the fort as fast as she could. Grayish morning light shone through the windows. She was quivering from the inside out, her legs shaky and her core pulsing. She hurried to the bathroom and splashed cold water on her face.

She needed to get a grip, and not the sexy kind. She'd learned the hard way that physical attraction was shallow and not to be trusted. She wanted to be attracted to a potential boyfriend, of course, but not at the expense of trustworthiness, loyalty, and true, devoted *romance*.

Sam may have awakened all her latent desires, but she couldn't get so blinded by her erotic urges that she forgot her goals for the new year or her vow that she'd prioritize an emotional and intellectual connection with a man over physical attraction.

Then again, it wasn't as if she wanted a relationship right now anyway, regardless of the "connection." She was starting *her* future, wherever that might lead her. It was a time of immense change and possibilities. Admitting her deep attraction to Sam didn't automatically translate to a *relationship*.

Indulging in that attraction wouldn't, either.

After using the bathroom, she went into the kitchen to start the coffee. The blanket fort door opened, and Sam emerged—a gorgeous specimen of rumpled, unshaven man with messy hair and his T-shirt still exposing an inch of firm, tanned flesh.

A quick glance downward assured Brooke that the other situation appeared to be somewhat contained.

More's the pity.

"Coffee will be ready in about five minutes," she said in an over-bright voice.

He grunted and strode to the bathroom.

Brooke busied herself making eggs and unwrapping a package of blueberry muffins. Only when Sam came out and walked to the window did she realize something had shifted outside, like the air itself had grown quiet.

"Did it stop snowing?" She put down the muffins and hurried to his side. "Is the storm over?"

"Looks like it." He rubbed away a patch of condensation on the glass and peered outside. "It's still snowing, but the sun is starting to break through."

Sure enough, the world was covered in a thick, pristine coating of snow. The tall pines looked as if they'd been frosted, and faint sunlight glittered on the treetops.

"It's beautiful," she breathed.

Sam moved away from the window. "I'll call the ranger station."

As he twisted the dials and spoke through the crackly static, Brooke returned to the kitchen to finish making breakfast. She overheard the ranger telling Sam they were dealing with power outages and fallen tree branches and to expect the road to be cleared tomorrow morning or early afternoon.

"It's New Year's Eve." She set the muffins and coffee on the table. She'd thought she might feel a little sad that she wasn't spending this year celebrating with her friends and family, but that had been when she'd expected she would be alone. Instead, she was trapped in a cabin with a man who was making her increasingly *zingy* both inside and out.

"What do you usually do for New Year's Eve?" She sat down and pushed the muffins toward him.

"Nothing." He pulled out a chair and sat opposite her.

"Nothing?" She blinked. "No parties or traditions or anything?"

He reached for his coffee and shook his head. "I don't celebrate holidays."

"You don't celebrate holidays?"

"I don't like holidays."

"You don't *like* holidays?"

He shot her a mild frown. "Never heard anyone turn so many statements into questions."

"I'm turning statements into questions?"

He laughed, and the deep, rumbling sound spread a pleasant warmth through her belly.

"Really, what's with the dislike of holidays?" she asked. "Were you traumatized by Santa or the Easter Bunny when you were a kid?"

He bit into a muffin. "Just never celebrated them much."

She recalled his confession that he'd been alone a lot when he was younger. Sorrow collected in her chest. The bits and pieces of himself he'd given her over the past day and a half were like tempting little water droplets falling into a bucket. She was increasingly thirsty for more.

She passed him the eggs. "Well, given that Bliss Cove celebrates everything from artichokes to Valentine's Day, moving there must have been a shock to your system."

"Not so much." He shook his head. "I like all the festivals. Good food."

"I noticed you like food." She mashed her eggs with her fork, wishing she could think of a way to ask him more about himself without being afraid he would shut down. "Hey, let's go outside later. I brought my camera, and I'd love to take some pictures."

He slanted his gaze to his computer. "You go ahead. I need to work."

"I'm sure payroll can wait, considering you have one employee." She finished off her eggs. "What else do you need to do?"

"Other stuff."

"What *stuff*?"

A sigh of exasperation escaped him. "Bookkeeping."

"Well, it's not quite tax season yet, so I think you have time."

He muttered something under his breath and shoved to his feet. "I'll go outside with you for an hour. No longer.""

"Great. Maybe the fresh air will improve your mood."

He waved her out of the kitchen so he could do the dishes. Brooke took a quick shower and dressed in jeans and snowpants. After Sam went into the bathroom to get ready, she tried very hard not to imagine what he looked like naked.

When he emerged, her heart did its usual bump up against her ribs. His faded jeans molded to his long legs. His T-shirt, washed so many times it had faded to light blue, clung to his muscular shoulders and chest as if it had been made just for him.

How the heck did a crossword-puzzle-doing bookstore owner get such a superhero body?

She'd slept with this man—literally. In the past two days, despite having minimal interactions with him since he'd moved to Bliss Cove, she'd pressed her body against his. She'd wrapped her arms around his neck.

She'd inhaled lungfuls of his delicious, wind-and-rain scent. She'd confessed her biggest failure to him with an innate knowledge that he wouldn't judge her. She'd started to go beyond being intrigued by him to actually...*liking him*.

"Ready?" He pulled open the back door and stepped aside to wait for her.

Brooke retrieved her camera from her suitcase, and they stomped out into the snow.

"It's like a whole other world." She breathed in the crisp air, awed by the untouched beauty and complete silence. "I've never been a person who needs to be alone much, but a place like this makes me see the appeal of solitude."

She started snapping pictures of the snow-covered trees, the smoke curling from the chimney, the mountains silhouetted against the gray sky.

She convinced Sam they could still have fun, and they spent an industrious hour packing snow and gathering sticks and rocks to craft a lopsided, grinning snowman. She scattered dry oatmeal for the birds, Sam cleared a path to the woodbin, and they scraped away the ice that had crusted around the windows.

By the time they went back into the cabin, Brooke was sweaty and pleasantly tired. As she closed the door, the wind gusted against the fire. The blanket fort swayed. After hanging her coat up, she tossed a log in the fireplace and prodded it with the poker until the bark caught flame.

"Instead of coffee, let's have hot cocoa." She straightened the blanket walls of the fort. "It goes great with animal crackers."

Sam started toward the kitchen. Setting the poker down, she caught sight of several typewritten papers scattered on the floor. She bent to pick them up, and her gaze fell on the lines typed in the center of the first page.

She gasped.

CHAPTER 9

Sam looked up sharply at Brooke's quick intake of breath. His heart stuttered. She was standing near the blanket fort, staring at a sheaf of papers in her hand.

His *manuscript pages.*

"Don't bother with those." He strode quickly toward her. "I'll deal with them."

She was still staring at the title page, which prominently displayed the words *Tripwire: A John Kane Novel by Sam Harris.*

Brooke lifted her head, her eyes widening. "Sam Harris? Is this *you*?"

A rock fell in the pit of his stomach. He searched his brain frantically for an explanation, and all he could manage was, "The…um, I'm a copyeditor."

As if she'd believe that.

She looked at the title and author name again, then suddenly smacked him on the arm with the papers. "This is your secret, isn't it? You're Sam freaking Harris."

No one had ever said that to him before because no one knew.

"You do know that Bliss Cove residents have been speculating about more than just your love life." Brooke shook her head in disbelief. "You're in witness protection, you're a double agent. Aria thinks you're the royal prince of a small European country in disguise. Darker imaginations have wondered if you're everything from a serial killer to a money launderer. But I swear, not a single person has wondered if you're secretly the famous author of an internationally best-selling series of thriller novels."

Sam tried not to wince at the effusive description. "I'm not—"

"No *wonder* you're such a recluse!" Brooke began pacing, her whole face lighting up with sudden delight. "This is why you keep such weird hours at the bookstore, isn't it? You're always going off to write. And why you never take part in any town events or date anyone. When I started my Brooke's Books column at *The Gazette*, I got the whole *'Who is Sam Harris?'* package from your publisher before I reviewed *Stone Cold*…favorably, I might add…and it's like you're a combination of Lemony Snicket and JD Salinger with the anonymity and mystery."

She paused to take a breath. "I mean, it's a huge part of your publisher's marketing campaign, right? You never do book tours or in-person interviews, your fan groups are always speculating about who you really are…and I remember once your publisher was going to do this whole 'The Revelation of Sam Harris' thing, but for whatever reason, they scrapped it. Why did they do that?"

"The executives got cold feet." He collected the rest of

the papers from the floor. "They were worried if people knew the truth, they'd lose interest in my books. So they wanted to keep the mystery going."

"And the revelation of your secret would be a huge coup." She nodded vigorously. "If that rumor ever started in Bliss Cove, it would totally make its way to *The Gazette* staff."

Sam tightened his jaw. That right there was the reason he'd avoided her for all these months.

He didn't care if people knew he was "an author," but if people discovered he was *Sam Harris*, his publisher's entire marking strategy would collapse. He was a good writer, but he also knew the value of a smart publicity campaign, and this one had been unexpectedly successful.

For ten years, only three people had known his true identity—his agent, his editor, and his lawyer. He'd intended just to be a pseudonymous author, but early in his career, a reporter had nosed around trying unsuccessfully to get an interview with him.

The reporter had then published a scathing article about his efforts to communicate with the "pretentious and ungrateful Sam Harris," which the publishing marketing team had spun into a campaign about the "mysterious and enigmatic Sam Harris."

The mystery had suited the tone of his books, and speculation had quickly taken root in fan groups and with reviewers. Soon the "Who is Sam Harris?" campaign had become part of both the overall marketing and his public persona. With every new release, the gossip and speculation rose to the surface again, fueling both sales and his popularity.

Though at first he'd thought the whole thing was silly,

he'd come to highly value the anonymity and subsequent privacy. He'd been able to travel, to visit dozens of cities and towns, to not be tied to anyone or anything. He'd never had to answer questions about his family or why he rarely saw his brother anymore.

After ten years, no one had discovered Sam Harris was really Sam Donovan—which was saying something in a world so connected by technology. Not for anything did he want to give up his anonymity.

"This is the granddaddy of all secrets, Sam." Brooke waved the title page. "I'm a *fan* of your work. I've read the first five John Kane books. *Huntsman* was probably my favorite. I cried when Elijah died after he and John rescued Patricia...I didn't see that coming from a mile away."

She spread her hand over the manuscript. "That's just one of the things that makes you such an amazing author, the way you throw these curveballs that keep the reader in such suspense. And yet everything is so well thought-out, like how John's father ended up marrying the woman from the... sorry for fawning, but I love good books."

Sam cleared his throat. Discomfort needled him. He didn't mind hearing such praise from Brooke—in fact, he liked it a lot—but he'd hated the idea of being in the spotlight the way his brother was. Unlike Lincoln, who'd never hidden behind another name, the mystery of Sam Harris had protected him.

"I appreciate that, thanks."

"That friend of yours...the Whistling Dixie woman..." Brooke's eyes narrowed slightly. "Was she your editor?"

Her reporter nose was working overtime now. Sam

sighed. "That was Lynette Hanover, my agent. She was visiting from New York last fall."

"Ah." She nodded as if that made perfect sense. "Where did you live before you came to Bliss Cove? Did you move there because you wanted a quiet place to write?"

"I'd rather not get into it." His tone came out colder than he'd intended.

Brooke drew back, and her eyes clouded over. Smothering his guilt, Sam shoved the manuscript into his backpack and zipped it up.

"You came here to work." She eyed his laptop. "Are you on a deadline?"

With a short nod, he glanced at the clock on the wall. Irritation speared him. He didn't have a minute to spare if he was going to make his deadline, but he'd been letting himself get distracted by Brooke with her blanket forts and snuggling.

Hell, he'd been *enjoying* it. Way too much.

"Yeah, I need to get some work done," he muttered.

"Okay." She indicated the table. "I'll just...um, stay over here so you can write in peace."

He groaned inwardly. She must think he was a jerk, which wouldn't be far from the truth. "Look, about the Sam Harris thing..."

"I know, I'm not supposed to know the truth." She started toward the kitchen. "I won't tell anyone, even if this is the biggest news story Bliss Cove has had since the high-school football team won the regional championships."

Sam sank into the chair and rested his elbows on his thighs. A headache pressed against his temples. He knew Brooke wouldn't intentionally tell anyone, but things had a way of slipping out. He didn't care how the revelation would affect his career—but he dreaded the idea of people digging up his family history and reviving all the shitty gossip.

"You don't believe me." She studied him, wariness rising to her eyes. "I'm a reporter, but I don't compromise my integrity or sell people out for the sake of a story."

Of course she didn't. Reporter or not, Brooke was...*good*. Too good for *The New York Times*. She was the hometown girl whose positivity and charm deserved a much better place in the world.

"I would never do that to you," she added.

Sam pushed to his feet and went to put his boots and parka back on. "I'm going to shovel some more."

"It's snowing again." She gestured to the window. "Besides, you can't go anywhere."

He grabbed the shovel and walked out the front door. Even if he couldn't leave, he needed as much distance from her as he could get.

He no longer thought he was in trouble. He knew he was.

CHAPTER 10

*S**am Harris.***

Brooke peered through the front window at Sam shoveling through the snow to his truck, like he was digging an escape route out of Alcatraz. Though the snowfall had started up again, it was much lighter than before.

She took a swallow of lemon-cayenne tea, feeling a flush heat her cheeks. She'd landed in the arms of an international bestselling author. She'd coerced him into helping her make a blanket fort. She'd accosted him in his sleep. She'd put her hand on his groin and hadn't exactly been in a hurry to take it away.

It might have been embarrassing, if her knowledge of Sam the man hadn't superseded her knowledge of Sam the author. Though the pieces of the puzzle fit together—it made perfect sense that he'd fiercely guard his privacy—she had many more questions.

Sam might have been a famous author, but what was *his* story? Where was his family? Why had he come to Bliss Cove?

Aside from needing to maintain his anonymity, she could guess at the answer to the last question. Due to the natural beauty and slow-paced lifestyle, her hometown had been a longtime haven for creative types, and it had even housed a colony for artists and writers at the beginning of the twentieth century.

So it wasn't difficult to believe that Sam had come to Bliss Cove to write—Brooke imagined an author could live wherever he or she chose—but what about *him*? Was he planning to stay indefinitely or move on as soon as he finished his next book?

Not that any of it was her business—nor did Sam want it to be. He was clearly frustrated by the fact that she'd inadvertently discovered his secret, and she had no intention of annoying him further by sniffing around for more information.

She sat at the table with her notebook. To prevent her mind from overflowing with all her questions and no answers, she forced herself to concentrate on her list of story ideas for Michael.

Romance for the Old Soul.

Thirty is the New Twenty-One.

What You Can Learn from a Sea Lion.

Sam came back in the front door, stomping snow off his boots and shaking it from his parka. Snowflakes dusted his dark hair, and his face was reddened from the cold. He hung his parka on the coat rack and shoved his boots off before going to the kitchen.

Brooke's heart thumped as the air itself seemed to part to make way for him. She imagined he spent a ton of time sitting in front of the computer, but one wouldn't know that from looking at him. He had the body of a star athlete and the energy of an outdoorsman who needed to move.

He poured hot water into a mug and added a packet of instant coffee. He glanced up and caught her gaze. "Want some?"

"No, but thanks for asking."

Picking up his mug, he walked past her to the sofa. He sat down and opened his laptop. After scrolling, he frowned darkly at the screen.

Wariness gripped her. She wanted him to trust her. She also wanted to know more about him, which unfortunately was exactly the thing that would make him *not* trust her.

"I do believe you," he muttered.

She blinked. "About?"

"You'd never sell someone out for a story." He hit a button on his keyboard, and the screen cast shadows and light over his strong features. "I know you'd never tell anyone I'm a writer. That was never an issue."

Relief flooded her, easing the tension in her shoulders. "Thank you."

He nodded, his attention still on his computer. Brooke turned back to her notebook. She suppressed the thousands of questions bubbling up inside her about how he became an author, what he'd done before that, everything about *him*.

So much had happened between them in such a short time that now they could use a few hours to refocus on their reasons for being at the cabin in the first place. Blanket forts and snowmen aside, they both had work to do.

For the next hour, they sat in a compatible silence broken only by the occasional tap of Sam's keyboard and the scratch of Brooke's pen.

Books that Changed My Life.

Soup: The Taste of Home.

Fear is Not Your Friend.

Sam expelled his breath in a long rush and drummed his fingers on the table. Tuning the noise out, Brooke focused on her list.

My Week at a Buddhist Retreat.

Birding – What's the Appeal?

He pushed his laptop aside and stood. He strode to the fire and poked at the flames, then added another log. He walked to the window, cracked his knuckles, returned to the radio, and fiddled with the knobs.

Brooke wrote, *The Art of the Blanket Fort.*

"Station twenty?" Sam shouted into the mic. "Do you read me?"

He turned up the volume, and a flood of static filled the room. She listed a few names of psychologists as possible expert sources about birding.

After trying for another five minutes to reach the ranger station, Sam put the mic down. He leafed through the old paperbacks, opened the board games to poke at the contents, and shook a deck of cards into his hands. Then he wandered around shuffling the cards.

What about stories of women who'd changed their lives after the age of fifty? Or families who'd decided to take their kids and start traveling full-time? People who took a leap of faith without knowing if there would be a safety net.

Sam stopped pacing, still shuffling the cards. "What're you working on?"

"My freelance story ideas." Her gaze was drawn unwillingly to his hands, which were large and dexterous. The cards almost danced in his capable grip. He flexed his fingers with unconscious effort, letting the cards fall in a perfect arc before straightening them with a flick of his palms.

What would his hands feel like on her bare skin?

The thought bloomed hot and hard. A shiver raced over her.

Determinedly, she positioned her pen over the paper. *Dating the Zodiac Way.*

With a mutter, Sam tossed the cards on the shelf and walked to the kitchen. He opened the fridge. Bowls and spoons clinked, cabinet doors slammed, water ran, and the microwave whirred. Foil crinkled as he tore open a bag of chips.

Pacing from the kitchen to the door and back again—which for him was all of five strides—he crunched noisily through handfuls of chips.

Brooke took a sip of tea. Maybe she could talk to Destiny about an article on how to incorporate wellness practices into a daily routine. Or what about rune casting? That had a mystical history extending back to the druids or something.

Sam shoved another handful of chips into his mouth.

She wrote, *Self-Soothing Techniques for Riled-up Men.*

"How can you just sit there?" he suddenly thundered.

Brooke looked up. "I'm not just sitting here. I'm working."

"On what?"

"I told you, my freelance ideas." She set her pen down with a slight frown.

"There's a blizzard out there." He flung his arm toward the window.

"Yes, I know. It's eased up quite a bit, though."

"You shouldn't have come up here alone."

"Well, clearly I didn't know there was going to be a blizzard."

"*Clearly.*" He brushed crumbs from his shirt onto the floor and grabbed another handful of chips.

Brooke folded her arms. "Would you like to tell me what's wrong?"

"Nothing's wrong."

"Is it your book?" She tried another angle. "What's *Trip-wire* about?"

"It's the first book in a new trilogy. I'm not telling you what it's about."

"Is that because you don't know yet?"

His scowl deepened. "What makes you say that?"

"Writers *write*. They don't shuffle cards and eat chips by the handful."

"How the hell do you know what writers do?"

"In case you forgot, reporters *are* writers." She reached for her tea. "And the reason I've never missed a deadline, not even when I was working at *The New York Times*, is because I sit down and *write* the story."

"Writing a novel is a lot different than writing a news article," Sam retorted.

"Maybe so, but at the end of the day, you have to get the words on the page, right? Eating and pacing like a caged tiger isn't going to get the job done."

With an impatient grumble, he tossed the chip bag onto the kitchen counter and stalked back to the living room.

"I've never missed a deadline either. And no way in hell am I going to miss this one because of a storyline I didn't want to write in the first place."

She blinked. Was that the real reason he'd come to the cabin—because he was having trouble with his story?

She found the thought hard to believe. His books were fast-paced genre thrillers with an underlying structure so strong he could make the reader believe anything. His world-building was immersive, his plots intricate but not convo-luted, and his characters lived and breathed. You didn't read a Sam Harris novel—you *experienced* it.

Most of the time, anyway. Brooke hadn't loved Sam's recent books as much as she had the start of the John Kane series. Something was missing, but she hadn't pinpointed what it was.

"What…" She approached cautiously, as if he might leap up and bite her. "What's the storyline?"

Frustration tensed his every muscle as he flopped back down on the sofa. For an instant, she didn't think he was going to answer. When he spoke, he seemed to be talking to himself rather than her. "The romance."

"Er…what now?"

"The *romance*." He repeated the word as if it were a curse.

Brooke shook her head. "Between John and Patricia?"

"That's the one." He rubbed his hands over his face. "Word on the street…and from my editor and reviewers…is that the romance is badly written and underdeveloped. Which is ironic since I'd never intended to write a romance into any of my novels."

"So why did you?"

"Pressure." He twisted his mouth. "And popular demand. After the series started taking off, everyone—my publisher, my editor, my readers, the reviewers—started clamoring for John Kane to find a romantic interest. Finally, I caved and wrote in Patricia's character, along with an arc leading them to marriage. That's three books from now."

A puzzle piece snapped together in Brooke's mind. John and Patricia's relationship. *That* was the weak spot in Sam's recent novels.

"What do you have to do?" she asked.

"Fix it." He stared at the laptop screen. "Apparently the criticism is taking its toll. I've been told the romance is bringing the whole series down."

"Is your editor helping you?"

"I want him to be hands-off." Sam frowned at his computer. "I don't like feedback until I send him the final draft."

Brooke took another step closer and risked a glance at his laptop screen. A blank page was pulled up.

"Based on the card shuffling and potato-chip eating, I'm going to guess your improvement of the romance isn't going all that well," she ventured.

He let out a humorless laugh. "Your guess would be correct. Add to the evidence file the fact that I'm even telling you about this. I must already be going stir-crazy."

"Or you actually trust me."

He looked up sharply. Their gazes collided with a hot spark. Brooke's pulse accelerated. Curling her fingers into her palms, she sat slowly in the easy chair.

Though Sam had always made her feel off-balance, nervous, and sometimes even a little prickly, something inside her responded to his frustration. She knew instinctively that he wasn't the kind of man who asked for help—which was probably part of the reason he stayed away from people. If you didn't get close to anyone, you didn't have to rely on them.

"I can help you." The offer came out in one breath, and her heart knocked anxiously against her ribs.

He narrowed his eyes. "With what?"

"John and Patricia's romance." Her throat went dry. She darted her tongue out to lick her lips and indicated the stack of romances on the table. "I've been reading romances since I was thirteen. I still read at least one or two a week. I've written articles about the romance industry, and when I was working for *The Wisconsin State Journal*, I did a profile piece on a local bestselling romance novelist. I'm exceedingly familiar with the arc of a romance, all the different plot points that make up a good love story, how to show that your characters are falling in love. I can help you make the romance better."

Though Sam didn't respond, he didn't look as if he were about to fall off the sofa laughing. He was watching her, his forehead creased.

"Why would you do that?" he finally asked.

"Have you ever heard Destiny say there are no coincidences? I think this is the reason you and I ended up in this cabin together."

With a huffed groan, he lowered his head and pinched the bridge of his nose between his thumb and forefinger.

Okay, she couldn't do the "fates and furies" thing with him.

She reached out and grabbed his arm. Her breath caught

at the sensation of his warm, muscled forearm under her palm. His body heat burned clear through his sweatshirt sleeve.

"My point is that I *know* romance." She tightened her grip. "You *know* I know romance. Not only have I read a metric ton of romance novels, I'm the chair of the Valentine's Day Festival. I wrote my senior thesis on the most famous lovers in history. I've been on more bad dates than I can count, to say nothing of my lousy break-up, which means I also know exactly what comprises a *good* date and a great relationship. I've even been known to assist Destiny with her matchmaking efforts since I have a knack for divining romantic energy."

He rolled his eyes. Barely, but definitely a *roll*.

"Hey." She gave him a little shake. "I know you're a bigshot author and I'm...*not*, but I wouldn't be so quick to dismiss me, if I were you. Do you know why I didn't review the last two John Kane novels for my Brooke's Books column?"

"I suspect you're about to tell me."

"Because of John and Patricia's romance...or lack thereof." She curled her fingers into his rock-hard arm. "Do you work out? Because, really, you have the most...anyway. I totally agree with your editor and fans and whoever else is telling you that John Kane is brilliant, super sexy, and brave as hell, but he treats Patricia like a cardboard cutout rather than a *woman*.

"Which isn't really a surprise since when she's with him, she gets so...one-dimensional, you know? She doesn't react to him like a real woman would, which is no wonder considering he's such a dolt around her. And their sex scenes?

Don't get me started. People are *right*, Sam. The romance is bringing everything down when it should be lifting the story *up*."

He was silent. A muscle ticked in his jaw.

"You can't be surprised that people wanted you to bring in a romantic interest," she added. "How else were you going to have John overcome his fear of personal connections?"

Sam frowned. "Well, he adopted a dog. And there's his relationship with his grandfather."

"A dog isn't a person, and he and his grandfather don't like each other. John needs someone to love who loves him in return."

"You mean a One True Love?" His tone held just enough derision to spark her irritation.

"Patricia *could* be his One True Love, if he'd start treating her like an actual swoon-worthy man should."

He snapped his eyebrows together. "A *what* man?"

"A man who's worthy of swooning over," Brooke explained. "Basically, a romance hero."

"Like your ideal man, who is apparently perfect."

Brooke slowly shook her head. She was beginning to think her definition of an "ideal man" rather inexplicably involved a grumpy, unshaven thriller-writer-turned-book-store-owner who indulged her blanket-fort obsession and whose glowering looks made her toes tingle.

"Sam." She took a breath, trying to pull them both back to the subject at hand. "I can help you with John and Patricia's story. If there were a Romance Expert job, I would be a highly qualified candidate."

"Being an expert on romance doesn't make you an expert on novel writing."

"Which is why *you're* writing the novel," she persisted. "I might not write fiction, but I know good writing when I read it. I can help you."

He narrowed his eyes. "What do you want in return?"

For a moment, the question startled her. "Nothing."

"Nothing?"

"Help doesn't have to be reciprocal."

He sat back, his mouth turning downward. "I don't take something for nothing. Ever."

Brooke experienced a stab of sorrow over the idea that he was more accustomed to transactions rather than kindness. But instead of turning her down, he was moving slowly toward a negotiation. And while she *would* help him for nothing, she wasn't a fool.

"Okay." She pursed her lips. "You can pay me."

He lifted his eyebrows. "Pay you."

"We can first do a trial run. If you think my advice is working, then we can continue the arrangement as a business transaction. If not, we'll just part ways."

"How much do you want?"

"Your call." She twisted a loose thread of her T-shirt around her finger. "I'm not getting my *Gazette* salary anymore, and I haven't yet had any other opportunities. And obviously I can't live on air, so if you feel you need to reciprocate, then you can pay me what you think my advice is worth."

Maybe he'd even pay her enough to help offset the costs of attending the Freelancer's Convention in New York. If they were even out of here by then.

Sam shifted his gaze to the window. She could almost see the cogs and wheels turning around in his razor-sharp mind.

"I'm not going to tell anyone your secret." She rubbed her hands over her thighs, not sure if she could articulate all the reasons she needed *proof* that she was moving forward toward self-sufficiency and independence. "But if it helps, you're the only person who knows I've been rejected from a few dozen jobs already. No one...not my family or my friends, not even Aria...knows that I've even applied anywhere yet. Like I said, I need to have something to show people. So you and I both have good reasons to keep this arrangement a secret."

With a mutter, he pushed to his feet and stalked to the window. Tension lined his shoulders. Silence stretched between them. Brooke tapped her foot, her nerves jittery.

"All right." He turned, folding his arms over his chest. "We can work together for a day or two as a trial period."

"Deal!" Excitement flared through her, and she smiled so widely that her cheeks hurt. "During the trial, I'll give you unlimited sessions about romance. Fictional, that is."

"Why unlimited?"

"Given the fact that you had John take Patricia on a fishing trip *date* where he showed her how to *gut a trout*..." Brooke shook her head in remembered despair. "We have a lot of work to do."

CHAPTER 11

welve hours ago, he'd woken up to the torturous pleasure of Brooke's touch. Her hand hadn't just been resting on his groin, either. No, god help him, her fingers had been curving tentatively around his shaft, practically squeezing—

A groan collected in his chest. He smothered yet another painful surge of lust.

This was such a fucking mistake.

He shuffled the deck of cards again. His physical need for Brooke aside, he was a solitary writer. He didn't even talk about his process to his editor. And here he'd just agreed to let a reporter help him with a story arc.

A reporter whose light, curious touch was burned into him like a brand. Why was he prolonging the torture by agreeing to let her teach him about "romance"?

Because his deadline was looming like a tsunami, and he'd never been this *stuck* before. Brooke was throwing him a lifeline. He wasn't convinced she could pull him out of the quicksand, but he had to let her try.

Tossing the cards aside, he went to stoke the fire. The blanket fort was still in the way, though he saw no good reason to disassemble it yet.

Brooke made them a dinner of microwaved pizza, which she ate at the table and he ate standing in the kitchen. Then she turned to a new page in her notebook and began writing industriously.

A *Romance Expert*.

What the hell did that mean? Okay, so maybe she was into hearts and flowers and all that kind of stuff—which he admittedly knew nothing about—but what was with her eye-rolling over his sex scenes?

He wasn't romantic, but he sure as hell knew how to turn up the heat in the bedroom. In fact, sex and writing were the only two things he'd ever been entirely confident about. He just hadn't done a great job of putting the two together. He'd never had to before now.

When he'd submitted his first Sam Harris manuscript ten years ago, he'd known what his strengths and weaknesses were. He'd written his novels focusing on his strengths—strong characters, solid action scenes, unexpected plot twists.

He'd intended for his protagonist, John Kane, to remain a solitary, crime-fighting, ex-CIA agent with no ties to a specific place or person. Unfortunately, the publishing machine had insisted that change. While Sam could appreciate the challenge for his character, he had little faith in his ability to fix the "weak link" in his writing.

Which meant Brooke might be his only hope.

She looked up, catching his stare. His heart thudded. He jerked his chin toward her notebook. "Article brainstorm?"

"What?" She glanced at her pages. "Oh, no. I was just

writing down some ideas for my romance tutorial. If you want to get started, I'm ready when you are."

Great.

Despite his reluctance, he was curious about what, exactly, she had to "teach him" about romance. He also wanted to try and figure out how she'd managed to hold on to even the idea of love and romance after having been betrayed so badly.

Because she's Sunny Side Up.

Brooke Castle was probably the only woman in the world—the only woman Sam knew—who could seamlessly put back together the shattered pieces of her romance illusion and still believe in it with her whole heart.

He pulled a chair away from the table and sat across from her, folding his arms.

"Go ahead, then." He indicated her notebook. "Start."

"I have your books downloaded onto my tablet." Brooke reached into a canvas bag beside the table. She took out a small tablet and powered it up, then scrolled through an e-reader app.

Her forehead furrowed with concentration. "Okay, so I really loved the whole arc of the John Kane story and how he infiltrates the mafia to recover the stolen coin...you did such a brilliant job of showing him make the shift from working for himself to helping others. But honestly, that made it so much more disappointing when he texts Patricia to meet him at O'Grady's Pub."

Sam frowned. "What's so disappointing? He wanted to get a beer and be with his girl."

"Oh my god." Brooke thunked her palm against her forehead. "Patricia hates O'Grady's! That's where she found her shitty ex-boyfriend had been taking the woman he was cheating on her with. John knew that, and not only did he not bother to *call her*, he just assumed she'd be okay with meeting him there. Then she actually shows up!"

She compressed her mouth in disapproval. "Really, Sam, Patricia has way too much backbone to just be at John's beck and call. She's a Krav Maga expert with a degree in psychology. No way would she not take issue with texting and that dank, smelly O'Grady's."

Sam rubbed his chest and sighed. "So what should John have done?"

"He should have called her because he needed to hear her voice, asked if she was busy, and then if she said no, he should have requested permission to come over."

"Requested permission?"

"Not in a dorky way, but he should have asked politely if he could come over. Then he should have asked if she'd eaten dinner, and again if she said no, he should have asked if he could bring something over."

"Don't you mean *requested permission*?"

She scowled and poked him in the arm. "I don't mean you should have written this exact scenario. My point is that John should have taken her thoughts and feelings into account instead of just assuming he knew what she wanted... which, of course, was totally wrong. He should have gone to her house with a special takeout dinner...maybe Indian food since that's her favorite...and a bottle of wine. Then he should have noticed something about her, like that she looked tired."

"Yeah, telling a woman she looks tired goes over real well."

"He should have said it in a loving tone while rubbing her shoulders, which would have been a prelude to a full massage after the Indian food and the wine."

"Sounds like a lot of work for a man who just narrowly escaped a gunfight after infiltrating the mob."

"Well, it might've gotten him a lot closer to getting laid than ordering Patricia to meet him at O'Grady's." With a huff, she slapped the tablet on the table and pushed her chair back. "That seems to be all he wants from her anyway."

"Why the hell would you think that?"

"Because he doesn't *consider her needs*, Sam." Brooke spread her arms out, a flush of indignation rising to her cheeks. "He only thinks about himself and how she can fit into his life, not how their lives can fit together. Gutting a trout on their second date? They're supposed to be One True Loves, not fishing buddies."

He barely smothered a groan. Brooke's eyes flashed.

"I know you don't believe true love exists, but for the sake of your novel, you have got to *pretend that it does*," she snapped. "What about their first kiss? You didn't even describe it."

"What's to describe?" he retorted. "It's a kiss."

"Readers want to know how it *feels*."

"It feels like a kiss."

"Do you see what your problem is here?" Brooke paced to the blanket fort and whirled back around, her arms still outstretched. "The romance isn't working because you're failing to show readers what it feels like for both John and Patricia to be attracted to each other and eventually fall in love."

She paused and clucked her tongue. "Honestly, you keep

going like this and no one is going to understand why they get married. Your readers should want to *be* either John or Patricia so they can experience all the intense emotions of lust and love. Obviously you have the talent to immerse your readers in the experience of John's world, so you just need to do that with his and Patricia's love story. That means you need to describe their feelings and senses."

Though he could see her point, he doubted his ability to do any of that well. He'd never thought he knew everything there was to know about writing, but he did know what he was *good* at writing. Feelings and senses weren't on the list.

"Okay, listen." With an impatient sigh, Brooke sifted through her stack of romance novels and plucked out a well-worn paperback with a half-naked couple embracing on the cover. "This is one of my all-time favorite romances. Here's the couple's first kiss."

She cleared her throat and read, *"He tangled his other hand in her hair and cupped the back of her neck. His grip was certain, gentle, as if he were securing her rather than holding her in place. Then he lowered his head and pressed his mouth to hers.*

"A slow, billowing sensation filled her, like molten lava flowing through her veins. Her body came alive, every nerve ending lighting up. Clouds spun in the middle of her soul.

He moved his mouth with deliberate ease over hers, urging her lips apart so he could dip his tongue inside. Her pleasure blossomed outward, filling her veins with heat. He slid his tongue over hers, nibbled at her bottom lip, and licked the corners of her mouth. It was a delicious, prolonged seduction, carrying the promise of so much more. Her whole body swayed toward him as she—"

Brooke stopped abruptly and rubbed her neck. Her cheeks were still flushed. Sam was starting to feel a little warm himself. And he experienced a stab of discomfort over how badly he wanted her to keep reading.

"Do you see what I mean?" She set the book down. "He's kissing her, but it's also about what she's *feeling*."

Sam shifted and scratched his head. "Yeah, but her feelings don't make sense. Molten lava? Clouds spinning in her soul? What does that even mean?"

"Oh my god, Mr. Bestselling Author." Brooke pressed her fingers to her temples. "It's a *metaphor*. Hasn't a kiss ever made you feel like you were lighting up? Like stars were whirling all around you? Like *the earth was moving*?"

Before he could respond—with an emphatic *"No"*—Brooke held up her hand. "Don't answer that. Given that you don't appear to have a romantic bone in your body, you wouldn't recognize that kind of emotion if it bonked you over the head. When you kiss, you're probably busy plotting how to get to second base. No offense."

He frowned. "I'm offended."

Her lips twitched. "Why, because I speak the truth?"

"Just because a romance subplot is giving me trouble doesn't mean I'm a selfish bastard about kissing. I take the lead, yeah, but I'm not always trying to get a woman's clothes off. Not at first, anyway. Not all the time," he added.

She crossed her arms, narrowing her eyes skeptically. "So on the rare occasions when you're enjoying kissing as an act in and of itself rather than a means to an end, what are you feeling?"

Sam mumbled a curse and rested his head in his hands.

"I don't dissect my feelings when I'm kissing a woman. I'm too busy *kissing her*."

"But you have to feel something besides…um, aroused."

He lifted his head. She was watching him, her eyes darker than usual. The firelight shone behind her, casting her in a golden glow. His heart thumped.

"I mean." Brooke tucked a lock of hair behind her ear. "There's physical arousal, of course, but there's also….emotional and intellectual arousal. Things that go on in your mind."

He pushed to his feet and deliberately approached her. She parted her lips to draw in a breath. He stopped in front of her, aware that he was crossing into dangerous territory but not caring all that much.

"If you tell me you're thinking about clouds and hot lava when a guy is kissing you," he said slowly, "then he's doing it all wrong."

"My point is…" Her attention drifted to his mouth. "There has to be *romance*."

"Actually, there can just be kissing."

"All right, then." She lifted her chin and nodded toward his laptop. "If you don't want to involve their feelings, then you at least need to describe the kiss itself. A woman just doesn't fall in love with a man who smashes his lips against hers. John has to have a certain *technique* that resonates with Patricia. Like a bird responding to a mating call."

She looked so serious that Sam smothered his instinctive laugh.

Brooke wasn't fooled. She *tsked* in exasperation. "A man needs to know *how* to kiss, Sam."

"You think I don't know that?"He watched the delicate muscles of her throat work with a swallow.

"Well, if one were to gauge your knowledge by reading your books, then no." She raised her dark eyebrows. "In fact, one would deduce that your kissing technique is sorely lacking."

"One would be wrong."

"An amazing kiss from a man who knows what he's doing is hard to find."

"I know how to kiss." He curled his fingers against his palms. "I could kiss you right now."

Two spots of color rose to her cheeks. "And I could be unimpressed right now."

"Challenge accepted."

He lifted his hand before he even realized what he was about to do—what he'd been wanting to do for longer than he cared to admit. In one movement, he slipped his hand around her nape and touched her mouth with his.

Though he was careful to keep the contact gentle, almost nonexistent, pleasure exploded through him like a firestorm. Her lips tasted exactly the way he'd imagined, like light, sweet things—cotton candy, meringue, whipped cream.

She inhaled in quick surprise, the back of her neck tensing. He started to pull away. She curled her hand into the front of his T-shirt and tugged him closer.

Goddamn.

Bracing one hand on the loft support behind her, he increased the pressure of his mouth. Yeah, he'd missed sex, but not until this instant did he realize he'd also missed *kissing.*

Not just any kissing either. Kissing a woman like

Brooke, who responded as if the entire world had slipped away. She threaded her fingers through his hair, parted her lips under his, and answered every press of his lips with warm eagerness.

His heart hammered. She shifted, and low murmur slipped from her throat. Her breasts brushed against his chest. Lust jolted through him. He was already getting hard, and they hadn't been kissing for more than thirty seconds.

Cupping the back of her head, he eased his tongue into her mouth. He wanted to slide his hand under her shirt to her naked breasts, to feel her body arching against his and—

He broke away, his breath rasping through his lungs. Brooke brought a hand to her lips, her skin flushed and eyes wide.

"Um…" She gave a quick shake of her head. "That was…I mean, okay, so you know how to kiss."

"So do you." He couldn't stop staring at her mouth, now reddened from the pressure of his.

Her flush deepened. "Well, it's one thing to kiss a stranger. It's totally different when you're kissing someone you love."

Her remark twisted inside him the wrong way, like a corkscrew. He couldn't stop his sudden anger over the ideas of her both seeing him as a stranger and kissing another man.

"You would know, huh?" His voice had an edge. "What about when you find out the guy you *love* is a dirtbag?"

Her eyes widened. Sam groaned. *Way to be an asshole yourself, genius.*

"Brooke…"

She held up a hand and backed toward the blanket fort. "At least I know what it feels like to be in love. Maybe that's a big part of your problem right there. You've never been in love. You can't write what you don't know."

She pivoted on her heel and ducked into the blanket fort, snapping the door closed behind her.

Sam dragged his hands over his face. He'd never bought the idea that writers had to know everything they wrote about. But he hated the idea that Brooke might be right.

CHAPTER 12

*B*rooke curled up in the blanket fort, still feeling the press of Sam's mouth against hers. She'd meant it when she'd said there was a big difference between kissing a stranger and kissing someone you love. But she hadn't known the difference would be like...*this*.

She'd once enjoyed kissing Michael, and they'd had a satisfying physical relationship, but his kisses had never made her feel so sparkly and shiny, like sun-drenched glitter. She'd never actually *experienced* all the things she'd dreamed about and imagined—her thoughts dissolving into a swell of pleasure, her knees weakening, her body humming like a plucked violin string.

She had now.

And though she'd always been aware of her physical attraction to Sam, not until the past twenty-four hours had she realized how much she liked him. She liked his dry sense of humor, his resourcefulness, his intelligence, and his willingness to go along with her ideas, even if he wouldn't have chosen them himself. She liked the way he listened. She really liked the way he kissed.

With a soft groan, she hugged her unicorn pillow and told herself not to get carried away on flights of fancy.

Aside from her crash-and-burn two years ago, she'd never had much of a struggle between her practical journalist side and her romance-loving, optimist side. Most of the time, they'd coexisted peacefully, ready to be called upon when the situation warranted.

But there was nothing remotely practical about her increasingly intense feelings for Sam—who, truth be told, was far from a "stranger." He wasn't "someone she loved" either, but he was…what the heck was he? Had these enforced circumstances turned them into friends, or was she letting her imagination get the best of her?

"Friends" didn't kiss each other with such passion, though. She hadn't wanted him to stop. She'd wanted him to keep kissing her, to slide his tongue deeper into her mouth, to tilt her head back and—

A rapping noise came from outside the fort.

"Yes?" she called.

"I'm requesting permission to enter," Sam said.

A touch of nervousness tightened her belly. "Permission granted."

The blankets parted, and he crawled in—his hair a disheveled mess, and that stubble giving his strong features a sexy, dangerous look.

Had she really once thought of him as *unkempt*? He was by no means a tailored suit and silk tie kind of man, but his rumpled look was so…*Sam*. Familiar and real.

"I'm sorry." Regret glittered in his eyes. "You're trying to help, and I'm being an ass."

"Actually, I think you're scared." Brooke moved aside to make room for him.

Letting the blankets fall shut behind him, he flopped against the pillows. "I don't get scared."

"You don't *know* you're scared." A little lightbulb went off in her head. "You're like John Kane. Tough, alone, self-sufficient, hard-working, and used to being that way. But deep down inside, you're scared of changing who you are. I'm not saying that to be mean. Believe me, I know what it's like to be scared."

He brushed his fingers across her *Courage* bracelet. "Is that why you got this?"

She nodded. "I want to be brave this year. I have to be. And honestly, I do understand why you're having trouble with John and Patricia's story. You have a process, a vision of your characters, and you're trying to wrench in a storyline that doesn't feel natural to you. You don't even believe in love. It's not much of a surprise that you're fighting it tooth and nail."

A heavy sigh escaped him. "Obviously that's not going to get the job done."

"Fighting love is often a futile endeavor." She poked him with her foot. "Just ask Romeo and Juliet."

"What's the alternative?" He slipped his hand down to her bare foot, his warm fingers settling on her toes. "Surrender?"

"I don't think we should surrender to love." Brooke pulled her knees up to her chest, her breath escaping as he ran his forefinger over her big toe. "Surrendering is like giving up. Throwing in the towel. We should *win* love. Achieve it. We should fall in love with being in love."

He smiled faintly and wrapped his hand around the top of her foot. "I'll confess that I've always liked you. But I didn't know before this weekend that I also admire you."

Despite a little internal *squee* at the acknowledgement that he liked her, Brooke kept her voice controlled as she asked, "Admire? Really?"

"Yeah." He spread his hand out as if he wanted to encompass everything she was. "You have this resiliency... not just with your optimism, but the way you hold on to what you believe in. Even though that asshole messed with you, you still have this perfect vision of love and romance."

"It's not just a vision." She lifted her shoulders. "It's the truth."

"Your truth."

A twinge went through her. He didn't just keep himself physically closed off from the world. He'd closed off his heart, too. With that kind of shield, he must have been lonely for most of his life.

"People can break your heart." She caught her breath slightly when he slipped his hand up to her ankle. "But they don't have to break your visions or your beliefs. They don't have to break you."

He studied her for a moment, his hand still wrapped around her ankle. "I've spent a lot of time and energy trying to stay away from you."

"Whoa." She pressed a hand to her chest. "Be still my beating heart."

He gave her a mild glower. "Even though I wanted to get closer to you."

Her pulse quickened. "So why didn't you? Oh, wait. I get it." She gestured between them. "Secret bestselling author. Reporter. Oil and water. Hatfield and McCoy."

He twisted his mouth in regret. "Stupid of me."

"Don't say that." She hugged the pillow to her chest and searched for any *hurt* over the idea of Sam purposely avoiding her, but there was nothing but understanding. She'd learned the hard way how necessary it was to protect yourself. "I have journalistic curiosity in my blood, so honestly, if I were you, I'd have avoided me too."

His eyes grazed hers before he shook his head with faint disbelief. "There's a saying that the strongest trees have the deepest roots. You're proof of that."

Her throat tightened unexpectedly. "I'm very lucky to have my family and the life they gave me. But I haven't proven I'm strong and resilient. Not yet, anyway."

"You don't have to prove it." He reached back to tuck a pillow under his neck. "You already are."

No, she wasn't. Strong, resilient people didn't stick their heads in the sand and try to ignore all the scary uncertainties of the world. Of their own lives.

But she was trying to change that, and it gave her great pleasure to think that Sam already saw her as strong and resilient. She just needed to prove it to herself.

He slid his fingers under the hem of her yoga pants. His T-shirt rode up again, exposing the taut band of muscles that she could see herself touching. And kissing. And licking…

Clearing her throat, she jerked her attention back to his face. "So you've really never been in love? Not even a little bit?"

He made a noncommittal noise. "Nothing that ever stuck."

Brooke half laughed and half groaned. "Love isn't flypaper, Sam. It doesn't just *stick*. Two people have to work to hold on to it. With both hands. That's how it lasts. How it endures through changes, heartbreak, and crises. Through *time*."

"You learned that from romance novels?"

"From true love stories. My parents and grandparents, my uncle who stuck by my aunt's side as she struggled with a pain-killer addiction. My cousin and her husband who've been trying to have a baby for the past five years. I love romance novels and happily ever after, but real-life love stories don't end there. There's a whole lot of *after* after happily ever after."

"Exactly." Lines appeared at the corners of his mouth. "That's when it all goes to hell. In the *after*."

"Not always." Brooke rested her chin on her folded arms. "The *after* is when you really discover you've chosen the right person. The one who won't leave your side. The one who will weather all storms with you."

Even sudden blizzards.

She pushed that thought quickly away.

He gave her ankle a gentle tug, easing her foot out from under her. Brooke let him pull her down onto the pillows next to him. He was lying on his back, and she gazed at his strong profile that was softened only by the thick half-moons of his eyelashes.

Though she found his resistance to even the idea of romance to be both frustrating and baffling in equal measure, there was no denying her pleasure in unpeeling the layers of his mystery.

"I have an idea," she said.

"Uh oh."

She poked him in the side. "You need to stop thinking about John and Patricia for a while and…wait for it…*get in touch with your inner feelings*."

"I'll send them a postcard. *Having a great time, wish you were here*."

Brooke huffed out a laugh and propped herself up on her elbow. "You could have an even better time if you'd acknowledge your emotions."

"Like I said," he muttered. "You're ruthless."

"Which means you have no choice." She pulled another pillow under her head and settled onto her side facing him. "Keep your eyes closed. I want you to think about how you're feeling physically. Are you cold, warm, uncomfortable, at ease? Are your muscles relaxed or tense? What's the pace of your heartbeat? Is your breath deep or shallow? What do you hear…I mean, besides my voice. What do you smell? Process how your body feels in its current environment."

She almost expected him to scoff and mutter something about getting back to work, but he remained silent, his eyes closed. The firelight burnished the tips of his eyelashes with gold. His hands rested loosely on his abdomen, strong and tanned against his worn T-shirt.

"Are you doing it?" she asked.

He murmured a noise low in his throat, a kind of rumble that she somehow felt right to her very center.

"Don't fall asleep," she warned.

"I'm processing."

"How are you feeling?"

His forehead crinkled. "Itchy."

"Itchy."

"Yeah." He opened his eyes and fumbled around underneath him. He pulled out the unicorn pillow. Flecks of glitter fell from the silver horn.

"Glitter is itchy." He scratched his lower back.

"Okay, that's legit." Brooke set the pillow aside. "What else? Start with *I feel…*"

"I feel *warm*." He settled back against the pillows and closed his eyes again.

"Good! What else?"

"I feel relaxed."

"Excellent." Pleased, she skimmed her gaze over his body. No visible tension that she could discern. "See, this isn't so hard. What's the pace of your heart?"

"My heart is racing."

"Oh. Well, maybe that's because of all your show shoveling." She resisted the temptation to press her hand against his chest and feel his *racing* heart for herself. "What do you smell?"

"You."

Her breath caught in her throat. Before she could reprimand him for being facetious, he opened his eyes and looked right at her. Maybe it was a good thing he was reclusive. He could captivate anyone with those penetrating dark eyes. If he were actually sociable, he'd have all of Bliss Cove spellbound.

Instead…it was only her.

"You smell like strawberries and powdered sugar." He

shifted onto his side, and his voice turned slow and lazy. "You smell like sunshine, snow, and rainbows."

Her own heart thumped so heavily it echoed in her bones.

"Hmm," she murmured. "You're more poetic than you let on."

"Secrets of the blanket fort."

"You're getting off topic." She infused a mildly scolding note into her voice. "Secrets aren't part of the exercise."

"I'm processing your scent." His eyes crinkled with warmth. "And how you look with your hair spread over the pillow and your cheeks pink with a blush that I can see even in the dark."

A soft heat filled her. She reached out and touched his chest, seeking the beat of his heart against her fingertips.

"Tell me what you're feeling." She pressed the area between his pecs. "Right here."

"Like I want to kiss you again."

Anticipation sparked through her. A smile tugged at her lips. "That's what you want, not how you feel."

"I feel like I want to kiss you again." He leaned closer, slipping his gaze to her mouth, and the rest of their surroundings faded from her vision.

"Still what you want," she whispered.

"I *feel*…," he closed the distance and brought their lips together, "good."

A light surged underneath her heart. He slid his hand to her lower back, urging her closer and fitting their bodies together. Everything inside her weakened at the sensation of his muscular frame pressing against hers.

He rolled them both so she was lying back against the

pillows and he was hovering over her, big and heavy. She gripped his shoulders and arched up against him. He kissed her thoroughly, sliding his tongue over hers, licking the corners of her mouth as if he wanted to devour her. She ran her hands over his chest, her heart hammering wildly at the thought of what he looked like naked. Fully clothed, his body was a work of art. Naked, he must be...*mindblowing*.

"You..." he pressed kisses in a hot trail over her cheek to her ear, "feel incredible."

He planted one hand beside her head and rested the other on her belly, edging his fingers just under the hem of her T-shirt. Her heart skipped a thousand beats. His palm was warm and slightly callused against her bare skin as he stroked upward. He cupped her breast and edged his knee between her thighs.

With a quick intake of breath, she brushed her fingers against the growing hardness in his pants. Desire unfurled like a ribbon through her blood.

He lifted his head suddenly, his breath heavy. A palpable restraint tensed his shoulders. "Didn't mean to go this far. I'm sorry."

"Hey." She fisted her hand in his shirt. "You say *sorry* when you make a mistake. Consensual kissing and touching isn't a mistake. At least, not in my world."

His eyes darkened. "I don't live in your world."

"You should come for a visit, then." She arched an eyebrow. "The weather's mostly sunny."

Faint amusement lit in his expression as he tugged a lock of her hair. "From where I'm sitting, the weather's always beautiful."

"Aw." She smiled and brushed her fingers across his jaw. "You might be a teensy bit romantic after all."

"Don't count on it."

"I'm not an optimist for nothing."

She tugged him closer, and he kissed her again. The tension eased from his muscles. She fell into a slippage of time and space, where nothing existed but the press of their lips and increasingly eager, curious explorations. She lifted her arms and let him take off her shirt, then wiggled out of her pajama pants. He groaned, raking his hot gaze possessively over her bare body, and a thrill of feminine power shot through her.

"Your turn." She grasped his shirt and tugged.

He eased away from her only long enough to pull his shirt off.

She parted her lips in astonishment. His chest was a sculpted landscape of hard planes and ridges sloping down to taut, washboard abs and that V of muscles that she'd only ever seen on men in underwear ads. The firelight gleamed off his broad shoulders, creating a bronze glow that made him look otherworldly.

"Good lord," she murmured. "You're like... *Thor.*"

He gave a self-deprecating laugh and planted his hands on either side of her. "If I'm Thor, then you're Venus or Aphrodite, and that's mixing up mythologies. Let's just be us."

"Yes." She drove her fingers into his hair, pulling him down to her and pressing her lips to his. "Sam."

"Brooke." He sounded as if he were savoring the taste of her name in his mouth.

Their kiss grew hotter, deeper. He glided his hands over

her as if he already knew exactly where she liked to be touched. He whispered his awe against her skin, dipped his tongue into her bellybutton, caressed her thighs. Fireworks sparked and flared inside her.

Though some distant part of her mind was shocked by the ease of such intimacy—certainly she'd never done anything like this in a blanket fort before—she felt as if they'd been converging toward this moment for months.

She managed to muster up a smidgen of strength to pause his sensual ministrations so that she could indulge in some explorations of her own. After urging him to lie on his back, she straddled his thighs and ran her fingertips across the powerful band of muscles lacing his abdomen. With unhidden fascination, she curved her palms over his biceps, stroked his smooth shoulders, watched the flex and pull of his pectorals as he shifted underneath her with barely leashed restraint.

He gripped her hips. His eyes were dark with lust. She squirmed. Her pulse pounded at the sensation of his considerable arousal throbbing against his pants. She cupped her hand over the heavy length. Her belly tightened with sudden anxiety.

"We don't have any protection," she whispered.

He rolled her off him and pressed her into the mattress, his gaze hot but steady on hers. "I'll keep you safe."

Pleasure billowed up like steam. He trailed his fingers over her body and found the soft place between her thighs. Brooke gasped. His touch was so precise and perfect that she responded like a feather curving into the wind. He murmured sexy words of encouragement against her lips. A sweet, hot ache expanded outward from her core. As the wave washed over her, he swallowed her cry with his mouth, open and hot.

He eased the final sensations from her body and rolled onto his back. His chest heaved. She shifted against him, giving his pants an impatient tug. After he'd pulled them off, she drank in the sight of his nakedness with both awe and excited delight.

Trembles coursed through her as she wrapped her hand around his shaft and urged him to the blissful completion that he'd given her. His groans of pleasure seemed to match her racing heartbeat. The sensation of him pulsing and shuddering at her touch elicited a fresh wave of arousal.

When he fell back against the pillows with a deep exhalation, she curled up beside him. Firelight flickered through the blanket walls. Their breath mingled in a heavy rhythm.

"Well." She rubbed her cheek against his shoulder. "That was fun."

He gave a hoarse laugh and patted her ass. "Indeed."

Easing away from her, he hauled himself out of the fort and returned with a warm, damp towel that he used to clean them both up. Tossing the towel aside, he settled back beside her and pulled her close.

For all her conviction about starting the new year in thoughtful solitude, Brooke would never have felt like *this* if she were alone. She'd have been peaceful and calm, yes, and maybe a bit lonely. She'd never have felt all warm, electric, and jittery. She wouldn't have this soul-deep satisfaction or an undercurrent of excitement running through her veins, as if she were poised on the brink of something unexpected and thrilling.

The microwave suddenly beeped.

"Oh!" She lifted her head. "It's almost midnight. I set the timer earlier so I wouldn't forget the champagne."

"You want me to get it?" He twisted a lock of her hair between his fingers, studying the reddish-brown strands.

"No, it's okay." She folded her arms on his chest and rested her chin on them. "I don't like champagne all that much, actually. I just brought it because I felt like I should ring in the new year with a tradition."

He released her hair, his expression sobering. "I hope this year gives you everything you want."

For some reason, his tone caused a rustle of unease. Shaking it off, she smiled and patted his chest. "Thank you. I hope the same for you, too."

She meant it, even if she didn't know what he wanted beyond finishing his book revisions. Funny how she still didn't know much about him, but she trusted him on what felt like a cellular level. Deep and certain. She'd never felt this way about a man.

"If you don't want the champagne, we can still celebrate with another new year's tradition." He cupped her nape and drew her closer.

"What's that?"

"The midnight kiss."

As their lips met, the world shifted from one minute into the next.

Just like that, a new year began.

CHAPTER 13

*D*espite the soporific effects of carnal pleasure, a blanket fort, and Sam's body heat, Brooke woke from a light doze a short time later. The fire had died down, but inside the fort, all was warm and cozy. She was pressed seamlessly against him from head to toe. They were both still naked, which was a little nerve-wracking and a lot mind-blowing.

Sam.

And her.

Like…*this*.

A hot blush fired her cheeks. She lifted her head to look at him. Her heart jumped. He was watching her, his expression unreadable but his eyes soft.

She swallowed. "Hi."

"Hi." He moved his fingers almost absently up and down her side in a gentle caress.

"Did you sleep?"

He shook his head. "I don't sleep much."

Odd, considering he was physically a model of incredible

health and strength. She ran her finger over his wrist, across the sinews of his forearm, and up to his biceps. "How does a thriller author get muscles like this?"

"Boxing."

She lifted her eyebrows. "Boxing?"

"I've been doing it for years." He stroked the underside of her breast. "I train at a gym over in Glendale."

"Are you a pro?"

"No. Amateur bouts sometimes, but mostly I just spar."

"Is that another reason you open the bookstore whenever you want?" Brooke's pulse accelerated as he skimmed his hand back down to her hip. "Because you're sparring?"

"Sometimes, yeah. Mostly because I'm writing, though."

"How did you start boxing?" She cupped his bicep, smiling slightly when he twitched in reaction.

"A police officer suggested it to my father when I was twelve."

She stilled. "A police officer?"

"Yeah." He opened his eyes, a wry smile twisting his mouth. "I wasn't a good kid. I was a *troublemaker*, actually. I'd been ditching school, vandalizing, committing petty theft... Once, after I was caught stealing, the police officer said boxing might give me a constructive outlet or whatever. So my father signed me up for training. I wasn't interested at first, but two lessons in, I was hooked."

"So was the police officer right? Did it become a constructive outlet for you?"

"For a while." He grasped her waist and pulled her on top of him, fitting their bodies together. "At least I trained in the gym instead of getting into fights at school. Well. I got into fights less often."

Though the sensation of lying on top of him had her arousal fluttering to life again, Brooke disliked the picture of the lonely, troubled boy that was forming in her mind.

"Why were you an angry kid?" She propped her chin on her hand.

"I wasn't lucky enough to have a family like yours." His expression grew pensive. "But there was nothing about my life that makes me special or different. Like countless other people, I just had shitty parents."

She couldn't imagine it. Didn't want to. "Where did you grow up?"

"New York." He slid his hands down to cup her rear. "My parents weren't married…which wouldn't have been a big deal if they hadn't had a fucked-up relationship. Nothing romantic there, believe me. They couldn't stand to be together, but they couldn't split up either. They lived in separate apartments, which was a nightmare because sometimes my father would stay at my mother's or vice versa, and other times there was a revolving door with random people coming in and out whenever they wanted. But no one knew who was going to be where, so my father would come to stay the night and find out my mother had a man over…and then all hell would break loose."

God. No wonder he had a hard time with the idea of love and romance, if that had been his childhood model.

"Which parent did you live with?" she asked.

"Both of them." He gave a humorless laugh. "My brother and I were shuttled back and forth all the time…well, when my brother was twelve or thirteen, my father wanted to take him in full-time. Which upset my mother. They got into a massive fight, my father won, and my brother went to live with him. But after that, neither of my parents would let me live with the other. So I still ended up with whoever was around. Or rather, whoever wasn't around."

"Is that why you were alone a lot?"

"Yeah." He let out his breath. "Neither of them was home much, if at all, so I fended for myself. It was easier when my brother was there, even though he and I never got along. After he went to live with our father, it was just me. I'm sure a psychologist would say I started acting out for attention. They'd probably be right."

"I'm so sorry."

He shrugged. "I could've had it a lot worse. My parents had money, and plenty of it, so it wasn't as if I didn't have any food or shelter. Most of the time."

Brooke blinked. "*Most* of the time?"

He patted her hip. "That's another story."

Another secret.

If she'd been in her reporter mindset, she'd have searched for a new angle or a question to convince him to keep talking. But her mindset was entirely focused on him. She wanted to know more about him—almost painfully so— but she wouldn't try and force the information out of him. She wanted him to talk to her because *he* wanted to.

Because he liked her as much as she liked him.

Because he was *feeling* things for her that he hadn't expected, as she was for him.

She stroked his stubble-coated jaw with her fingertip. "How often do you shave?"

"Whenever I remember." He ran his knuckles over his neck. "If I shaved as often as I should, I'd be doing it twice a day."

"Hmm. Twice a day is pretty sexy."

He lifted an eyebrow. "Are you hitting on me?"

"Maybe." An irrational jealousy nudged her. "That must happen a lot to a big, famous author like you."

"Sometimes, yeah, but not because I'm an author." He moved his hand in slow circles over her hip. "Only a few people know I write as Sam Harris, so any action I get isn't based on fame or whatever."

Brooke twisted her mouth. "Can we not talk about you getting *action*?"

A distinct male satisfaction rose to his eyes. "Are you jealous?"

"While I pride myself on being charitable and gracious toward people...or at least, trying to be...the idea of you with other women makes me feel like a hissing cat." She groaned and put her hand on her forehead. "Not to sound like a stalker or anything."

"I thought I was the one acting stalkerish."

"What do you mean?"

"You haven't noticed how I always stare at you whenever you walk by?"

"You stare at me?"

"All the time...well, whenever I see you." He smiled wryly. "It's how I know you bring coffee to *The Gazette* offices every morning and buy daisies every Friday afternoon. You also might be part of the reason I go to all those damned festivals."

"Really?"

"Yeah." He stroked his hands up her back. "I know you're going to be there, running around taking pictures, talking to people, smiling at everyone. I like seeing you."

"Aw." Her whole body softened with tenderness and warmth. "I was wrong. You *are* sweet."

A scowl creased his forehead. "Don't tell anyone."

"Don't worry. Blanket fort secrets get locked in the vault."

"Then let's make some more." Cupping the back of her head, he pulled her closer for a warm kiss.

A thousand fireflies took flight inside her. She fisted the sheets on either side of his head. He rolled her over, trailing his lips across her cheek, down to her neck, and lower. He licked her nipples and bit down gently on her collarbone. He moved his hands over her body, seeking all her hot, quivering places, rubbing and teasing until she was gasping with need.

As he urged her toward the peak again, she looked into his lust-darkened eyes and felt her heart crack.

If he could give so much physically, if he could read with such fluency the unspoken shifts and arches of her body, if he could be so perceptive and passionate when they were fooling around in unexpected circumstances…his capacity to *love* must be immense.

He would love with his whole being, with everything he was. For him, loving would be like breathing.

If he didn't believe it was a lie.

CHAPTER 14

*B*rooke woke when morning light crept into the blanket fort. Sam was gone, but the sheets and pillows were still warm from his body heat. She buried her face in the penguin pillow, inhaling the scents of citrus, soap, and male before reluctantly pushing the covers aside.

After pulling on her pajamas, she crawled out of the fort, lifting a hand to block the sunlight. He was seated at the table, frowning at his laptop.

"Morning." He rose and went to the kitchen, returning with a cup of hot coffee.

"How's it going?" She nodded toward the laptop.

He crouched next to her, balancing on the balls of his feet. His eyes crinkled with a smile. "I'm managing to get the words on the page. Good advice, by the way."

"I know it's not always that easy." She accepted his hand as he rose and helped her to her feet. "I have a bunch of freelance ideas on paper, so the words are there, but the ideas suck."

"What ideas do you have?"

After sitting at the table, Brooke took a sip of coffee and opened her notebook. "*Debt-Free by Forty. Bucket List Adventures From Your Sofa. Inside Your Sewer System.* Suffice it to say, if I were an editor, I'd reject myself."

He smiled slightly. "You're targeting lifestyle magazines?"

"And society and culture." She nodded. "Both online and print. My grandpa says that print magazines and newspapers are on an upswing, so it wouldn't be a bad idea to get my foot in each door."

"You said you have a deadline?"

"Mid-January. Michael wants me to think *outside the box* and come up with a list of *click-baity, grabby* ideas. I'm pretty sure sewer systems isn't what he had in mind."

Sam suddenly went very still. "Michael?"

Her stomach dropped. In all her confessions, she'd somehow managed to leave this one out. Maybe because she was still struggling with the whole thing herself.

"Michael." She swallowed and laced the pen through her fingers. "The same Michael who...well. Yes."

"What are you talking about?" Sam's voice hardened. "You're in contact with him?"

"More than that." She dropped the pen and pressed her fingers against her temple. "Michael is the editor of *Empire* magazine."

Shock poured off him like cold from a glacier. He backed up a step. "You're working with your ex? After what he did to you?"

"I'm not working with him *yet*." Her nerves began to tense. She didn't expect Sam to be delighted by this revelation, but the thunderous look descending over his face was almost alarming. "I'm just sending him freelance ideas. You said it yourself—*Empire* is doing really well, and being one of their freelance writers would be a good boost for my career. Which, if you recall, is rather pathetic at the moment."

"That doesn't mean you need to rely on an asshole who lied to you," he snapped.

Brooke pushed her chair back abruptly. "I'm not relying on him. I'm doing what I need to do in order to advance my career."

"You're giving him power over your career." Sam paced to the kitchen and back, his hands fisting. "Over *you*. You're not trusting your own abilities and talent."

"I'm not giving him power over me." Her voice sounded unconvincing, even to herself. "Look, I didn't talk to Michael for months after we broke up. It was all I could do to hold myself together, and then when I discovered I *couldn't* anymore…when I resigned from the dream job and moved back home, I had to convince everyone, myself included, that I'd done the right thing.

"But I was so angry for so long…at myself, at my colleagues, at Michael, at the woman he'd been seeing, at the whole *world*, that even though I was happy to be back in Bliss Cove, the anger and guilt were making me sick inside. So I went to therapy and I did all the things you don't believe in—meditation, yoga, aromatherapy—to try and find positivity again. That path also meant I had to try and forgive Michael."

Sam's mouth compressed into a thin line. "What he did to you was unforgivable."

"I didn't try to forgive him for *him*." She spread her

hands out. "I tried to forgive him for me. Last fall, he read something I'd written online and he emailed me telling me he liked it. We exchanged a few messages, and he asked me to send him some freelance ideas.

"At first, I wasn't going to, but then my rejection letters started rolling in, and I figured I didn't have much left to lose. So I sent him a few proposals. He didn't like the first batch, but he asked me to come up with more ideas. Honestly, he's giving me more of a chance than anyone else has yet."

"You don't need him," Sam retorted. "You're smart, talented, resourceful, a fantastic writer...a fucker like that doesn't deserve to even talk to you, much less publish your work."

Though his praise expanded like a balloon in her heart, Brooke hated that he was making her doubt her decision all over again. She straightened her spine.

"This really is none of your business." She gestured to the blanket fort. "Telling you my secrets doesn't mean you're allowed to criticize what I choose to do. And it's not as if I'm being totally selfless in trying to forgive him. I want a contract to write for *Empire*."

"*Empire* is not the only periodical out there! In fact, it's not even in the top ten. You can do so much better than relying on a—"

A knock sounded at the door, stopping his words. Brooke pressed a hand to her thumping heart. She and Sam stared at each other, as if they were both stunned by the evidence that there were other people in the world.

The knock came again, louder.

Muttering a curse, Sam stalked to the door and yanked it

open. Two stocky forest rangers, clad in khakis and dark jackets, stood on the doorstep.

"Morning." The older, grizzled ranger nodded at Sam. "You Donovan?"

"Yeah."

"Larry Owens, ranger station twenty. This is my colleague, Warwick."

The men exchanged greetings. Larry glanced past Sam's shoulder at Brooke.

She rubbed her bare arms, wishing she was wearing more than her pajamas. She gave Larry a little wave.

"You okay, miss?" He waved back and skimmed his gaze over the blanket fort.

"Fine, thanks, officer…ranger…sir."

Sam stepped in front of the ranger, blocking her from the other man's sight. "Can we help you?"

"Just letting you know the road's clear all the way down." Warwick jerked his thumb over his shoulder. "Suggest you head back before nightfall. There's another storm front turning in our direction. Doesn't look as bad, but you never know."

"Okay, thanks."

"You need help with anything?"

"Not at all."

"You, miss?" Warwick craned his neck to see around Sam's shoulder.

"We're fine." She tucked a lock of hair behind her ear. "Thanks for stopping by. Would you like some coffee?"

"No, we've got other stops to make." Larry tipped his hat to her. "Drive safely."

Only after Sam had closed the door behind the two men

did Brooke realize that a weight was starting to press down on her heart.

Obviously, she'd known they'd leave the cabin at some point, but part of her wished for just a little more time here with Sam. It felt as if they had a whole mess of unfinished business, and she had no idea how they would figure any of it out back in Bliss Cove.

Where they'd been polite, distant acquaintances.

Silence stretched between them, taut and thin.

"Well." Forcing a bright note into her voice, she gathered up her notebook and walked to her open suitcase. "Finally, huh? I was beginning to think we'd never get out of here."

She began refolding her clothes. Her hands were shaking.

She wasn't exactly naïve…at least, not anymore. She'd experienced desire, lust, and what she'd thought was love. Her heart had been scorched, and she'd cried bucket-loads of tears over more than one man.

She knew quite well that sex didn't *need* romance to be good, as she and Sam had both so eagerly proven last night. It was a lovely enhancement, icing on an already delectable cake, but it wasn't a requirement. For a fictional romance, yes, but not in real life.

Not even in hers.

She felt Sam's tension as if it were palpable. She suddenly wished he would settle his hand on the back of her neck. She wanted him to press his lips against her forehead and assure her that though their circumstances had been a mistake, *they* were not.

Which, all things considered, was just the wrong thing to want.

"I'll dig the cars out." There was the shuffling noise of him pulling on his boots. "We'll be on the road before noon."

Her stomach twisted. She had enough uncertainty and loose ends in her life without needing Sam to be one of them.

"Sam." She got to her feet and turned to face him. "Just to reiterate, you don't have anything to worry about. What happened in the blanket fort stays in the blanket fort."

He yanked the laces of his boots, his expression shuttered. "I thought you were an open book."

"I am." She swallowed hard. "Unless I have a reason to keep a secret."

"Seems to me the only secrets you *have a reason* to keep are the ones you're ashamed of."

A cloud descended on her. This was how he wanted it, then? A fateful weekend, a hot, intimate night, whispers in the dark...and it all disappeared in the blinding light of reality?

Then again, what else did she expect? Aside from having known from the start that Sam wasn't a relationship kind of guy, she had a laundry list of things to work on for herself this year. A relationship—or, God forbid, an *epic romance*—wasn't one of them.

At least...not with a man who'd made it clear he wanted to be alone.

"I'm not ashamed of what happened here," she said. "Not in the least. I just don't want you to think I expect anything more. We have very different ideas of relationships, and while I still think you need help with your romance plotline, I'm not about to try and change your mind about real-life love. I want you to know that."

"Good." He stood from the bench and folded his arms. His eyes were so opaque they looked almost black. "Thanks for the head's-up."

Brooke ran her hands over her thighs. She'd intended her statement to lighten the air between them. Instead, the tension thickened. "So we'll just go back to being…um, acquaintances."

"Fine."

His abrupt agreement was a blow to her heart. She took a breath and reminded herself that they didn't have to be *distant* acquaintances anymore. They had a reason to keep seeing each other.

"I still want to help you with John and Patricia's story." She rubbed her hands together. "I can tell you about some of my favorite characters, and I think you'd really benefit from reading a few good romance novels so you can see how the authors structure the—"

"Actually, I've got it figured out." He grabbed his parka and shoved his arms into the sleeves. "Thanks for your help, but I'm better off working alone."

"Oh." The weight pressed down harder on her heart. "Okay. So the trial period is over, then."

"Yeah." He zipped up his parka and turned. His boots rang out against the hardwood floor as he strode to the door. "It's over."

CHAPTER 15

*a*fter a couple of silent, determinedly efficient hours packing their belongings and loading their cars, Brooke preceded Sam down the winding mountain road. He'd insisted on following her all the way back to Bliss Cove, which she thought was both endearing and annoying.

Why bother acting as if he wanted to look out for her when he would retreat into his corner as soon as they got back into town?

Making an effort to ignore his big truck right behind her, she navigated the road toward the highway. ABBA blasted from the speakers. The snow thinned, melted, and then disappeared completely as they drove farther west.

When Brooke's gas tank indicator flashed, she put on her turn signal and headed toward the off-ramp. Sam followed. She pulled into a gas station, and he eased his truck beside the pump opposite hers.

"You doing okay?" He started toward the convenience store. "Do you want something to drink?"

"I'm fine. Nothing, thanks." She pushed the nozzle into the gas tank.

As the pump worked, she took out her phone to call her mother and let her know she was heading back. Notifications popped up on the screen like bubbles in a pot of water—emails, texts, social media.

Brooke's heart stuttered.

From Aria: *Oh no! I heard the news. I hope you're okay. I feel terrible, but...really? Sam is stuck there too?*

From her mother: *I'm so glad Sam is there with you. I'd be so worried otherwise.*

From Destiny: *No wonder. Venus is moving through Mercury, which means your sexual energy is intense. Lucky for you...Sam is an excellent match. I still say he's a Scorpio. ;-)*

From Aria again: *Ooo. Lots of buzz about you and Sam. This is so interesting. I can't wait to hear the deets.*

From her mother again: *The "snowstorm" has people talking. You know the busybodies. Just wanted to warn you.*

Brooke groaned. All she needed was for both her and Sam to get hit by a blizzard of gossip.

She finished filling the gas tank and got back into her car to call Aria. "What in the world is going on over there?"

"The first big romance story of the year." Aria's voice rose with intrigue. "There is no way you can tell me that you were trapped in a cabin with Sam Donovan for a whole weekend and nothing happened."

Brooke rubbed her forehead. "This is all a very big misunderstanding."

"Sweetie, even over the phone, you're terrible liar," Aria reprimanded. "You especially can't lie to your best friend who is keenly aware that you've been harboring a secret fascination with a certain hot bookstore owner."

Brooke sighed. "This is the kind of thing that happens in a Regency romance, not in 21st century California. Say, the Duke of Whatever and Lady Whatzit end up trapped in a snowstorm, and when they return to polite society, everything thinks they've been boinking and the lady is compromised, and it's all a big scandal until the duke is forced to marry her."

"Nice try changing the subject."

"How did this news get out anyway?" Brooke tapped her fingers impatiently on the steering wheel. "We were the only two people there. And it was a booking error, not as if someone were setting us up. Oh my god. Did you set us up?"

Aria laughed. "I wish. Unfortunately, if I tried to set you up with Sam, I'd have arranged a dinner at the Mousehole, not some elaborate scheme involving a freak snowstorm and a double-booked cabin."

"Then how did the *whole town* find out?"

"From the way I heard it, the grapevine went like this." Aria cleared her throat, and Brooke could picture her friend holding up each finger as she made the points. "Sam told one of the forest rangers to contact Felix Milford. So the ranger did, and he told Felix you guys were alone up at the Eagle's Nest, and to please call your mom. And the rental company hadn't told Felix about the booking error yet, so he thought you and Sam were up there *together* for a romantic retreat. You know, like Hunter and I had planned.

"So Felix called your mom, and your mom was obviously gobsmacked, and then Felix went to work his shift at Metalworks, and apparently he mentioned it to Joe...who told Destiny, who, by the way, was in Joe's office at the time, and word on the street is that they weren't just whistling Dixie. You can guess how it all unfolded from there."

Oh, Brooke could guess, all right. "This is terrible."

"Hey." A contrite note entered Aria's voice. "I'm sorry if I was being flip. Is this all a bad thing?"

"Yes." Brooke ignored a tiny voice in her heart clamoring to be heard. A voice countering that no, it hadn't been a bad thing at all. Just the opposite. It might have been one of the loveliest things that had ever happened to her.

"Aria, I need your help."

"Of course. What can I do?"

"I know the whole *snowbound with a hot guy* thing is intriguing, but you know Sam." Brooke glanced at the store, where Sam's tall figure was visible through the window as he paid for his purchases. "He's private. He doesn't want anyone digging into his life. He'll hate knowing that people are gossiping and speculating about what happened at the cabin."

"What, exactly, *did* happen at the cabin?" Aria asked.

"Nothing!" Brooke suppressed a surge of guilt over lying to her best friend. "We just sat around, bored out of our skulls. He played solitaire, and I read novels…and really, the most interesting thing that happened is that the ladder to the loft broke. Other than that, it was totally mundane. Nothing romantic or sexy happened. We are not together. Please, *please* tell people that. Squash the rumors. Eighty-six the tall tales. Get me and Sam off the Gossip Train."

Aria was silent for a second, as if she were processing Brooke's dramatic pleas. Finally she said, "Okay."

"Please."

"I got it." Aria's tone turned brisk. For all her sweetness and warmth, Aria Prescott was a woman who got shit done. "I'll call your mom and let her know what's going on so she can douse the flames. Callie and Rory will get on it, too….Rory's helping Grant at the Mousehole this week, so she's in a great position to play defense."

The tension in Brooke's shoulders eased. "Thank you."

"You and Sam are nothing but casual acquaintances who had a little adventure together," Aria said firmly. "That's the narrative we'll spread."

Casual acquaintances.

She ignored the pang in her chest. "Okay. Thanks."

"But, girl, when you're settled back in, we're going out for drinks," Aria said. "And you're going to tell me what *really* happened."

"Considering nothing happened, that will be one boring happy hour." Brooke forced a laugh. "I gotta go. Love you, Crazy Cat Lady."

"Love you back, Dogged Newshound."

After thanking her friend again, Brooke ended the call. She watched Sam leave the convenience store. He paused to hold the door open for a woman entering. A breeze rustled through his dark hair.

She'd keep her promise. She wouldn't even tell Aria what had really happened. She and Sam would go back to the way things had been for the last year.

Even if she couldn't help wishing that he would go forward with her instead of back.

He reached into a bag as he approached her car. She rolled down the window.

"I'll fill the tank, and we'll get going." He handed her a

bottle of lemon-cayenne iced tea and a box of Barnum's Animals crackers. "We should be back before dark."

He strode toward his truck, the bag cradled loosely in the crook of his elbow.

Brooke set the tea and crackers in the console. After Sam had paid for the gas, he climbed into his truck. The entire drive back to Bliss Cove, whenever she glanced in the rearview mirror, he was there.

CHAPTER 16

*T*he ocean waters glittered with morning sunlight. Boats glided away from the harbor toward the open expanse of the Pacific, sails unfurled to catch the wind.

Brooke pulled open the door of the Java Works coffee-house. After placing her order, she walked to the pick-up counter to wait.

Two days after her and Sam's return from their snow-bound adventure, she still felt as if she were an astronaut struggling with reentry. The cabin owner, Felix Milford, had apologized profusely, refunded Aria and Hunter the full cost of the rental, and offered them a free stay for a future booking.

He'd also offered Brooke another ten-day stay at no charge. Despite the fact that the snowstorm had been no one's fault, Aria felt guilty about Brooke's shortened visit and promised her a springtime spa retreat.

Brooke hadn't told her friend that she needed a retreat from her retreat.

Thankfully, Aria's rumor-suppressing strategy appeared

to have worked—aside from a few questions from people about the storm and "glad you're okay" remarks, no one interrogated her about anything to do with Sam.

"Here you go." The Java Works barista set a tray loaded with six coffees on the counter.

"Thanks, Janie." Brooke took the tray and headed back outside to Starfish Avenue.

Balancing the coffee tray, she greeted several acquaintances as she continued walking. Shopkeepers opened their doors and pulled up window shades. People strode up and down the street with a purpose, whether it was work, shopping, coffee, or breakfast.

She turned onto Poppy Lane and entered the old stone building that housed *The Bliss Cove Gazette*. The room bustled with noise and conversation—keyboards clicking, phones ringing, printers churning out stories. Since Brooke's departure, the staff consisted of three staff reporters, the sports writer/editor, ad sales manager, and the formidable editor-in-chief.

Senior reporter Frank Ferguson, who had been with the paper for twenty-five years, lifted a hand to her in greeting as he spoke into his phone. Brooke set his coffee on the desk and distributed the others before walking to the editor's office. A pane of smoky glass perforated the door and was etched with the words: *Charlie Castle, Editor-In-Chief.*

Brooke knocked, pushing the door open at her grandfather's gruff, "What?"

"Morning, Gramp...er, Charlie." Brooke set his black-coffee-better-be-strong-don't-even-think-of-putting-sugar-in-it on the desk. "Got your coffee."

"You don't need to be bringing us coffee, girl."

"I don't mind." For the two years she'd been a reporter on staff, she'd brought everyone their morning coffee. No reason to stop now.

She rounded the desk to give her grandfather a quick hug. She also stopped by a few times a week to chat with him, both because she liked to and to let him know that she bore no resentment over his attempt to keep her gainfully employed.

Though it still upset her to think he'd spent his own money on *her salary*, she understood why he'd done it. He'd never been demonstrative, and she'd never actually heard him express love, but he would do anything to take care of his family.

With a grunt, Charlie tolerated her embrace before turning back to his computer.

Brooke sat in one of the chairs opposite his desk and sipped her mocha with whip. "What's the latest news?"

"Got Ferguson covering the trial over in Glendale. Looks like it could go either way."

Snapping his heavy eyebrows together, he studied the spreadsheet on the computer. Though he wasn't particularly tall or big, Charlie had always radiated a powerful, deter-mined energy that made him seem larger than life. He'd had an extraordinary career covering everything from political rallies to wars, and he had the battle scars to prove his dedication.

He'd been threatened, stood in the line of fire, watched people get killed, and suffered an IED injury that left him with a prosthetic leg. Brooke had been sixteen when he'd returned and purchased *The Gazette*, and the return of her reporter-hero grandfather had ignited her own passion for journalism. She'd wanted to be like him.

But she hadn't lasted more than three years in the big leagues before she'd crashed and burned.

She slid her gaze to the photo of Charlie and Ruth that rested on his desk. Charlie had had an incredible, memoir-worthy career, but it was also true that he and Ruth had a beautiful love story in their own right. With their model of love and devotion, Brooke's mother had settled for no less than her own true romance.

"Gramps, who do you have covering the Valentine's Day Festival this year?"

"Rogers. You're chair of the festival again, aren't you? Didn't she call you for an interview?"

"Not yet. Have you ever considered running some profiles on Bliss Cove's longtime marriages? You know, the divorce rate in his country is half or something like that, so it might be nice to showcase some lifelong romances around Valentine's Day."

He frowned, which meant he was processing the idea.

"You could start with your own," Brooke added.

"I write and publish the news." He shot her a scowling look. "I don't make the news. What's going on with you? You started applying for other jobs yet? I can still contact the editor of *The Chronicle*, if you want to talk to him."

Brooke shook her head, suppressing a stab of guilt. "I don't want to get another job because you contacted an old friend for me. I can do this on my own."

"You applied anywhere yet?"

"A few places," she hedged, picking up a flyer from his desk.

The flyer advertised the upcoming annual Bliss Cove Book Fair, which took place every February and included book sales, poetry readings, creative writing workshops, and kids' programs. Though she wasn't officially on staff, Brooke had always volunteered to help with the fair's organization and set up—which included her unsuccessful attempts to get Sam to participate.

This year, all Book Fair funds would go toward The Reading Project, which supplied books and literacy education to local underserved communities. Bee Delaney, the Bliss Cove librarian, who was hoping to raise enough money to purchase and outfit a mobile library truck.

Brooke waved the flyer at her grandfather. He'd been the main sponsor of the Book Fair for the past twelve years. "Are you on this year's fair committee?"

He nodded. "You and Aria going to do your kids' read-aloud program?"

"We'd love to." Brooke thought about Title Wave again. The former owners of the bookstore had always participated in the fair, but last February, the store had been on the verge of closing, and Sam hadn't yet taken charge of it. So Title Wave hadn't had a presence at last year's fair…and it wouldn't this year either, if Sam had anything to say about it.

"Have you talked to Sam Donovan about participating?" she asked her grandfather.

"You said he turned you down."

"He did, but maybe you could try talking to him."

Charlie shook his head. "If he's not interested, nothing I can do."

"Gramps, he owns the only bookstore in town. It's

ridiculous for him not to be involved in the *book fair*. He could just sell books, if nothing else, or at least provide them to other vendors."

He could also probably connect Charlie with a bunch of other authors for signings and readings, though Brooke would never bring that up.

"Please?" she asked.

Her grandfather eyed her with a hint of exasperation. "I'll see what I can do."

"Awesome, thank you." Brooke tucked the flyer into her backpack. "Are you coming to Sunday night dinner at Mom's?"

"Maybe." He peered at his computer again. "Make your pecan pie, and I'll consider it."

"I'll make two." Standing, she leaned across the desk and kissed his cheek. "Love you."

His responding grunt indicated that he loved her, too.

Brooke left his office and checked in with the other reporters about their weekends and their assignments.

Out of both habit and a touch of desperation, she then walked around town on the "reporter's beat" route that she'd done while working for *The Gazette*. Her daily check-ins with town employees, business owners, the police, even the school crossing guards had led to many of her stories.

Maybe now they'd inspire more creative freelance ideas that didn't involve sewer systems or the angst of turning thirty.

I Was Trapped in a Snowstorm with a Thriller Writer.

It was kind of like that Stephen King book, except instead of broken legs and an axe-wielding psychopath, there was hot naked snuggling and a man who doesn't know how much he needs to believe in love.

If Brooke had a complete lack of scruples, that story might get an editor's attention.

Forcing her mind back to the task at hand, she waved at a police officer who was approaching his vehicle. "Hi, Scott."

"Hey, Brooke." He smiled warmly as she approached. "Heard about your adventure up in the Sierras."

"It was all an unfortunate mistake." Even now, her heart twisted at the implication of calling anything that had happened in the cabin a *mistake*. "Anything interesting going on? I'm doing some freelancing and looking for ideas. Fundraisers, great police dog stories, maybe an inspiring story like the one last year when the department bought Annie Garrett a new bike after hers was stolen?"

Scott creased his forehead in thought. "Can't think of anything recent. Mrs. Barthes gave us a call when a seagull flew into her house and got trapped. Hank used a bucket to get it out safely. Had to break up a party up in the Fog Forest over the weekend. Group of high-school kids, as usual. That helpful?"

"Possibly." Brooke tried to inject an enthusiastic note into her voice. "Let me know if anything else comes up, okay?"

"Sure thing."

After wishing him a good day, she paused at a park bench to scroll through her work-in-progress list of ideas. The most promising one was a feature on a local food education program for underserved communities in rural areas.

Grant Taylor, owner of the Mousehole, had started the

program a few years ago, and he'd recently expanded it into neighboring counties. Maybe it wasn't incredibly "click-baity," but it would be a solid, feel-good story about people helping others.

She'd email Michael about it later.

You can do so much better.

Sam's words rang in her ears as she returned to Starfish Avenue. Easy for him to say, with his successful career and apparently steady income. She didn't have either one—and for longer than she'd even realized. Getting an income from your grandfather when you were almost thirty didn't exactly qualify as success.

Giving him power over you.

With effort, she shut Sam's voice out. After she'd gone through all her texts and emails from the past three days, she'd discovered two more rejection letters from online magazines.

Though she didn't love this level of contact with Michael, at least he was giving her a shot to advance her career. No one else had.

And she was choosing this route. She was finding a way to give herself a step up instead of hiding in a job that had almost been like receiving charity.

No longer. She'd earn her way through talent and hustle, not a handout.

She caught sight of Title Wave across the street. The Open sign hung in the door.

After a quick internal debate, she crossed the street and entered. A little bell over the door jingled.

Sam was studying a sheet of paper at the front counter,

his dark hair flopping over his forehead, his jaw unshaven as usual, and his shoulder muscles all bunched up and practically straining his T-shirt. His strong features were set with concentration, and his thick eyelashes created shadows on his cut-glass cheekbones.

Warmth pooled in her lower body. Like every other woman in town, she'd always *noticed* Sam's good looks, but now that she had up-close-and-personal knowledge of both his strength and *him*, her awareness was at a whole new level.

"Hey." She tried to sound casual as she approached him. "I didn't think you'd be open again so soon."

He glanced up, faintly wary. "Why not?"

"With your deadline and all." She waved her hand to indicate the store. "I'm surprised you're here instead of pounding away furiously at your keyboard."

"I'm still recovering from the weekend," he replied dryly.

"Yeah, me too." She hitched her backpack further over her shoulder. A sudden shyness overcame her. It was one thing when she and Sam were in the alternate, isolated reality of the cabin where normal rules didn't apply. Now they were back on familiar territory. Real life.

A quizzical light appeared in his eyes. "You okay?"

Part of her registered it wasn't the first time he'd asked her that. She liked the way he asked, too—not as if he were merely being polite. There was an undercurrent to the question, as if he really wanted to know the truth. As if her response, whatever it was, would have a direct impact on him.

"Yes, thanks." She reached into a pocket of her backpack. "I wanted to return this."

She pushed an envelope across the counter, scrawled with her name. She'd found it in her mailbox yesterday afternoon.

"Why?" Sam frowned as if the envelope were poisonous.

"It's too much." She pushed it closer to him. "When I said you could pay me what you wanted, I didn't mean a small fortune."

"Take it." He shoved the envelope back toward her. A muscle ticked in his jaw. "If money is the reason you went to your ex for help, then I'll give you even more. How much will it take for you to tell him to go to hell?"

Beneath a swell of reactive indignation, a tiny flame flickered in her heart. No one had ever been angry on her behalf. She'd never given them a chance to be. Her family and friends had been upset and sympathetic to know that she'd suffered a break-up on top of everything else, but she hadn't wanted to burden them with the sordid details of how badly she'd been deceived. So the secret had festered inside her like an infection.

She'd told Sam, though. The confession had come so easily there in the warmth of the blanket fort, with his dark gaze unwaveringly on hers. She'd known instinctively that she didn't have to protect him from the raw, stripped-down truth. A man of his strength and fortitude could take it. In fact, he'd want to shoulder the weight himself.

Brooke let out her breath slowly. Was that why she'd told him? Because her renewed contact with Michael and opening herself up for his rejection again was starting to weigh heavily on her? Had she wanted—needed—to lighten the load?

Sam shoved the envelope at her with a decisive movement, as if the matter were not up for debate. Brooke put her hand over it.

"I helped you for a few hours, if that," she reminded him. "And since you're here rather than at your computer, it seems I didn't even help you all that much. This is an unjustifiably excessive amount of money to pay me."

He lifted a box of books onto the counter. "Take the money, Brooke."

She wanted to, very badly. But she'd left *The Gazette* because she couldn't take Gramps' handout. There was no way she could accept Sam's either.

On the other hand, this wasn't entirely a handout. And even a portion of it would go a long way toward covering her costs for the Freelancer's Convention.

"I'll take half," she finally said. "But please understand this doesn't mean I'm going to withdraw my ideas from *Empire*."

"Your call." He turned away from her.

Brooke let out her breath slowly. "Look, can we not fight about this? I know the cabin was a…mistake, but obviously stuff happened that I'm *not* sorry about, and I think that makes us a little more than acquaintances now. I'd hate to think you're judging me after all that."

The muscles of his back tensed. "I'm not judging you."

"You think I'm being stupid."

"I think you've convinced yourself you have no other choice." Facing her, he planted his hands flat on the counter. "But you know that twenty, thirty…hell, fifty rejections for a writer is nothing on the road to getting what you want. *Empire* is just one of thousands of opportunities out there."

Brooke rubbed her hands together. True as that was, she didn't have an infinite amount of time to start making money and establishing her career. And *Empire* was no third-rate magazine.

They paid well. They hired well-known writers and authors, so she'd be in excellent company. She'd have a by-line, which would restore some of the credibility she'd lost when she'd left *The New York Times*. Even if she did score a full-time job interview somewhere, she'd have to explain why she'd left such an illustrious journalistic position.

"My point is that you need to trust the fact that you have other chances." Sam set a stack of romance novels in front of her. "These are promo copies, so take whatever you want."

If only it were that easy.

She looked over the titles, selected a few, and slipped them into her backpack. "How's John and Patricia's romance going?"

"Fine."

"Are you sure you don't need my help anymore?"

"I'm sure." He lifted another stack of books from the box and began inputting them into the computer system.

"Okay." Brooke stepped away from the counter. "I'll see you around, then."

"Yeah."

She started toward the door. From the instant she'd collided with him in the cabin, she couldn't remember a time when she hadn't *felt* his attention on her in multiple ways—warm, sharp, penetrating, curious, irritated, atten-tive. Even when he wasn't looking at her, she'd sensed his regard, as if he had an internal antenna directed right at her.

But now, as she left the bookstore, a trickle of cold ran down her spine. Sam had retreated back behind his stone wall and intended to stay there. She couldn't feel anything about him anymore.

CHAPTER 17

Kane kissed her. She kissed back. He felt...

Sam dragged his hands over his face. His eyes burned. His jaw hurt from clenching his teeth. He'd been working nonstop since he'd closed the bookstore at two and gone for a workout and shower, which had been...

He squinted at the clock on his computer. Nine and a half hours ago.

He'd spent most of those hours dicking around with the main plot of *Tripwire*, which was already solid, and ignoring the holes where he was supposed to stick the romance. Finally, he'd forced himself to tackle the problem.

Kane felt...

He fucking *felt*...

Sam cracked his knuckles and typed, *He felt hot. Like he was burning up.*

Christ. Sounded like the guy had a fever.

He could almost hear Brooke. *"Love is like a fever, but a*

good kind. It spreads through your body and heightens everything—your temperature, your heartbeat, your excitement, your senses. It means you should pay attention because something out of the ordinary is taking place."

With a groan, he shoved away from his desk and stalked to the kitchen. The place he'd been renting for the past year was a two-story house on an isolated plot of land near the Bliss Cove Library. Aside from his two desks, computer, and a few pieces of dirt-brown furniture, the place was empty.

The surroundings had never bothered him before now. He just needed a place to work and sleep. But now, as he stood in the linoleum-floored kitchen with its florescent lights and fake-wood cabinets, he had a visceral urge to be back at the Eagle's Nest.

Not just the cabin, but...*the cabin with Brooke.*

He couldn't stop thinking about all her ridiculous bedding in the cozy little blanket fort, or the dining table that was so small their knees bumped every time they sat down. He even missed the narrow sofa and the easy chair positioned at such an angle that the firelight flickered through Brooke's hair whenever she curled up with one of her romance novels.

He was losing his mind. Worse, he was losing his focus —if he'd ever had any to begin with. He couldn't let one aberrant weekend screw up his progress.

What progress?

Fisting his hand in his hair, he gave himself a good tug and returned to the computer.

He felt...

"Tell me what you're feeling." The memory of Brooke's voice drifted into his ears. He remembered her fingertips on

his chest as she prodded at the area where his heart was supposed to be. *"Right here."*

"Like I want to kiss you again."

A slow smile curved her pretty mouth. *"That's what you want, not how you feel."*

"I feel like I want to kiss you again." He'd been aching for it.

Even now, his body reacted to the memory of her soft lips parting under his, and her warm body yielding to his touch.

He rubbed the back of his neck.

Hot. Horny. Incredulous. Carnal. Eager. Impatient. Jacked up.

Though accurate, none of those words conveyed what he'd felt when he'd slipped his hand between Brooke's bare thighs, or when she'd driven her fingers into his hair and breathed his name against his mouth.

He stared at the computer screen. The lines of his manuscript were as fuzzy and knotted as his brain. Two and a half weeks left. His attempt to isolate himself at the cabin had been thwarted in ways he could never have imagined. He sure as hell hadn't gotten anything done there.

Except...

Letting out his breath, he rolled his chair back and went to put on his running shoes. A run usually helped clear his mind.

He grabbed his keys and headed down to the darkened beach. The cold, salty wind whipped against his face, and moonlight shone through a thin marine layer. He jogged over the pathway bordering the shoreline, forcing away all thoughts of Kane and Patricia.

It pissed him off that he was having such trouble with a subplot thousands of other authors had successfully written before him. Hell, there were romances in Greco-Roman literature. In mythology, medieval manuscripts, Shakespeare. Writing Kane and Patricia's romance shouldn't be like reinventing the damned wheel.

He ran harder, faster. His muscles worked. His breath burned his lungs.

He hated failure. He'd spent too much of his childhood and teen years *failing*.

But he'd never failed with his own romance. He'd never had one. Not the kind that Brooke believed in so hard. The kind she said was *truth* and that he knew was a lie.

"Maybe that's a big part of your problem right there. You've never been in love. You can't write what you don't know."

Her voice tangled in his head. Images of her flashed in front of him—Brooke hugging her unicorn pillow, biting down on her pen, folding her legs into the lotus position.

She couldn't hide her feelings if she tried—she was too open, too transparent. He saw her joy when she talked about her family, and her sadness and regret over the New York part of her life. He saw her disappointment when she realized he didn't believe in love.

Sam veered away from the beach and into an older neighborhood on the south side of town. He ran on the sidewalks in front of modest ranch houses and duplexes until he came to a rundown, four-unit apartment building. A faint light burned in the second-story windows facing the street.

He came to a halt in front of the glass-paned door. Chest heaving, he pressed the buzzer beside the name *Castle*. After a minute, a door at the top of the stairs opened, and Brooke appeared. His heart jackhammered.

Squinting beneath a mass of disheveled hair, she came down the stairs. She stared at him through the window before unlocking the door and pulling it open.

"Sam?" Her eyes widened. "What in the world are you doing here?"

"I'm...I..." He couldn't grab hold of the right word. His brain was spinning. "I need—"

"Come in." She reached for his hand and urged him into the foyer.

Swiping his arm over his sweaty forehead, he followed her upstairs. The other day, she'd refused his help unpacking when they'd gotten back from the mountains, so he hadn't seen the inside of her apartment. Now, as he stepped into the warm, inviting space, he took a deep breath.

"Were you at the gym?" Brooke closed the door behind him.

He shook his head. "Out for a run."

"Ah." She sniffed the air around him. "Windy and salty."

"Sorry."

"No, I like it." She slipped her gaze over his sweaty T-shirt, a puzzled crease appearing between her eyes. "Why did you end up here?"

He shook his head to try and think straight, but all he could do was stare at her. Her hair spilled over her shoulders in messy waves, and she was wearing a wrinkled pink T-shirt printed with a cartoon of a pug dog and the phrase *Snug as a Pug in a Rug*.

"You were sleeping." He ran a hand down his face. "I thought...I saw the light on."

"I keep a nightlight on in the living room, just in case I need to get up." She nudged him toward the purple sofa. "Sit. I'll get you some water."

He sank onto the sofa. The overstuffed chairs and sofa were covered with multi-colored pillows in various shapes and sizes. Plants in macramé holders hung from the ceiling, and the walls were decorated with prints of Impressionist artwork. It was an apartment-sized version of the blanket fort.

His heartbeat began to slow. Brooke returned from the kitchen with a glass of cold water. He downed half the glass in two gulps and wiped his mouth with his arm. "I'm sorry, I...I wasn't out to...I mean, I didn't plan to come here at first, but—"

"Sam." She sat on the sofa beside him and rested her hand on his knee. "It's okay. You don't have to apologize or explain."

But he did.

He took another swallow of water and set the glass down. For a guy who made his living with *words*, he was doing a shitty job of figuring out how to string them together in a sentence.

"I do need your help," he finally said. "I don't know how to write the romance. You're right...all that stuff about feelings and why they love each other. I've got nothing."

"You don't have nothing." She tightened her hand on his knee. "You're an incredible writer, and you know it. And it's not as if you can't write relationships...the struggle between John and his grandfather is one of the most poignant father-son story arcs I've ever read."

She paused, her voice softening. "Honestly, Sam, you

really just need to open yourself up to the idea of romance. Both its building blocks and nuances. You need to acknowledge that even if you don't believe in love, most people think of it as life's greatest joy. We believe in it. We want it. Can you understand that?"

He rested his elbows on his thighs and stared at the blue throw rug patterned with big yellow daisies. "Yeah."

"Good. And it's not...um..."

He looked up at her hesitation. A faint blush colored her cheeks.

"What?" he asked.

"It's not as if you don't know what you're doing on the physical side of things." She ran her hand over the arm of the sofa, her flush deepening. "You're really good at kissing and...er, other sexy stuff, so it shouldn't be too much of a leap to translate that to the page."

Though her comment created a vivid flashback of them naked in the blanket fort, Sam shook his head. "That's not love or romance."

She blinked and averted her gaze.

Oh, shit. He was such an ass.

He put his hand out. "I didn't mean what happened—"

The words crammed in his throat again. He had no idea how to tell her that the blanket fort was beyond anything he'd ever experienced. And he'd experienced a lot.

"I think we're...outside the norm," he finally said.

Amusement creased her eyes. "I suppose that's better than *weird*."

"Christ." With a low laugh, he rested his head in his hands. "I suck at this. I should write a horror novel."

"Actually, I think you just need a thesaurus." She nudged

her foot against his leg. "*Outside the norm* can also mean remarkable. Rare. Extraordinary."

The tightness in his chest eased. He lifted his head to find her watching him, her eyebrows drawn slightly together. His heart knocked against his ribs.

"I have an idea." She leaned closer. "You need an education on the *romantic* part of romance. The little gestures and rituals. So I think we should date."

He lifted an eyebrow. "Date."

"Not seriously." She held up her hands, as if she were either warding him off or reassuring him. "Just for fun and for research until you finish your revisions. It appears as if dating isn't really your thing, am I right?"

Without waiting for a response, she continued, "Whereas I could probably write a book about my dating experiences, both good and bad. And since dating is usually part of love and romance, I think you should get an idea of what constitutes a *good date* so you can send John and Patricia off on some romantic evenings. We'll have to be somewhat undercover so people don't think we're actually together, but we can manage that."

She smiled. "What do you think?"

He thought he'd walk through fire as long as she kept smiling at him like that.

"I'd love to date you." Frustration pushed at his chest because that sentence didn't convey everything he still wanted to tell her. About why he was such a failure at this, and why he knew he could never be the kind of man she wanted.

She regarded him, the smile fading from her rosebud

mouth. Heat flicked in the air. He reached a hand up and touched the pinpoint mole at the corner of her eye.

Forget words, descriptions, and fumbling for the right phrase. He would *show* her how he felt.

He closed his hand around her wrist and tugged her closer. When her face was only a few inches from his, when he could breathe in her sweet, cinnamon scent and look into her brown eyes, he stopped.

If she showed one instant of doubt, hesitation, uncertainty—

She kissed him. Like a sparrow swooping across the sky, she closed the scant distance between them and pressed her lips to his. He couldn't have been more surprised if the earth had opened under his feet—and it felt as if it had.

Her mouth was warm, tasting both salty and sweet, like caramel popcorn. Whatever he'd been thinking fell away. Pleasure exploded through him. Every time their lips met, he was reminded that he'd never before experienced a kiss that was so affecting, as if their point of contact could generate an electrical charge strong enough to power the entire country.

It's one thing to kiss a stranger. It's totally different when you're kissing someone you love.

Her words echoed through him, settling in his blood. He lifted his hands to the sides of her head, tilting her mouth to just the right angle before delving inside. Together they sank back against the sofa cushions. He stroked his tongue over her lower lip and trailed kisses across her cheek and down to her neck.

She fisted her hands in the front of his shirt and arched her body against his with an unspoken invitation. He ran his hands over her soft curves. Her nipples hardened against his palms. Heart hammering, he grabbed the hem of her nightshirt.

She broke away from him and lifted her arms to help him pull it off. The sight of her full, perfect breasts and rounded hips sent his pulse into overdrive. Pulling him back to her, she moved her hands under his shirt and stroked his chest. Her touch was hot and cool at the same time.

He lost all track of time and thought. She tugged off his shirt and track pants, and within seconds, her naked body was shifting and writhing against his, every movement firing his lust hotter. He forced himself to go slow, to take his time exploring every inch of her, from the hollow of her throat to the arch of her foot. She was so soft everywhere. Her fragrant skin was addictive, her sighs of pleasure like music.

At one point, she pushed him to sit up so she could straddle his lap and touch him in return, her hands gliding with eager curiosity over his chest and lower. When she enclosed his shaft in her warm fist, he knew he wouldn't last much longer. He gripped her waist.

"Brooke…"

She kissed him. "Bedroom."

They managed to make their way to her bedroom, and she stopped along the way to retrieve a box of unopened condoms from the bathroom cabinet.

"A practical but clearly unnecessary purchase." Breathlessly, she pressed a foil packet into his hand. "Until now."

He tumbled her onto the bed. He couldn't get enough of her warmth and softness, the little moans emerging from her throat, the way she wrapped her arms around him as if she didn't want to let go. By the time he put on a condom and urged her thighs apart, he was burning with need. With a groan, he eased inside her. She gasped, hooking her legs around his thighs as he sank fully into her heat.

She was heaven. He moved slowly until she matched his rhythm, and then they began rocking and thrusting together. Even through the hot, panting lust, Sam had a faint realization that *this* must be what it felt like to have wildfire in his blood and stars shooting through him. He'd never felt this kind of blinding intensity with another woman before.

He knew the instant Brooke started to come. Little ripples coursed through her body before building into a wave that wrenched a cry from her throat. The pressure sent him over the edge. He sank into her again and again before giving in to the explosive release.

Spent and exhausted, they fell back against the pillows. *Clouds in his soul. A kaleidoscope of glittering colors. A woman curling up against him like a kitten.*

He put his arm around her and pulled her closer, gliding his hand over her smooth, damp back. She eased across him so she was lying fully on top of him. He loved the position— her feminine weight on his body, her face so close that he could look into her eyes forever.

"Like I said…" she ran her finger across his lower lip, her expression soft, "you don't need an education on the sexy stuff."

He rubbed her ass. "But now that we're dating, we get to go to the movies together and have a milkshake at the soda fountain?"

"That would be a start." A line formed between her eyebrows. "When was the last time you went on a date? A real one, not one meant for educational purposes."

He deflected a stab of unease over the idea of them dating only for "fun and research." He couldn't even remember the last time he'd been on a real date. He'd never really done the courtship ritual, which he supposed was just one of a thousand reasons he'd been failing so badly with Kane and Patricia's romance.

"I guess that depends on your definition of a date," he finally said.

"Like when you asked a woman out and then picked her up, brought her flowers, kissed her good night. That kind of *date*."

"I don't know. A couple of years, I guess?"

"I figured." She patted his chest. "This is why you need a Romance 101 course."

He frowned. "So where does sex fit into that? We're just having fun?"

"Well…yes." She lifted herself up to look at him, uncertainty rising to her eyes. "What else would it be?"

He couldn't let his brain go to *what else*.

"Right, because we're not actually together." He couldn't stop the edge to his voice or the increasingly powerful feeling that he didn't want to be with Brooke for the sake of a fictional romance. He wanted to be with her for *them*.

But then what? He'd never be her epic romance, and she'd never settle for less. And not for anything would he make her promises he couldn't keep.

She was still watching him, her lower lip caught between her teeth and her forehead creased. Shoving all his frustration down deep, he put his hand on the back of her head and drew her closer.

"Bring it," he murmured. "I was a lousy student, but I'm all in for your class."

He pressed his mouth to hers. Her body softened, her curves fitting so damned perfectly against him that the phrase "made for each other" came unexpectedly to mind.

He deepened the kiss and rolled Brooke onto her back, his desire sparking all over again at the sound of her throaty moans and the way she arched against him in a wordless plea. He trailed his mouth to her neck, licking the hot pulse at the base of her throat before easing down to her breasts. He stroked his hand between her legs, urging her thighs apart as he trailed his lips over her belly and lower.

Her breath caught in her throat. He nudged her legs wider and positioned himself between them.

"Sam…" It was a half-gasp, half-cry. "Oh, my god."

He used his fingers and mouth to open her up, penetrating her in a way that had her squirming and moaning loudly. Her response spiked his lust again.

She fisted her hand in his hair and bucked her hips upward. He took her right to the brink and let her ease back down several times before a precise stroke of his fingers sent her over the edge.

As she was still shuddering, he rolled on another condom and surged into her with one thrust. She wrapped herself around him, matching his movements and clinging to him with such eagerness and trust that he experienced an intense rush of possessiveness.

Mine.

The thought dissolved into mind-numbing pleasure and a release that left them both gasping for breath.

They fell back against the pillows again to recover.

Brooke nestled up against him. He threaded his hand into her hair and absorbed the feeling of her in his arms.

Life's greatest joy.

We should fall in love with being in love.

Do you really believe that love is a lie?

In his experience, it was. People who professed love, then hurt and cheated on each other sure as hell hadn't been telling the truth.

As a kid, he'd been quick to paint people with the same brush—his peers, his teachers, the press, his parents' friends. His years of traveling had changed his perceptions, but it hadn't changed his belief that marriage was for other people. *Love* was an empty word. Romance was fiction.

In *his* world.

He'd seen it in others, though. He hadn't acknowledged it, hadn't given it a name, but…yeah. He'd sensed love between spouses, couples, lovers. Women had said the words to him. But he'd always felt as if he were behind a wall where the actual physical feeling of love didn't reach him. He lived on one side, and people like Brooke lived on the other.

He'd experienced everything else tenfold—desire, lust, affection, caring. But he'd always stopped short, blocked by the wall, when love, with all its weaknesses and vulnerability, loomed. He'd never thought much about what would happen if the wall crumbled.

But in that moment, he did.

CHAPTER 18

a pressure on his chest woke Sam with a start. He opened his eyes and found himself staring into the unblinking green eyes of a hefty calico cat who, whiskers quivering, was apparently inspecting the big, strange creature taking up more than half of her mistress's bed. Sam suspected he'd probably usurped the cat's usual sleeping spot.

"Hey," he greeted.

Jojo pawed at his chest and let out a little mewl. Sam glanced beside him, where Brooke was nestled underneath four layers of bedding and surrounded by half a dozen pillows. Her hair spilled in all directions, and there was a mark on her smooth, bare shoulder from his overzealous attention.

Since he'd already woken her last night, he forced aside the urge to touch her again. He plucked the cat off his chest and went to retrieve his T-shirt and track pants from the living room. Jojo meowed, more stridently this time.

"What?" Sam returned to the bedroom and studied the cat. She meowed again.

In the event that Jojo began caterwauling and woke Brooke, Sam hefted the cat off the bed and carried her out of the room. He closed the door behind them and set Jojo down in the hallway. The cat darted into the kitchen and began stalking around two purple ceramic dishes on the floor.

Ah. Message received.

He rummaged in the cupboards and refilled the cat's food and water. He couldn't find any coffee, so he scribbled a note and put it beside Brooke's pillows. He took her keys from the table by the door and headed out to a nearby café.

As he waited for the order, his phone buzzed. A text from his agent popped up:

The main investor was Fred Pierson, Omnibus Corp. Daughter Candace Pierson.

His spine tensed. He typed *Candace Pierson* into a search engine. Sure enough, images of the polished blonde appeared. In many of the photos, a blond guy was at her side —blinding white smile, curly hair, movie-star features.

Sam cleared the browser history and stuck his phone back into his pocket. Though he wasn't surprised by the confirmation, it fueled his anger all over again.

An anger that was shocking the hell out of him.

Any decent human being would be upset knowing that good-hearted Brooke with her loving family, blanket forts, and plucky attitude had gotten taken by a dickhead opportunist. No one liked to see the bad guy win.

But Sam couldn't stop thinking about the fact that, in this

case, the bad guy winning meant that Brooke lost. She'd picked herself up and gotten on with it because that was what she did, but she shouldn't have to fight so hard. She shouldn't have to rely on her shitty ex to open a door for her.

He picked up his order and returned to the apartment. The water was running in the bathroom. Jojo slinked around his legs as he set the muffins on a plate and put it on the table with the coffee tray.

"Morning." Brooke's voice slid over his skin.

Sam turned. The breath rushed out of his lungs. He'd seen her disheveled and sleepy before, but now...with her hair a tumbled mess, her eyes heavy-lidded with satisfaction, her lips still reddened from his kisses...the sight of her hit him like a bolt of concentrated sunlight.

He almost went weak in the knees.

Crossing the room, he grabbed her hips and pulled her hard against him. She widened her eyes the instant before he kissed her. He intended for it to be a warm, "good morning" kiss, but the instant he touched her soft lips, his control snapped like a twig.

He tightened his grip on her hips, urged her mouth open, devoured her with hot, greedy possession. A murmur escaped her throat. Backing her up against the wall, he caged her in with his arms and kissed her thoroughly. Her strawberry scent filled his head. She curled her fingers into his shirt.

He couldn't get enough of her. He didn't want there ever to be *enough*. She was his golden ticket, and he was the kid running as fast as he could into the chocolate factory with its endless treats and prizes.

A loud *meow* broke his intense fervor. He lifted his head,

his breathing hard, and stared into Brooke's dazed brown eyes.

"Oh my." She darted her tongue out to lick her lips. "I'm going back to sleep."

"Back to sleep?"

"So I can wake up and get another *good morning* like that." She patted his chest and gave him a smile filled with both warmth and desire.

Sam huffed out a laugh and straightened her robe, which had started to slip from her shoulders. "Next time, I'll try to be more polite. No promises, though."

"No need for politeness when it comes to good-morning kisses." She stood on tiptoe to kiss him when Jojo yelped again. Brooke glanced past his shoulder to the kitchen. "Oh, she needs her viewing spot. Excuse me."

She slipped away from him and hurried into the living room to open the blinds. Sunlight streamed into the room. Swishing her tail, Jojo jumped on the windowsill and peered out on to the world like a queen surveying her domain.

"Thanks for feeding her." Brooke returned to the kitchen, eyeing the coffee and muffins. "And me."

"Anytime." He had the strange feeling he meant that word in ways he couldn't articulate.

"So, are you ready for Romance 101?" After sitting down, Brooke took the lid off her cup and blew on the coffee to cool it.

"I'm not only ready." He pulled out the chair across from her. "I intend to get an A."

Amusement curved her lips. "That kiss got you off to a pretty good start. So did last night, for that matter."

"I'll keep that in mind." He rotated the plate toward her. "I got you a blueberry."

"How did you know blueberry muffins are my favorite?" She plucked the muffin off the plate and began unpeeling the wrapper.

"You had about four boxes of them at the cabin." He bit into a banana-nut muffin. "Easy guess."

"Paying attention." She lifted her eyebrows. "That's one of the key qualities of a swoon-worthy romantic hero."

Though Sam took the remark as the compliment it was, he couldn't prevent a surge of unease. He'd never intended or wanted to be any woman's "romantic hero," and even if he had, he didn't fit the mold of Brooke's perfect guy.

When it did come time for her to get married—and having been surrounded by such shining family examples, there was no doubt in his mind that day would come, even if the idea scorched him with jealous anger—she'd settle for no less than what she'd read about in all her novels. Especially after that bastard Michael had burned her...Brooke would take no chances and offer no compromises.

As well she shouldn't. A woman like her deserved everything she wanted.

And a man like him...well, he'd just have to enjoy every second he spent with her, like soaking up the sun before nightfall.

"So what's the plan?" he asked.

"Leave that to me." Brooke shot him a smile that turned on a light in his heart. "You're on my turf now."

Sam couldn't think of any place he'd rather be.

CHAPTER 19

*T*hough she'd have liked to spend the full day with Sam, especially after the explosive heat of last night, Brooke sent him home with instructions to review the trajectory of John and Patricia's romance.

She busied herself with her own work, which included job searches, proposal revisions, and a few hours' worth of research about romance novel structure. She printed out worksheets and stuffed them into her backpack before heading out at dusk to meet Sam down by the beach.

The Bliss Cove boardwalk had always been one of her favorite places. She loved the whirling carnival lights, the sticky-sweet smells of cotton candy and funnel cake, the mechanical sounds of arcade games, and the bustling, cheerful crowds.

As she caught sight of Sam standing by the pier railing, her heart did a little cartwheel. The wind rustled through his dark hair, and he wore jeans and a long-sleeved, cotton shirt that hugged his broad chest. He turned as she climbed the stairs, as if he sensed her approach. His slow smile made her all soft and gooey inside.

"Hey." He stepped forward, bending almost as if he were about to give her a kiss hello. Then he caught sight of her face and stopped. He pulled his eyebrows together. "What?"

"We're, um…" She indicated the crowded boardwalk. "I just realized we might run into someone we know. They're going to wonder what you're doing here. What we're doing here together."

He frowned. "None of their business."

"I know, but you don't need people wondering any more about you than they already do. And I don't want to be responsible for someone discovering your secret superhero identity."

"Okay." He glanced past her. "We'll tell people you're doing a story about independent bookstores. You're interviewing me."

She chuckled. "After the half-dozen times you've turned me down for an interview?"

He scratched his jaw, looking slightly abashed. "We'll say you made me an offer I couldn't refuse. Which wouldn't be far from the truth."

He winked at her. A pleasurable glow lit in her belly as they started toward the carnival.

She was determined to keep her head on straight where this thing with Sam was concerned—she was helping him out and they were indulging in some fun, sexy times with no expectations—but she was "in touch with her feelings" enough to recognize how much she enjoyed being with him.

The sex had been spectacular, as she'd anticipated it

would be, but she also liked waking up beside him, drinking coffee across the table from him, talking about the latest news and weather, even watching him scratch Jojo behind the ears.

The warm, fuzzy feelings might even be the roots of full-fledged love—a notion she had to keep locked away deep inside her. Though she wished they could explore all the nuances of a *real* relationship, she would never coax him into something he didn't want.

Not to mention, he was under pressure to get his book finished. He didn't need the distraction of her growing feelings for him. She'd be happy just to continue the camaraderie that had started so unexpectedly in the cabin.

Even on a Thursday night, the carnival at the end of the pier was in full swing. Multicolored lights shone against the dark sky, and the Ferris wheel spun like a kaleidoscope. People sat at picnic tables eating burgers and corndogs, while others crowded around the game booths, trying their hand at ring toss and balloon popping.

They ate deep-fried pizza for dinner, played several games, and went on a roller coaster, an airplane ride, and the Ferris wheel.

As the gondola ascended up the side of the wheel, the earth below became a constellation of bright lights and distant noise. The ocean stretched out from the pier like a pool of ink, and the cold wind rocked the gondola back and forth.

"I've always loved it up here." Brooke dragged her fingers through her wind-whipped hair and peered down at the roaming crowd. "After I moved back to Bliss Cove, one of the first things I did was come on the Ferris wheel. Even though my life was in shambles, coming up here and just looking at the ocean reminded me that things were still good at home. Maybe my life would be good again one day, too."

"Did it turn out that way?"

"For the most part." She straightened and shifted to face him, admiring the contrast between his strong features and the thickness of his eyelashes. "I felt guilty and kind of weak that I couldn't handle the big leagues, but like I said, coming back here was one of the best things I've done. It just took a while for me to figure that out. I spent a lot of time wondering if I'd made a huge mistake."

Sam settled his hand on her thigh. "I cheated on the SATs in high school."

She lifted her eyebrows. "Really?"

"Long time ago, obviously." He gazed out at the ocean. "Junior year. I paid another kid to take them for me. Got caught. My father cut a deal with the school to keep me enrolled, but I didn't want to stay. So I dropped out."

"I had no idea."

"Not many people do." He gave her a faint, humorless smile. "But I've done a lot of other things worse than that. So have thousands of other people. Leaving a job that was running you into the ground wasn't anything close to a mistake. And you had a place to come back to. Not everyone can go home again."

She put her hand over his. She'd learned many hard, often heartbreaking truths about people's lives during her years as a national news reporter, but she also knew—to the center of her being—that hope and *home* could always be found.

Not that Sam needed or wanted to hear her philosophizing. She squeezed his hand as the gondola began its descent to the other side. After it stopped, they exited the ride and walked back to the midway.

"You should give John and Patricia a Ferris wheel scene," she suggested. "Or at least a carnival ride scene."

"What for?"

"So he can make a BRG." She stopped in a short line leading to Sugar Spun, a food wagon advertising multiple flavors of cotton candy.

"A BRG?" Sam glanced at her skeptically. "Kane making a *burg* sounds neither romantic nor sexy."

"A Big Romantic Gesture." She nudged him in the side with her elbow. "Like in the movie *The Notebook*."

"Never seen it."

She stared at him. "What?"

"I've never seen *The Notebook*."

"You've never seen *The Notebook*?"

"There you go turning statements into questions again." He half-smiled and reached into his pocket for his wallet.

"How many romantic movies have you actually seen?" Brooke asked.

"I don't know." He counted out a few bills. "I don't watch a lot of movies."

"*The Proposal. Titanic. You've Got Mail. Roman Holiday. Serendipity. Sleepless in Seattle.*" Her eyes widened as he shook his head. "*Gone with the Freaking Wind*?"

"Yes." He held up one hand in defense. "And *Casablanca*. That's romantic, right?"

"Well, *yeah*." She made a scoffing noise. "We're having a movie marathon soon. Or at least a clip marathon, where I can show you all the best romantic movie moments. You need ideas because John has got to give

Patricia a BRG as an expression of how much he loves her and wants her."

To his credit, he nodded in agreement rather than arguing. They reached the window of the truck, where a woman in her fifties wearing a white baseball cap peered out.

"Brooke, honey!" She reached out to squeeze Brooke's hand. "Dan, c'mere, it's Brooke."

A plump, bearded man pushed up to the window. "Hiya, Brooke. How've you been?"

"Great, thanks." Brooke smiled and indicated Sam. "Do you know Sam from the bookstore? Sam, this is Mary and Dan. They've been running Sugar Spun for...what, ten years?"

"Eleven, now," Mary said proudly, patting the counter as if it were a beloved pet. "Couldn't be happier."

"Dan used to be the CEO of a tech company up in San Jose, and Mary was a lawyer," Brooke told Sam. "Then one day they decided they'd rather run a cotton candy truck."

Sam blinked. "Just like that?"

"Just like that." Dan snapped his fingers.

"We were sitting in our huge house, both of us on our computers, and I couldn't remember the last time we'd gone anywhere." Mary leaned her elbows on the counter, her expression growing distant. "We were tired all the time, stressed out, snapping at each other. And you know, Dan and I were college sweethearts. When we met, we had no money, but somehow we managed to *do* things all the time."

"Road trips, weekend getaways, concerts." Dan looked fondly at his wife, a smile appearing in the tufts of his beard. "We did it all."

"We had so much fun." She gave his beard a light, affectionate tug. "And then twenty years later, we had all this money and no fun whatsoever."

"So you decided to buy a cotton candy truck?" Sam asked.

"We sat down and each thought of ten things that we considered especially fun." Mary's eyes twinkled. "G-rated, of course. *Cotton candy* was sixth on my list. *Carnivals* was third on Dan's list. We put the two together, sold the house, and bought the truck."

"They travel to carnivals and fairs up and down the coast all year." Brooke glanced behind her to make sure no other customers were waiting to place orders. "But Bliss Cove is their favorite, right?"

"Hands down." Dan beamed at her. "We come here, what, four, five times a year? Usually we're here for most of July and August. Oh, we added some new flavors to the menu for the new year. What can we get for you?"

He slapped his hand on the menu board, which listed over thirty flavors of cotton candy, including bubblegum, caramel, mango, and peach. Brooke requested a strawberry cone, and Sam—remarking that he'd never heard of it— chose habanero pepper.

Dan treated them to an elaborate demonstration of how they made and spun the cotton candy before handing over two large cones of light, airy fluff. After paying and thanking them, Brooke and Sam walked toward the beach while plucking at the spun sugar.

"How is it?" Brooke ate a bite, enjoying how the sweet floss melted in her mouth.

"Not bad, actually." Sam tore off a large piece and ate it. "Sweet and spicy at the same time. Just like you."

Brooke smiled. "That might have earned you an extra credit point."

"I'll take whatever I can get." He tilted his head back toward the food truck. "They have a great story."

"Yes, they do. Sugar Spun Love." The phrase tickled the back of her mind. It was a feeling she hadn't felt in so long that she'd almost forgotten it.

The tiny, flickering flame of inspiration.

"Remember when I told you I know a lot of people who have lifelong love stories?" she asked Sam. "Mary and Dan are one of them. Not many couples could take a leap of faith like that and make it work. Plus, they're still so steadfastly in love with each other. I'm sure they've had rough times, too…how could they not?…but you only have to look at them to see how happy they are."

"So does buying the truck count as a BRG?" He ate another piece of cotton candy.

"A BRG for their relationship, yes. They literally drove off into the sunset together. They're still driving. They have a framed quote on the inside of the truck, right above the cotton candy machine. *'In life, it's not where you go. It's who you travel with.'* Which is so true, except if you're traveling alone. Oh, dear." She winced. "I didn't mean you, specifically."

He chuckled and indicated a park bench where they could sit down and finish eating. "It's the truth. I traveled alone most of the time."

Brooke, on the other hand, couldn't really remember a time when she'd been completely alone. Her attempt at solitude in the cabin had been thwarted in ways she couldn't have imagined.

"You've been all over the world?" she asked.

"More or less." He extended his cone in invitation, and Brooke plucked off a tuft.

"How does Bliss Cove compare to the rest of the world?" She ate the spicy-sweet bite.

He was silent for a moment before he said, "One of the first things I did when I moved here was visit the Mousehole for artichoke soup."

"We are famous for that soup."

"I remembered reading about it on a food website or something." Sam gazed out at the dark ocean. "So I was sitting at the bar when suddenly I heard a woman laugh. It was like Christmas bells. It was the sound that light would make. I turned and saw this incredibly beautiful brunette sitting in a booth by the fireplace, laughing at something her friend was saying.

"For a minute, all I could do was stare at her. My heart was about to pound out of my chest. Then, to my amazement, she looked right at me. It felt like she'd reserved that smile just for me. In that instant, I thought Bliss Cove had to be one of the best damned places in the world."

Brooke almost couldn't breathe past the astonishment filling her chest. "Wow."

"Turns out I was right."

"You're a stealth attack, Sam Donovan." She wiped her sticky fingers on a napkin and tapped him on the nose. "All scowling, no romance…and then you toss out something like *that*. Did I really look at you?"

"You did." He finished off the last of the cotton candy and tossed the paper cone into a trash can. "And the first time you walked into Title Wave…to ask me if you could write a story about the bookstore…I remembered you. Hard."

"I can't tell you how much I want to kiss you right now."

A grin flashed across his face. "Show me."

"I will." She gave him what she hoped was a sultry look from beneath her lashes.

It appeared to work because he leaned toward her in anticipation. She put her hand on his chest.

"Later," she said.

He frowned. "How much later?"

Lowering her voice to a throaty purr, she said, "After you…"

"What?" His eyes darkened.

"…highlight each plot point of John and Patricia's romance."

"Ruthless." With a sigh, he gave her a quick, intense kiss. "Good thing I like you that way."

CHAPTER 20

"Thanks, Janie." Brooke picked up the coffee tray and walked to Poppy Lane. She smiled at everyone she passed, shared her croissant with a flock of birds, and felt as if she were radiating happiness.

To anyone else, she might have looked as if she was just being Sunny Side Up, but inside she was *so much more*.

Last night, she and Sam had parted ways at the boardwalk, though Brooke had been second-guessing her dictate before she'd even unlocked the door of her apartment. Jojo was calmly overjoyed to see her, but the place felt empty without Sam.

She knew it wasn't just because of their night together, either. They'd packed so much unexpected togetherness into their snowbound adventure that she'd gotten used to having him around. She'd gotten used to being around for him, too.

Still, she was distinctly aware of the warning signal still flashing beneath her happiness.

They weren't "really" dating. Sam had made his views about real-life love and romance abundantly clear, and

Brooke wasn't going to fall into the trap of believing she could change his mind. Aside from needing to protect her own heart, she didn't want him to think she'd suggested this whole venture because she thought he needed to be saved.

She headed up to *The Gazette* offices and distributed coffees to the reporters, pausing to chat for a few minutes and ask them about the latest news.

"Verdict coming down on the Sheridan trial later this week." With a nod of thanks, Frank accepted his large, one-sugar French Roast. "Looks like the prosecution might have done its job."

They talked about the details of the insurance fraud case, then launched into speculation about the town council's upcoming voting initiatives and the proposed new public arts funding.

"I'd better get this in to Charlie." Brooke indicated her grandfather's coffee. "Say hi to Linda for me, okay?"

"Sure will." Frank turned back to his computer.

Brooke paused, studying the photo of his wife and children. "Hey, Frank, how did you and Linda meet?"

He glanced at the photo, his grizzly face relaxing into a smile. "The laundry room."

"Really?"

"Uh huh. We were both in the dorm laundry room one morning, and I realized I didn't have any money for the dryer. So I dumped this sopping load on top of the machine and wandered around asking people for change. This stunning blond girl took pity on me and gave me four quarters. I told her I'd pay her back on Friday night at six, if she was available. She was. We've been together ever since. I still do all the laundry."

Brooke smiled, her heart softening. "That's incredibly sweet."

"Linda says it's the best dollar she's ever spent."

Love on Spin Cycle.

Leaving Frank to his work, she headed into Charlie's office. He was on the phone, and he lifted a finger to indicate she should wait.

Brooke set his coffee by his computer and sat down. Charlie ended the call and reached for the coffee. "You going to the Freelancer's Convention next week?"

"Yes, I just registered the other day." Brooke sipped her mocha. "It's been so long since I was on the market for a job that I'm a bit out of the loop. This will be a great way to network and learn what's new."

"Where are you staying?"

"The Granger."

"That's not in a great area." He frowned. "Why aren't you staying at the Marriott?"

"I can't af...the Marriot is booked." She injected an enthusiastic note into her voice. "The conference schedule is incredible. I'm going to have a hard time figuring out which panels to attend since there won't be time for all of them."

"I know a few people who will be there." Charlie turned to his computer. "I'll give you their numbers. Get together with them for lunch or something."

Brooke nodded, though she still didn't love the idea of using her grandfather's contacts to seek out an opportunity. She knew it was great to have a personal connection—in fact, networking was always helpful—but she didn't want to get a job because she was *"Charlie Castle's granddaughter."*

She got to her feet and went around the desk to give him a quick hug. Her gaze fell again on the photo of him and Ruth that he kept on his desk. Brooke's father also had a framed photo of him and Helen on his desk at the accounting office. In fact, most of the men she knew kept a photo or some memento of their wife and family close to them at the workplace.

Taking her coffee, she returned to the newsroom. She had always taken it for granted that people fell in love and lived out a lifetime together. They held hands, laughed, argued, enjoyed both life's daily routines and extraordinary moments, and they didn't give up on each other.

She knew couples who had gotten divorced or broken up, but in her close circle, that was the exception rather than the norm. She'd always been surrounded by people whose love and trust proved stronger than any storm.

But not everyone had such a love story. And most people —like Sam—probably hadn't been exposed to the level of deep commitment that was the foundation of Brooke's life.

How many people didn't even know what a long-term love relationship looked like? Even if they did, in the midst of the world's problems, they might benefit from a reminder that love didn't just exist. It was alive, dynamic, ever-changing. It bound people together through life's celebrations and tragedies, over vast distances, across time. Love would always be the most powerful force in the universe.

After asking Frank if she could use one of the newsroom's computers, she sat at a spare cubicle and typed up a proposal about Bliss Cove's "real-life love stories." Charlie and Ruth, Mary and Dan, Frank and Linda, her parents.

Other couples came easily to mind—Len and Nancy

Tomkins, who were in their eighties and had met as teenagers. The innkeepers of the Outside Inn, Hilda and Hank Higgins, who'd been married for forty-two years before he passed away.

Brooke changed the couples' names until she could get their permission for in-depth interviews. The story would be perfect for *Empire*'s February edition, but even if Michael didn't like the idea, she could still write it for *The Gazette* free of charge. Maybe she could make it a series, with individual profiles published each week.

She typed "Lifelong Fling" into the subject line and sent the email to Michael.

Pleased, she gathered her belongings and headed back outside. The mixture of excitement, satisfaction, and anticipation told her it was a good idea. A *great* idea. She hadn't had this feeling in longer than she cared to remember. She couldn't wait to tell Sam.

She hurried across the street to Title Wave, but the shutters were drawn and the Closed sign hung in the window. Getting into her car, she drove to his house tucked away in the woods a few miles from the Bliss Cove Library.

Both his truck and his car were in the driveway. She parked and rang the front doorbell. Through the glass window in the door, she saw his tall figure approaching. Everything inside her lit up.

He pulled open the door, looking deliciously rumpled and a bit lumber-jacky in faded jeans and a wrinkled gray T-shirt under a red flannel shirt.

"Hey." His face relaxed into a smile. "I didn't know we had class this morning."

"Oh, shoot. Am I interrupting? Are you in the middle of a big writing session?"

"No, I was just taking a break. Come in." He stepped aside, holding the door open.

As she entered, he slipped his arm around her waist and pulled her in for a kiss. Unlike the intense, powerful kiss he'd given her yesterday morning, this one was light and gentle, an *I'm glad you're here* rather than an *I need you now.*

Brooke loved all of Sam's kisses. She wanted to experience the entire range of them. Knowing his depths and layers, that could take a lifetime.

Deflecting the thought, she preceded him into the living room. Not surprisingly, the furnishings were as basic as an interstate motel room, aside from two large desks and a computer. The second desk was littered with notes and papers, a bookshelf held worn paperbacks, a big-screen TV sat against one wall, and a massive whiteboard was scribbled with ideas and hasty graphics.

Sam disappeared into the kitchen as Brooke set her backpack down. She studied a chart on the whiteboard, which appeared to list emotions for John Kane.

A soft feeling – tenderness, affection
A hot feeling – lust, desire, anger
A feeling he's never experienced before – ???

"*Love*, Sam," Brooke murmured.

Until Patricia, John hadn't known what love felt like. He didn't even appear to know what it *looked* like.

"Did you say something?" Sam came back into the living room.

"Just thinking out loud." She turned to face him, and he extended a cold bottle of lemon-cayenne iced tea.

Brooke took the bottle, faintly surprised. "I thought you didn't like iced tea."

"I don't."

"But you…" She twisted off the cap. A light glowed in the back of her mind, like a sunrise.

"I got those for you." Sam rested his hands on his hips, a puzzled crease appearing between his eyebrows. "What, you're not drinking iced tea anymore?"

"No, I am." She took a long swallow, suppressing the urge to smile. "It's just nice that you thought of me. It's romantic, one of those little gestures that means a lot."

He still appeared somewhat confused, as if trying to make the connection between romance and iced tea.

"Uh, I just thought you might be thirsty," he finally said.

"I was. Thanks."

He walked to his desk and leafed through a stack of wrinkled, scribbled papers. "So you're here to check up on me? You'll be glad to know I got a lot of work done last night."

"Excellent." Brooke shrugged out of her hoodie and tossed it onto the sofa. "I also wanted to tell you I came up with a fantastic story idea. I want to write a series about Bliss Cove's long-time couples…real-life love stories, like Mary and Dan. I'm calling it *Lifelong Fling*, based on the Over the Rhine song."

"That sounds like a great idea. Have you written the proposal yet?"

She nodded, not bothering to tell him she'd already pitched it to Michael—likely Sam would assume that she had, anyway.

"I'm going to ask my grandfather for the first interview. He'll grouse about it, but he knows deep down that his and Grandma Ruth's story is special and unique. And speaking of stories, how's the progress with your revisions?"

"I'm going forward rather than backward, which is always a good thing." He smiled ruefully. "What's on the class syllabus?"

"We need to review your work, but first things first." Brooke walked to the TV and picked up the remote control. "We're going to the movies."

CHAPTER 21

While Brooke had indulged in many movie marathons over the years, she'd never enjoyed one quite as much as she did this time with Sam. He microwaved popcorn, she queued up a movie list, and they settled on the sofa together.

As they sat through several full movies and a bunch of carefully selected scenes that were heartwarming, romantic, bittersweet, funny, and sad—sometimes all at the same time —she half-expected him to sigh heavily and groan occasionally.

Instead, he got a notebook and pen and sat on his end of the sofa, writing industriously. During a bathroom break, Brooke glanced at the notebook he'd left on the coffee-table and discovered he was scrawling *notes about the romances.*

When Lloyd serenades Diane with a boom box. When Noah climbs the Ferris wheel to get to Allie. When Rick tells Ilsa to get on the plane. When Carl discovers that Ellie's life with him was her adventure. Whenever Westley *looks* at Buttercup.

"Have you thought of a BRG for John Kane?" she asked when he sat back down next to her.

"A BRG." Sam rubbed a hand through his hair. The sleeves of his shirt were rolled up, revealing his muscular forearms. "I guess I thought it was the trout-fishing date. Or Kane always wanting to take Patricia to O'Grady's."

"How are those big, meaningful gestures?"

"I don't know that they are." He frowned and studied the paused image on the TV screen. "But maybe they're small, meaningful gestures. He took her fishing because he remembered she'd told him that some of her best childhood memories were when her father took her fishing. And O'Grady's was the first place he ever saw her, so going back there with her reminds him of how lucky he is to be with her."

"Oh." The word escaped Brooke on a breath of air. "I didn't know that."

"I guess I didn't put those details in the books."

"You need to." She shifted toward him and patted his chest. "Your readers will love it. That's one of the foundations of their relationship right there. He listens to her. The best part of his day is when he gets to be with her."

"I'm starting to understand what that's like."

Her heart skipped a beat. So was she.

As if realizing he'd just revealed more than he'd intended, Sam stood and walked to his paper-littered desk. "Should we go over what I've done?"

"Sure."

He brought over a pile of notes. He'd retroactively plotted out the entire storyline from the moment John meets Patricia up until their shift into a serious relationship. After they reviewed the plot, they spent the next several hours working on fixing the weak points and outlining the future story. Together, they created a timeline, listed the main plot points, and mapped out the romance up to marriage.

Brooke managed to convince Sam that John had been guarding himself against love to avoid getting hurt, and that Patricia needed to be shown in all her complexity—intelligent, vulnerable, tough, confident, uncertain, and brave. Likewise, their romance wasn't a straight line from first look to wedding vows. It had peaks and valleys, challenges and joy.

Sam had planned for the marriage to take place in the first book of the next Kane trilogy. When Brooke pointed out he'd have to continue writing about John and Patricia's relationship after they married, he admitted that John Kane as a married man and even potentially a father would add multiple layers of complexity to the whole series.

By the time they wrapped up their work in the evening, the whiteboard was covered with freshly scrawled notes, they'd argued heatedly about whether John should take Patricia to Paris or the Bahamas for a vacation, Brooke had stood her ground on the incorporation of *love body language*, Sam had only groaned once, and they'd both agreed that he could forego metaphoric poetry about clouds and molten lava in favor of his powerful, action-driven prose.

"You're on to something here, Sam Harris." Brooke capped the dry-erase marker and sank down beside him on the sofa. "Just make sure you show their feelings through actions and body language."

"What about words?"

She glanced at him. "Words?"

"Yeah, like that exercise you made me do in the blanket fort." He shifted toward her, his dark eyes filling with both amusement and warmth.

A smile tugged at her lips. "Words are good."

"I agree."

"So." She touched his chest. "Tell me in words how you feel."

"I feel…" He leaned closer, his gaze slipping to her mouth. "Happy."

He brushed his lips across hers. A shower of sparkles fell through her. She edged closer as he increased the pressure of the kiss. Everything inside her tightened and loosened in time with her heartbeat. She slid her hand around to the back of his neck and parted her lips under his. He murmured a noise of approval deep in his throat, sweeping his tongue into her mouth.

An ache started in her core and expanded outward like the ripples in a pool of water. Sam cupped his hands on either side of her face, cradling her as if she were a treasure.

Slowly he lowered her back against the sofa cushions, their lips still locked together. Her heart raced at the sensation of his strong body pressing against hers.

God. She'd never felt like this before, all hot and glittery with melted honey sliding through her veins. She couldn't remember the last time she'd made a decision she didn't feel the need to question or overthink.

When she was with him like this, all of her misgivings and worries fell away. All that mattered was the friction of their bodies, the glide of his hands and press of his lips. All that mattered was them.

Sam lifted his head, his dark eyes burning into hers. "Okay?"

She nodded, too breathless to speak, and pulled him back to her again. He slipped his hand down to her breast, covering it with unmistakable possession. With a groan, she clutched the back of his shirt and arched her hips against the hard bulge in his jeans. Her heart jumped wildly. She tugged at his shirt.

"Take this off."

He pressed a lingering kiss to her mouth before easing away to shrug out of his button-down and pull off his T-shirt.

Brooke rose to her elbows. Heat unfurled in her belly as he revealed his smooth, muscular shoulders, and the gorgeous slopes of his pecs leading down to his rigid abdomen. A trail of hair led from his naval below the waistband of his jeans. She wanted to trace his muscles with her fingers and follow that trail right down into the forbidden zone.

She wound her arms around his neck as their lips met again. The temperature of the air increased by slow degrees until a trickle of sweat ran down her spine. Sam separated himself from her again, but this time to strip her of her clothes.

Glad that she'd had the foresight to wear her best bra and panties, she wiggled out of her pants and shirt. Tension coiled through his muscles as he raked his hot gaze over her body.

"Beautiful." He whispered the word against her bare shoulder before trailing his lips to her cleavage.

Electric sparks shot through her. She shifted to take off her bra, giving him full access to her breasts. He stroked his hands down her sides and captured one of her nipples between his teeth. She squirmed, yearning for him to fill her and ease the empty ache.

Time distilled to both a second and an eternity. To both her intense pleasure and slight frustration, Sam took his time exploring every inch of her body, touching and kissing her from the arch of her throat to her toes. They only parted when he made a quick trip to the bathroom to retrieve a condom. By the time he sheathed himself and eased between her legs, she was panting with need.

Bracing his hands on either side of her head, he pressed forward slowly. Oh, the easy, slick immersion was the sweetest torture. She moaned, writhing as he seated himself fully inside her, his head lowered and his chest heaving.

Then he eased back and pushed forward again, a slow rocking that fired her with urgency. She arched upward to match his movements. Streams of pleasure washed over her, filling her blood with heat.

She gripped his biceps, and a cry tore from her throat when bliss exploded over her nerves. He lowered his mouth to hers, sweeping his tongue between her lips. His muscles tightened. He surged inside her and stilled with a rough groan, his own body shuddering with release.

With a grunt of satisfaction, he rolled off her and adjusted their positions so she was sprawled on top of him. Stroking her hands over his powerful arms, Brooke sighed deeply with pleasure.

"Really?" she murmured.

"Hmm?" His voice was lazy and slow.

"You're happy?" She lifted her head to look at him.

A smile tugged at his mouth. "With you, yeah."

"I'm happy with you too." She propped her chin on her hand. "You know, a lot of reviewers have wondered if John Kane is a fictionalized version of you. Mostly because they have no idea who Sam Harris really is. And now that I know you're not a solitary, crime-fighting, ex-CIA agent...wait a second."

He huffed out a laugh. "Never even considered joining the CIA. I've never had a regular job. When I was on the road, I worked odd jobs or whatever I could get. But mostly I just wrote."

"When did you publish your first book?"

"Ten years ago." A shadow crossed his features. "I'd written one novel under my given name, but it went out of print pretty fast. So I created Sam Harris and tried again. Second time, I was lucky. The Sam Harris books didn't start taking off until the third one was published, but my publisher stuck with me until then. Thankfully, readers are still buying the books."

"Any plans to end John's story?"

He shook his head. "Maybe one day, I'll give him a happy ending. Not anytime soon, though."

Brooke stroked her finger over his beautifully shaped lower lip. She saw a lot of Sam in John Kane—his self-imposed isolation, his struggle with expressing his emotions, his difficult childhood, his preference for solitude, his rich inner life.

"How much of John's story is yours?" she asked.

His mouth twisted. "Remember that scene in *Cold Shot* when Kane is telling the diner waitress about getting lost when he was a kid?"

Brooke's throat closed over. "That happened to you?"

"A version of it did." He rubbed a spot in the middle of his chest. "Once when I was around eight, I was supposed to go to my mother's after school. She wasn't home. I didn't have a key, and we weren't supposed to talk to the neighbors...so I sat on the step and waited until long after dark. She didn't show up.

"I figured I'd walk to my father's house, but I got lost. Didn't know what to do. I couldn't find a policeman, and I'd have been too scared to go to one anyway. My parents were exceedingly protective of their positions...my father was a business partner, and my mother was a *patron of the arts*, as she liked to say.

"They kept certain parts of their relationship and our family life a big secret. My brother and I knew we were part of it. So I was scared it would blow up if anyone discovered I was lost. I guess that was where I drew the *troublemaker* line."

A thought occurred to Brooke. "Is that why you told me in the blanket fort you had food and shelter *most of the time*?"

He nodded. His jaw tightened. "I was gone for over a week. Nine days."

"At eight years old?" Brooke's heart constricted. "What in the world did you do?"

"At first, I just wandered. Slept in doorways. Stole food. Ran when anyone looked at me funny." He trailed his fingers up and down her spine. "Then after a couple of days, I passed by this cluttered little bookstore my grandmother used to take me to. The owner was this old guy who looked like he belonged in a book about wizards. White hair, glasses, old tweed suit. I thought he'd kick me out, but he didn't. Just left me alone. I was there for hours.

"Then when he was closing the store for the night, he asked me if I needed help. Turned out he remembered my grandmother and me. He offered to call my mother, but again she wasn't home. I begged him not to call the police and told him I couldn't go home because I didn't know when my parents would be back."

"So he let you stay at the bookstore?"

"He did. His name was Mr. Patterson. He brought me food and blankets, told me there was no bulletin about me in the police reports, and kept trying to contact both my parents. I spent all my time reading, mostly the Narnia books. Mr. Patterson said if he couldn't reach my parents, he'd take me home himself."

"But your parents must have been worried sick."

"They didn't know I was gone."

Brooke sat up. *"What?"*

"I told you I was shuttled back and forth between my parents." He adjusted the sofa pillow behind his head. "They both thought I was with the other parent the whole time. They were in one of their fighting phases and weren't talking to each other. The school had called about my unexcused absences, but they either didn't get the messages or ignored them. Plus I was always cutting school anyway, so they weren't surprised by school messages."

"How did you finally get home?"

"Mr. Patterson left me an envelope inside a copy of *The Silver Chair*. It had some cash and a note saying, *When you're ready, I'll take you home*. Finally, I decided I couldn't stay there forever, and I took him up on his offer. He hired a cab and brought me back to my mother's. She was home this time, but like I said, she hadn't known I was gone."

"Did you tell her what happened?"

Sam shook his head slowly. "Didn't see the point, I guess. Patterson didn't come in either, so she hadn't known where I was."

"Did you ever go back to the bookstore?"

"Yeah." He smiled faintly. "Often. Patterson and I became pretty good friends. He passed away a few years later. The store was sold, and the new owners turned it into a gift shop."

Brooke pressed her hand against his heart. This was why Sam took over Title Wave when it had been on the verge of closing down for good.

"That's an amazing story." She shifted and slipped her leg between his. "It must have been cathartic to put a version of it in John's book. I remember you used his experience as one of the reasons he became a drifter for so many years."

"Yeah." He ran his hands down her back. "But it's not why I did. Or maybe it was. By the time I was twenty, I'd had enough of New York. I never wanted to go back."

"That's when you started traveling?"

He nodded. "I stopped when I saw you."

Brooke lifted her head. A light clicked on deep inside her, as if his confession had turned a switch. "I'm very glad you did."

"So am I." His eyes were multiple shades of brown—golden like whiskey, warm and earthy like tree bark, deep like chocolate.

She rose to straddle his thighs and spread her hands across his chest. "Can I tell you a secret?"

"I dunno." He stroked her hips. "We're not in the blanket fort."

"This isn't a blanket fort secret."

"Then lay it on me."

She thought she should be a bit fearful of the confession, or at least nervous. But there was nothing except a deep, abiding certainty that she wanted him to know. She braced her hands on either side of his head and pressed her forehead against his.

"I *feel…*" she whispered, "like I'm falling in love with you."

He went still beneath her, his quick intake of breath his only movement.

"Brooke." His throat worked with a swallow. "You know I'm not—"

"I don't care what you're *not*." She threaded her hand through his hair. "I care what you are. And I'm not telling you because I expect you to say it back. I just want to give you the truth. My truth."

He pulled her closer and kissed her with an intensity that made her blood burn. When he lifted his head, his eyes were darkened to the color of the earth.

"Want to know what my truth is?" He curled his fingers against her waist.

She nodded.

"You."

CHAPTER 22

*B*rooke's default setting was *happy*, but the next week with Sam turned the dial up to a whole new level. Neither of them brought up her L-word declaration again, but Sam was excelling at the Romance 101 course.

He planned a picnic on a hill overlooking the cove, he brought her daisies because he knew they were her favorite flower, he cooked her an elaborate breakfast of French crepes, and he took her to a club featuring her favorite band. He helped her make chocolate-chip cookies and he bought her a necklace with a silver snowflake pendant as a memento of their snowbound adventure.

She was happy, all right. And certain that her *falling in love* feeling was making a smooth, straight landing directly onto the *outright love* runway.

She and Sam balanced their romantic dates with work, though evenings usually found her on the sofa in his living room while he hashed out another *Tripwire* plot issue. At night, they fell into bed, hungry and hot for each other.

Brooke had enjoyed sex with previous boyfriends, but it had never been *like this*. For all his "no romance" attitude, Sam was the most attentive lover she'd ever had. He was especially good at making her want it in any number of ways —sweet, dirty, tender, intense, and everything in-between.

Though the words *I love you* popped into her mind at any given moment—during sex, or when they were laughing at a bad joke, or even when she was watching him scowl in concentration at his manuscript—she didn't say them aloud.

The purple *Courage* bracelet on her wrist reminded her that the mere act of telling Sam about her growing love had taken bravery. Maybe it had even been her first real act of courage for the new year.

Late on Friday afternoon, she arrived at his house and found him on the back porch, his elbows on the railing as he gazed at a couple of squirrels rustling in a grove of trees. She slipped her arms around him from behind and rested her head between his shoulder blades. She'd never known a man who was so warm and strong.

He turned, gathering her into his arms and pressing his lips to hers in greeting. "You hungry? It's getting close to dinner."

"Sure." She squeezed him around the waist.

They headed out into the chilly evening in search of food. Always mindful of their need to maintain secrecy, which so far hadn't appeared to be endangered, Brooke suggested an Italian cafe in neighboring Rainwood. They indulged in a lengthy meal of wine and pasta, followed by a shared tiramisu that was so good Sam asked for one to be boxed up to take home.

While he paid the bill, Brooke excused herself to use the

restroom. As she was heading back, her cell phone buzzed. Pausing in the corridor, she took it out of her purse.

The name *Michael* flashed on the screen. Her nerves tensed as she answered the call. "Hello."

"Hey, B." His voice was cheerful and upbeat. "Got your email. I like this *Lifelong Fling* concept. It's great that you're focusing on Bliss Cove couples, but this has a lot of potential for our February edition, what with Valentine's Day and all."

Her heart gave a sudden, hard bump against her ribs. "Really?"

"Yeah, really. Let's talk when you get into town. Did you get your flight?"

"Yes. I'm arriving Monday morning and leaving Friday. I'm at the Granger Hotel."

"Call me when you get in. My panel is on Wednesday morning, but I'll see you before then."

"Okay. Thanks, Michael."

She ended the call. A sudden tension ran down her spine. She looked up to find Sam standing right beside a server's station, a cardboard box in his hand.

Her insides twisted, though she had no reason to feel guilty or ashamed.

"Ready to go?" She tried to infuse a light note into her voice.

"I was just getting the extra cake." He indicated the box, his eyes narrowing. "You gave him the story?"

"What did you think I was going to do with it?" Brooke started back to the table. "If I can't sell it to another periodical, I'll publish it in *The Gazette*. But I'd really like to get paid for it and to have a solid credit for my freelance work. *Empire* is a great opportunity."

"He doesn't deserve it." Sam sounded as if he were speaking through a clenched jaw.

"You don't get to decide that." Brooke pulled on her jacket, hating the old uncertainty rising in her chest. "In fact, you don't have any say in what I do with my career."

His features hardened. "I *should.*"

"Why, because we've been working together?"

"Because I—" He stopped and shook his head hard. "I hate that you're selling yourself out."

"That's not what I'm doing! *God.* You know how hard it is to break into publishing! Why shouldn't I use a contact to give myself a step up?"

"A contact is one thing. Your ex is another." Stopping beside their table, Sam shoved his chair back into place with an abrupt movement. "Aside from the fact that he's an asshole, that magazine is one of the reasons he broke up with you, isn't it? Candace Pierson's father invested heavily in *Empire* as a startup. Was that before or after your dickhead ex asked her to marry him?"

Brooke's stomach hurt. "I don't know, and I don't care. It's over."

"Is it?" His jaw tensed. "Then why are you giving him one second of your time, much less any of your talent? Why are you going to let him profit from your work?"

"Why do you care?" She hitched her purse over her shoulder, conscious of the other diners who, thankfully, were scattered at tables on the other side of the room. "He didn't do anything to you."

"He treated you like shit, which is a hell of a lot worse than anything he could ever do to me," Sam snapped. "I grew up with a lying, cheating bastard. I guarantee they don't change."

"I don't want to talk about this anymore."

"Too bad." He folded his arms, looking about as movable as a boulder.

"No." She shook her head. "Last I heard, we had a business agreement about your book. That's it."

Anger fired into his eyes. "That is not *it*."

"Oh, excuse me." She stepped closer and lowered her voice further. "An agreement *with benefits*. And nowhere in that agreement did I ask for your input about my career choices."

"Tough. I'm giving it to you anyway."

"Sam, *Empire* is a magazine! I'm a writer." She spread her hands out in frustration. "I'm trying very hard to separate what happened from the fact that I *need* a jumpstart for my career. And you giving me shit about it isn't helping."

"I'm not giving you shit. I'm telling you the truth because I—"

"Brooke?" A woman's cheery voice broke through the tension-filled air.

Brooke's heart sank. "Mrs. Bowers."

The mayor of Bliss Cove strode toward them, resplendent in a flowered purple dress and bright pink handbag embellished with roses. "Well, how nice to see you here. Is that…" Her eyes widened. "Sam?"

Brooke frantically tried to think of a reasonable, non-dating explanation as to why she and Sam would be having both an argument and an intimate dinner together. "Uh…"

"Nice to see you, Mayor Bowers." His voice even, Sam

extended his hand to the older woman. "Did you enjoy your dinner?"

"We haven't eaten yet." Mrs. Bowers skimmed her gaze over the empty wine bottle and glasses on the table. "I didn't know you two were acquainted."

"We're acquainted." Sam's clipped tone indicated he wasn't thrilled with the acquaintanceship at the moment.

"We're just…having dinner," Brooke added lamely.

"I see that." The mayor eyed the dessert plate and two forks. "Interesting. You know, I'm not a busybody, but it was impossible to avoid the rumors when we heard about the snowstorm."

Brooke tried not to wince. Sam's shoulders stiffened, and she tried silently to assure him she'd already headed things off at the pass.

"What rumors?" he asked the mayor.

"Oh, just nonsense about what kind of hanky-panky might have gone on between two young people trapped in a one-room cabin." Mayor Bowers waved her hand dismissively. "But never mind that. Your mother and Eleanor Prescott were indignant at the very thought, and everyone has been assured it was all unfounded speculation and conjecture. Honestly, the truth made more sense since it was a bit difficult to imagine the two of you actually *together*."

Sudden heat crept up Brooke's neck. "Excuse me, but why would it be difficult to imagine me and Sam together?"

The mayor blinked, as if startled by the edge to Brooke's voice. "Really, I meant no offense. Sam is just a bit…um, different from your usual dates."

"Which are what?" Brooke crossed her arms and narrowed her eyes.

"Your usual dates are nice, friendly young men who have been in Bliss Cove for ages." Mayor Bowers lifted her hands in defense. "Am I wrong in thinking it's unusual for you to be going out with Sam, who's always been a bit strange?"

Brooke's hackles rose. Sam stepped toward her, putting a hand out as if to remind her he'd never cared what anyone in town thought of him.

But she did.

"For the record, Mrs. Bowers," Brooke turned to the other woman, "you might think Sam is strange, but did you ever stop to think that maybe he keeps to himself because he doesn't want people in his business? And, of course, getting into other people's business is a Bliss Cove pastime.

"But if you'd like a rumor to spread, than I suggest you spread the news that Sam Donovan is amazing in every way. He's strong, kind, smart, caring, and more loyal than I think he even realizes. He would never admit it, but he'd do anything for anyone. So if that's your definition of *strange*, then he fits the bill perfectly."

The mayor opened and closed her mouth. Sam stared at Brooke, his expression faintly stunned.

"However…" Brooke grabbed her purse and spun toward the door. "You heard right, Mrs. Bowers. Sam and I are most definitely not together."

She stalked outside and hurried toward a cab idling at the curb.

So much for *happy*.

CHAPTER 23

Sam took a gulp of whiskey and wiped his mouth with his sleeve. The noise and music filling the Mousehole Tavern did nothing to drown out the *feelings* that had been ricocheting through him since his argument with Brooke last night.

He was mad at himself. He was mad at Brooke. He was really fucking pissed off at that *Empire* jackass. And he was especially angry at whatever goddamned "universal forces" had conspired to put him in the same cabin with Brooke during a freak blizzard.

If she hadn't been there...

If he hadn't been there...

He wouldn't have spent an hour picking out a snowflake pendant for her. He wouldn't have watched her stand on her tiptoes to reach a box of sugar in the kitchen cabinet and been so caught up in her *cuteness* that he'd hauled her close and kissed her like she was the air he needed to breathe.

He wouldn't have spent almost every night during the

past week buried so deep inside her that he never wanted to leave. He wouldn't have felt as if he were struck in the heart every time she flashed him a quick, private smile. He wouldn't have learned that *bellis perennis* was a common species of daisies, or that Brooke was ticklish at the base of her spine, or that—

He sure as hell wouldn't be thinking corny, romantic thoughts.

"I feel like I'm falling in love with you."

He still couldn't get his head around it. Her words sat like a glowing ball right inside his chest, so bright he couldn't even look at them. He didn't dare think about what would happen if he let himself believe her.

But Brooke didn't lie. She was the most open and honest person he'd ever known.

Which meant—

"Another whiskey, straight up," he said.

Grant Taylor, owner and head chef of the tavern, glanced at him with a raised eyebrow but poured the Jack Daniel's. He set the glass in front of Sam along with a bowl of peanuts.

"You want some dinner?" Grant asked.

Sam shook his head and swallowed half the drink. He didn't know what the hell to do next. He didn't know if he should call Brooke or if she even wanted to hear from him again. Messy entanglements like this were the reason he stayed away from people. His own damned fault for breaking the rule.

"Hey, man." Jake Ryan hitched himself onto an empty barstool. "You know Hunter?"

Sam nodded, extending a hand to the other guy who took a seat at the bar beside Jake. A property developer, Hunter Armstrong had descended on Bliss Cove last spring with the intention of demolishing the historic Mariposa district to make room for a shopping and condo complex. He hadn't expected to face a determined enemy in the sweet, cat-loving Aria Prescott.

Though Sam had followed the battle from the sidelines, he'd anonymously contributed several sizeable donations to Aria's renovation fund, which had eventually become a joint venture run by both her and Hunter.

Grant stopped by to deposit Jake's and Hunter's usual beers in front of them.

"Haven't seen you here in a while," Jake said to Sam, after taking a drink. "We're playing some pool later, if you want to join us."

Sam made a noncommittal noise and grabbed a handful of peanuts. A few minutes of polite small talk and he'd get out of here.

"Hey, sorry about the cabin screw-up." Hunter twisted his mouth ruefully. "I should've called about the reservation rather than relying on the website."

"No problem."

Jake huffed out a laugh. "Sounds like it was a big problem, if you walked in and found out Brooke Castle was there."

Sam frowned. "What does that mean?"

"Nothing, man." Jake held up a placating hand. "Just that we're all waiting for a personal essay about her snowstorm adventure."

Sam flexed his fingers. "Brooke wouldn't do that."

His tone came out harder than he'd intended. Hunter and Jake exchanged glances.

Hunter shrugged. "She's a great girl. She can turn anything into a story."

"That's her job." Sam took a swallow of whiskey. "But she doesn't sell people out."

"Why would she…" Jake pulled his eyebrows together. "Man, what went on with you two up there?"

Sam tightened his grip on the glass. A dull flush heated his neck. Since he was a kid, he'd made a point of not showing people how he felt. Now, apparently, Jake could see right through him. That's what *feelings* did. They made you transparent.

"Her family's been in Bliss Cove forever." Jake cracked open a peanut and popped it into his mouth. "That's why everyone was so worried when word got out that she was trapped up in the mountains. Then when people heard she was with you…"

"I know, I know," Sam muttered irritably. "Beauty and the beast."

"Destiny was taking bets that you'd come back engaged." Hunter grinned and reached for his beer. "At least, until Aria put a stop to the betting pool."

"We're not engaged." *Why did that thought make his heart skip a beat?* "We're not anything."

Anymore.

The other two men fell silent. Sam swallowed the last of his whiskey. The liquor burned down his throat, adding fuel to his frustration.

"New appetizer, gentlemen." Rory Prescott, Grant's girl, approached from the kitchen, carrying three plates. "On the house, in exchange for your honest opinion. Fried calamari with lemon-garlic aioli."

After thanking her, they all tried the crispy squid and made noises of thumbs-up approval.

"Are you cooking back there now?" Jake nodded toward the kitchen and ate another piece of calamari.

"Lord, no." Rory laughed as Grant came up beside her with drink refills. "I'm a helper and the official food-taster. I've applied to be the Mousehole's official IT manager, but the stubborn, technophobe owner still refuses to consider investing in a computer system that would greatly streamline his workflow and more than likely increase his profits."

She shot Grant a sweet smile. He patted her ass in response.

"Thanks for your help, guys." Rory headed back to the kitchen, her long black ponytail swinging. All four men watched her go appreciatively.

"She hasn't converted you yet, huh?" Hunter asked.

"I won't let her." Grant shrugged and began polishing highball glasses. "I mean, she's probably right about the workflow or whatever, but the battle is too damned much fun."

"Losing the battle can also be fun," Hunter said. "Trust me on that."

"Man, you didn't lose." Jake shook his head and ate another peanut. "None of us did."

"That's the truth," Grant agreed.

Another brief silence fell as the three other men contemplated their great fortune in winning the hearts of the

Prescott sisters. Jake and Callie had gotten married last year, Rory and Grant were engaged, and Aria and Hunter...

For whatever reason—probably the whiskey—Sam found himself saying, "So, you planning a Mariposa Street wedding?"

He half-expected Hunter to stammer out some excuse about why he and Aria weren't getting married anytime soon. Instead, the other man nodded. "I asked Aria to marry me last summer, but she wanted to wait until the Mariposa work was finished and we'd gotten Monarch Enterprises up and running. I hope it'll be this summer. If—"

He pointed his chin at Grant. "She doesn't want to steal your and Rory's thunder."

"No thunder to steal." Grant glanced toward the kitchen, as if he could see his fiancée through the doors. "I'd marry Rory tomorrow, and I'd wait a lifetime. Whenever it happens and whatever she wants, I'm in."

He suddenly shot a narrow look at the other men. "And if you tell me I'm whipped, you'd be right. No better way to be, as my wise kid brother once told me."

Jake chuckled. "No argument from me. Before Callie, I didn't have a clue that marriage could be this awesome."

"It can't *all* be hearts and flowers," Sam muttered, cracking a peanut against the bar top.

"No." Jake creased his forehead. "When I was single, I had a hell of a lot more closet and drawer space. Not to mention, I didn't have to store my shampoo under the sink because I actually had room on the shower shelf. Callie has so much crap in there now I barely have room for one bar of soap."

Despite the lengthy diatribe, Jake didn't seem too

annoyed by the surplus of feminine products in his bathroom.

"I hear ya." Hunter sighed and tilted his head back for another swallow of beer. "Then there's the makeup. The lip gloss. The hairbands. The underwear…though I don't mind that too much. Oh, and the healing crystals in every single room."

"That's just Aria." Grant smirked.

"What, Rory doesn't leave her girl stuff all over the place?"

"Rory doesn't have girl stuff." Grant set the glasses on the shelf. "She leaves gummy worm wrappers and dirty clothes everywhere. Then she always ends up stealing my shirts."

He, too, didn't seem particularly bothered by this.

"What about when they hog all the blankets?" Jake tossed another peanut into his mouth.

"Or take forever to get ready to go out," Hunter said.

"Or eat the food you were saving for the playoffs." Grant began wiping down the counter.

Or make you build a blanket fort.

Sam finished off his whiskey. He felt prickly and irritated. "So why do you bother?"

All three of them jerked their heads to stare at him.

Hunter looked faintly baffled by the question. "Man, I love Aria more than anything."

"Being married to the woman you love," Jake said, "is the greatest thing in the world."

"Why *wouldn't* you bother?" Grant shook his head in disbelief.

Sam broke apart a peanut shell and reached for another. If Brooke were here, she'd be glowing and dreamily telling him about how these three couples were all each other's *One True Loves* or whatever, and how they were destined to be *Lifelong Flings*.

Right, well…he could admit now that kind of thing happened for other people. The moony slobs in front of him were evidence enough.

"You staying for pool?" Jake asked.

"No, thanks."

Sam dug into his pocket for his wallet and tossed enough bills on the bar to cover the round of drinks, plus a few more for Jake and Hunter. He shoved off the barstool and grabbed his jacket from the wall rack.

A sudden, feminine laugh almost made his heart stop.

It was the sound that light would make.

He turned. His heart almost pounded out of his chest. Brooke was standing by the fireplace booth, talking to Max Weatherford, the local veterinarian. Whatever the guy was saying had Brooke smiling. Her eyes twinkled.

A knot tightened in Sam's chest. He wasn't stupid enough to think she'd moved on that fast, but the sight of her with another man was a cold dose of reality. Because Max Weatherford—an all-around good guy who was beloved by the entire town—was exactly the kind of man Brooke should be with.

Hell. Max was the kind of man Brooke *wanted*. Her ideal romance-novel hero with his easy sociability, all-American chiseled good looks, and probably a crap ton of "sweet noth-ings" in his repertoire.

Pulling on his jacket, Sam stalked to the door. The Romance 101 class had been unlike anything he'd ever imagined, but it was time for him to get back to both work and reality.

Class was over.

CHAPTER 24

*E*ven in the middle of an East Coast winter, Manhattan vibrated with energy. Nothing had changed in the years since Brooke had last been there— pedestrians crowded the streets, cars and taxis clogged the snow-covered roads, and everyone moved with the tense urgency of needing to be somewhere five minutes ago.

She checked into her single room at a budget hotel several blocks from the Marquis Marriott. Hating the way she and Sam had left things, she'd called him last night, but his phone had gone to voicemail. The only communication she'd had with him had been a "safe travels" text he'd sent her before she'd boarded the plane.

She changed out of her travel clothes and into a suit, then made her way to the convention. Though she felt her big-city anxiety surge back to life as she navigated crowds and crossed busy streets, she was looking forward to revisiting some of her favorite restaurants and shops. Her time in New York had ended badly, but she'd lived here for three years— long enough to establish a cache of good memories.

After registering, she spent the morning at various panel discussions and workshops. She took copious notes, ran into former colleagues and acquaintances, enjoyed the free coffee and pastries bar, and found the courage to introduce herself to several prominent editors.

By the end of the second day, she was glad she'd come. She texted her parents that everything was going well, and she pondered a text from Michael: *Dinner Wed? Want to discuss yr proposal.*

Dinner didn't mean she was agreeing to anything. Sam's criticism was still running through the back of her mind. Then again, so was her own belief that *Empire* was a step in the right direction.

She'd written out a list of the reasons why, and another list of Michael's more positive qualities, which included *ambitious* and *knows good writing when he reads it.* Plus, she knew her own strengths. She'd be an excellent contributor to *Empire*.

But for her own well-being, she needed to shift the dynamic and let Michael know that she would *choose* to write for *Empire*, and only if she wanted to. He didn't get to accept or reject her or her writing.

She texted him back. *6 works for me. LMK where.*

He responded with *Harvest*, a fine dining restaurant in Rockefeller Center. Brooke added it to her calendar. Before going to bed, she called Sam again, but he didn't pick up. She left a message and went to sleep with the hopes of waking up to a response.

The next morning, there was nothing.

Not that she was surprised. She should have seen it coming, actually. A man who didn't know what love looked like, who thought it was a lie, would naturally assume that one quarrel would sever all ties between them.

Not to mention, she knew he still had no idea what to do with her declaration of love. He might have been trying to widen the distance between them. She couldn't close it again until she got back and was able to talk with him face to face.

She showered and dressed, then headed out for her third full day of workshops, panels, and networking. As she was taking a lunch break and checking her phone, an email message sent a shockwave through her whole body.

The sender was Jillian Powers, who, as far as Brooke was concerned, needed no introduction. But Jillian introduced herself anyway.

Ms. Castle, I'm the senior editor of Clarity magazine. We received your application for our features writer position and would like to find out if you're available for an interview.

Please contact my assistant at the number below to set up a time. Thank you.

After riding out a wave of excitement so intense it was almost nauseating, Brooke called the number and spoke with Jillian's assistant, Mandy.

"We're scheduling interviews through the end of the month, Ms. Castle," Mandy chirped. "Would Thursday the twenty-first work for you?"

Thursday the forty-eighth would work for me, if that's what Jillian Powers wants.

"Yes, that works. I'll book a flight for the previous

day." Brooke twisted the strap of her satchel around her fingers. "I am in town right now for the Freelancer's Convention, if anything happens to be available within the next few days."

"Oh, Jillian's calendar is full this week." Mandy sounded regretful. "I'm so sorry. I can let you know if anything opens up."

"Of course, I'd appreciate that. You can reach me at this number."

"Lovely. We'll plan to see you on the twenty-first, then. Ten a.m. in Jillian's office on Liberty Street."

"I'll be there. Thank you."

She ended the call and immediately tried to reach Sam. Nothing. She didn't leave a message, wanting to tell him herself.

She resisted the urge to call her parents and grandfather —they'd be so excited and hopeful, but of course an interview was not a job offer. And no doubt there was a massive pool of candidates, so—

Brooke shook her head to stop the negative train of thought. An interview was one step closer to getting hired.

She sought out the workshop on the international freelance market. She also attended Michael's panel discussion on magazines, which involved him and three other editors.

Brooke sat in the back of the room, glad that she had the chance to at least see him before their dinner. He looked the same—lean and handsome with his blond hair cropped short.

He'd always been a snappy dresser with a penchant for expensive suits he couldn't really afford. That didn't appear to have changed either, as he wore what looked like an Armani suit and blue silk tie. If she wasn't mistaken, there was even a matching blue silk handkerchief in his breast pocket.

To her total lack of surprise, people converged on him like ants on a sugar bowl after the discussion, asking questions and probably flirting, too. She slipped out of the crowded room and went in search of the free coffee and pastries table.

After the day's events had concluded, she returned to her hotel room and changed into a green sheath dress and low-heeled pumps. She applied a layer of makeup and pulled her hair into a knot at the base of her neck.

Though the "dress up" regimen had never been her style, she needed to feel extra powerful and in control at this dinner. Knowing she had an interview with a top-tier life-style magazine in her back pocket gave her an even bigger boost.

She splurged on a cab to Rockefeller Center. Based on the website, Harvest was a pricey, fine-dining establishment located on the fifty-second floor. By the time the cab driver pulled up, it was a few minutes to six.

After paying, Brooke hurried into the building. The ice-skating rink swarmed with people, and bright lights twinkled from the trees. She passed through security and located the elevator bank.

As she neared the cluster of people entering an open elevator, her heart thudded hard.

Right in front of her, a tall, dark-haired man stood toward the back of the crowd. Under normal circumstances, he might not have caught her attention, but her nerves were jittery over both Michael and the interview request. And something about the man's posture and solid stance, as if he were holding the earth in place, elicited a surge of familiarity.

Sam?

Her breath caught. She increased her pace. Her thoughts darted in a thousand different directions. She swallowed the instinct to call his name.

The man stepped into the elevator and moved to the side. The doors began closing.

Brooke broke into a jog. The man shifted his gaze to her. He put his arm out to block the doors, holding them open.

She darted into the elevator and came to a stop, her pulse racing. She turned toward him. His name again formed on her lips, then died.

He wasn't Sam.

Of course he wasn't. Sam wouldn't show up in Manhattan without calling or telling you. Silly goose.

Brooke pulled in a breath. "Thank you."

"No problem." He released the doors, his fingers poised over the elevator panel. "What floor?"

"Fifty-two."

"Harvest, huh?" He smiled slightly, revealing a boyish dimple in his left cheek. "I recommend the halibut and the dark chocolate soufflé. In different courses. Of course."

She managed to smile at the small joke. "Of course."

Though she was being rude, creepy, or both, she couldn't stop staring at him. Up close, he was strikingly handsome. He looked as if he were in his mid-thirties, with fine lines radiating from the corners of his eyes and bracketing his mouth.

But he looked so much like Sam—strong features and high cheekbones sloping down to a wide, well-shaped mouth. Even his eyes, though a lighter brown, were a similar shape and framed by thick, dark eyelashes. He was an inch or two taller than Sam and maybe broader in the chest and shoulders, but the resemblance was uncanny.

He lifted his eyebrows, as if questioning her stare.

"I...I'm sorry." Brooke gave herself a quick mental shake and faced forward. "I thought you were...you look like someone I know."

His posture tensed. "Is that right?"

"Well, they say we all have a doppelganger." She forced a chuckle. "You must be his."

The elevator came to a stop at the twenty-first floor, and Brooke moved aside to let a few people exit. The doors closed again.

"Who is it I look like?" the man asked.

"Oh, just a...um, friend." Doppelganger or not, she wasn't about to tell a complete stranger about her complicated love life.

She glanced at him again, only to find that he was looking at her this time. Another flicker of *Don't I know you?* went through her.

The elevator doors opened, revealing the glass-paneled entrance to Harvest.

Brooke slipped her purse over her shoulder. The man held the door for her again.

"Enjoy your dinner," he said.

"Thank you." For some strange reason, she felt as if she should say more, but that, too, was silly.

She left the elevator and walked toward the restaurant. Another couple exited behind her. The woman edged up next to Brooke, leaning closer as if she were about to impart a secret.

"That was Lincoln Atwood," she announced in a conspiratorial whisper.

Brooke stopped. "The author?"

"The one and only. Isn't he gorgeous?" The woman fanned her face with her hand and gave a swoony sigh. "I heard him do a reading at the Met last year, and oh my lord, that *voice*. He had the whole room captivated. Most of the women were practically orgasmic."

"Honey." The man behind her shook his head in reprimand.

"What? It's the truth." The woman shrugged without apology. "I guarantee he's the only Pulitzer-prize winning author who looks and sounds like *that*. Anyway." She smiled at Brooke. "I overheard you saying he looked familiar. That's probably why."

"Probably." Brooke started toward the hostess station. "Thanks for letting me know."

She stepped aside under the pretense of checking her phone, allowing the couple to go ahead of her.

Lincoln Atwood.

He was an incredible author. She'd given his most recent book five stars in her Brooke's Books column. He'd been a literary prodigy, having published his first novel at twenty-four. The book, *Truth*, had received great acclaim and was a finalist for the National Book Award.

Since that illustrious debut eleven years ago, Lincoln had published half a dozen other novels that had both hit the bestseller lists and been lauded by critics. His most recent book, *Honor*, was no exception. The young prodigy had become an established, acclaimed author with countless awards for his work and a devoted international fan base. At thirty-five, he was legendary.

She'd seen plenty of photos of him in articles and book reviews. Heck, his headshot was in the back of all his books. No wonder he looked familiar.

Slipping her phone back into her purse, she left her coat at the coat check and explained to the hostess that she was meeting Michael Barnes. The woman nodded and led her past the linen-draped tables and sparking chandeliers.

Brooke had run into celebrities all the time when she'd lived in New York. Aside from a spark of recognition or internal fangirl moment, she'd never given them much thought. But Lincoln Atwood…she felt like that brief encounter would stick with her.

"Brooke Castle."

Her stomach tensed. She pushed Lincoln Atwood to the back of her mind.

Though she and Michael had spoken on the phone a few times, she was unprepared for the sound of his voice saying her name in person. He was standing beside a table glittering with silver and china. He was equally polished—his Hugo Boss suit and tie impeccable, his clean-shaven jaw and perfectly arched eyebrows emphasizing his noble features.

"Hi, Michael." She let him take her hand and pull her closer for a light kiss on the cheek. The smell of his cologne almost made her sneeze.

"You look beautiful." He ran his gaze admiringly over her.

"Would you like a cocktail, ma'am?" A server appeared as the hostess pulled her chair out.

Needing something strong, Brooke requested a gin and tonic. Michael waited until she'd taken her seat before he sat across from her.

"Thanks for joining me," he said.

She didn't bother thanking him for asking. This was a business dinner.

"Your panel discussion was quite informative." She unwrapped her linen napkin and spread it over her lap. "And I'm glad to know you like the *Lifelong Fling* idea."

Michael chuckled. "Way to get down to business. Can't we just talk first? It's been a long time."

She nodded. "Feels like a lifetime."

"Yeah." He sat back and slipped his gaze over her. "I mean, really, you look fantastic. All that sea air has been good for you. You were pretty messed up when you left New York."

"I had reason to be." She smiled tightly.

"I know." He chuckled and flicked his gaze to a nearby table. "That's one of the reasons I wanted to see you again, actually. To apologize."

Though it was too late for apologies, Brooke *had* made an effort to forgive him. She could give him credit for trying to make amends.

She waited as the server brought their drinks and departed before she said, "Go ahead. I'm listening."

"For what it's worth, I am sorry." Michael twisted his college ring around his finger. "We had a great thing going, and I screwed it up. Huge mistake."

At one time, she might have agreed. But now? If they hadn't broken up, and if she hadn't moved back to Bliss Cove…

No snowbound cabin.

No blanket fort.

No Sam.

Even with their precarious footing at the moment, she wouldn't have given up their time together for anything.

She let out her breath slowly. "Actually, Michael, you did me a favor. You weren't the right man for me. Not by a long shot."

A slight hardness tightened his jaw. "Did you find a guy who is?"

"I'm not going to talk about that with you." She reached for her drink. "How's Candace?"

"Okay, I guess." He rubbed his finger on the handle of a fork. "Actually, we're not together anymore."

"I'm sorry." She managed to make her sympathy sound sincere. "What happened?"

"Her father." He rolled his eyes and laughed. "He was supposed to be a silent partner in the magazine, but turns out he couldn't shut up about either *Empire* or our marriage. Candace was his little princess, and I couldn't do anything right. I should've seen it coming. I mean, I think I realized I'd made a mistake, like, five minutes after saying, *'I do.'* I did, but I shouldn't have."

"Well. Lesson learned."

The server approached again. "Are you ready to order?"

While Michael scanned the menu, Brooke said, "I'll have the halibut, and then the dark chocolate soufflé for dessert."

"Poached lobster for me." Michael handed his menu back.

After the woman had left, Brooke took a healthy swallow of the gin and tonic. "So let's talk about my proposal."

"Yeah, I like it." He leaned forward, skimming his gaze over her face and down to the v-neckline of her dress. "You were always a great writer, but you were never made for hardcore news. When I got your email about love stories, I thought, *That's so Brooke.*"

He was right, but that didn't stop her defenses from locking into place. Maybe it was the condescending note in his voice.

"It took me some time to discover my writing niche." She took another sip of her drink. "But I finally did."

"Yeah. It's a cool idea." He pursed his lips. "I mean, it needs some refining…like, you can't just talk about old people…but overall, it's solid. That sea air must've been good for more than your looks."

With a chuckle, he reached for a piece of bread from the basket.

"So what's the next step?" Brooke asked.

"Oh, you know…" He stuffed the bread in his mouth. "Toss it around to the other editors, brainstorm how to refine it, sharpen the angle, et cetera. Takes a while."

Tension crawled over her shoulders. "I understand, but I don't have a *while*. You said you were looking for your February edition."

"Yeah, but things are fluid, you know?" He swallowed a gulp of his martini. "Gotta shuffle and move them around. Did you color your hair?"

"No."

"Because you look amazing."

Brooke sighed. "Michael, the article."

"Okay, look." He twisted his neck and suddenly reached across the table to grab her hand.

She stiffened and tried to pull away. He tightened his grip. To avoid a scene, she didn't engage in hand-wrestling, but she hardened both her eyes and her tone.

"Let go, Michael."

"I know why you came to me." He leaned closer, his eyes gleaming in the low light. "It's brutal out there. You're getting chewed up and spit out, aren't you? Put through the meat grinder."

"Your point?" She clenched her fingers into a fist. "And I didn't come to you. You contacted me."

"My point is that you need me." He tugged her arm, forcing her closer and rubbing his fingers over her wrist. "Which is totally perfect because I need you back."

A heavy, sick sensation collected in her chest. "Let go of me."

"We have an editors' meeting on Monday." He shifted and tugged at his silk tie. "Play your cards right, and I'll run your article by the features editor first thing."

Brooke yanked her hand away from his hard enough to break free. The table rattled.

"Whoa, chill out." Holding up his hands, he sat back. "I'm not talking about anything serious. You're here for a few more days, so we can have a little fun for old times' sake, see how it goes. Monday I'll pitch your little love stories article and see what happens."

She gripped the napkin to stop her hands from shaking. "You asshole."

"Oh my god." He barked out a laugh and gulped more of his drink. "Have you seriously been teasing me all this time?"

She stared at him. "*What* are you talking about?"

"Come on, Brooke." He rolled his eyes heavenward. "We've been playing cat and mouse for months now. You didn't think I was just going to publish your work without you giving me something in return? Tit for tat, so to speak."

She studied his handsome face, searching for a hint of the love she once thought she'd felt for him. There was nothing but cold, dead ashes.

"You're pathetic," she said. "You can't have my work. And you'll never have me again."

He frowned. "You fucking wasted my time?"

"Tit for tat, Michael." With a smirk, she pushed her chair back. "For a while there, I did think we had a shot at being acquaintances again. I wanted your help because I was desperate *and* you owed me big time. But you are still the same little narcissistic toad you were two years ago. You'll never care about anyone but yourself."

She grabbed her purse and stood. A few patrons glanced in their direction. Michael grabbed her wrist.

"Sit down," he hissed.

"Let *go*." She twisted from his grip again. "You're never going to see or talk to me again. You can't have any of my ideas, and don't you dare think about stealing them because I have the paper trail proving they're *mine*."

"You…" His expression hardened suddenly. "You bitch."

"Call me whatever you want, Michael. When you're a bitter, lonely old man with no one to talk to and no one to love, you'll look back and remember that I'm the one who walked away. You'll know you never came close to deserving me."

She spun and headed toward the door.

"What about your fish?" Michael called.

"You eat it."

She strode to the elevators, her heart hammering and skin burning with anger. But when she stepped out into the cold winter air, a sudden laugh burst from her. The persistent unease in her chest was gone, replaced with a bright, glowing light that came directly from within.

She hurried toward a cab and climbed into the backseat, giving the driver the address of her hotel. As she settled back against the seat, her phone buzzed with a text from Jillian Powers' assistant.

Jillian had a cancellation for Friday morning. She can meet with you at 9:00am about the features writer position, if you are available. Please text to confirm. TY!

CHAPTER 25

John Kane had never put a name to feelings. Life moved fast, was too harrowing and complex. His body absorbed highs and lows. If he coasted on a midline for a couple of days, he was lucky.

But he knew rage. A black, suffocating storm. Watching Walker bleed out on the greasy sidewalk...the anger stole his breath. Iced his blood. He wanted a revenge that would kill. There would be no end.

Then Patricia put her cool hand over his. She rested her head on his shoulder and sat with him in silence.

This.

Sitting in the dark, breathing her in, as a slow, heavy peace quieted the storm...Kane called this feeling "love."

*S*am saved the manuscript and closed his laptop. Standing, he stretched out his arms and back. He shoved his feet into his boots, pulled on his parka, and went outside. He checked the gas level in the generator and hauled another load of wood into the cabin.

His deadline was tomorrow. As soon as he got back to Bliss Cove, he'd do a final pass of *Tripwire* and send it to his editor. He'd lived with John Kane long enough to know when one of his stories was finished.

And when it was good.

After stoking the fire, he went into the kitchen and uncapped a bottle of lemon-cayenne iced tea. Silently toasting Brooke, he took a swallow of the lousy stuff and opened a box of Barnum's Animals crackers. He ate them while leaning against the counter.

The broken ladder still rested against the wall, and a piece of duct tape—a remnant of the blanket fort—was stuck to a wooden loft support. He'd found multicolored glitter sprinkled on the floor in front of the fireplace.

He finished the crackers and tossed the box in the recycling bin. Tomorrow morning, he'd head back to town.

Brooke had been gone all week. Though her absence was a physical ache, isolating himself in the cabin with no one but his characters to talk to had put him at the finish line. He'd finally figured it out.

She'd be back tomorrow.

He'd be waiting for her.

~

JILLIAN POWERS WAS EVERYTHING BROOKE WOULD HAVE expected from the senior editor of a lifestyle magazine that boasted a circulation of over 2.5 million. With her Chanel suit, sleek hairstyle, and elegantly furnished office, she radiated both confidence and warmth.

She offered Brooke fresh gourmet coffee from a gleaming, stainless steel machine and conducted the interview in a corner seating area of her office.

Though Jillian started off with the usual questions about Brooke's strengths and interpersonal skills, Brooke soon felt the interview shifting into more of a conversation than a Q&A. She also grew increasingly sure of herself. Before applying for the features writer position, she'd done her homework.

She knew in-depth details about *Clarity's* target demographic, circulation numbers, brand mission, and content strategy. She was a true, loyal subscriber who'd read every monthly issue over the past five years and could tell Jillian exactly which articles she'd found the most valuable.

By the time the interview wound down, Brooke felt better about her life prospects than she had in a long time. Her showdown with Michael had finally forced her to cut all ties with her past, including the regret and shame she'd secretly carried.

No, she wasn't a hardcore news reporter who liked chasing stories about political unrest and crime, but she was most definitely a reporter who could write excellent, insightful articles about books, relationships, history, wellness, divination, fashion (okay, scratch that one), strength, and happiness. She wanted to write positive, uplifting stories that made people feel good about themselves and their lives.

"I appreciate you taking the time to talk to me." She gathered her things together. "I've been a longtime reader of *Clarity*, and I'd love to make the leap into becoming part of the writing staff."

"I'm very glad you could come in on such short notice." Jillian smiled and picked up the stack of papers that included Brooke's resume and copies of her past articles. "You're a wonderful writer, and the style of your features articles would fit our slate very well. You should expect to hear from us soon."

A knock came at the door, and Mandy poked her head in the room. "Excuse me for interrupting, but Lynette Hanover is running late for your meeting, so you have an extra half-hour, if you need it."

"Thanks, but we're just wrapping up." Jillian leafed through the papers.

Mandy gave a little nod and left the room.

Brooke stilled in the process of zipping up her purse. A strange cold suddenly prickled over her skin.

"I just love this article you wrote about the romance author in Chicago." Jillian tapped her finger on a printed copy of the article. "You wouldn't think that authors lead terribly interesting lives, but that makes it all the more fun to peek behind the scenes. So, do you have any other questions for me?"

Brooke's throat was dry. She took a sip of water before asking, "I'm sorry if this is inappropriate, but did Mandy say Lynette Hanover?"

"Oh, yes." Jillian's eyes brightened. "Lynette is a good friend. I'm so pleased she recommended you. How do you know her?"

"I don't." Brooke set her glass down. "I've just heard… isn't she a literary agent?"

"One of the top agents in the country." Jillian nodded emphatically. "She represents a number of bestselling authors."

"And you said she recommended me?"

"Yes." A touch of confusion darkened Jillian's eyes. "She called and said you'd applied for the writer position. Obviously, we get hundreds of applicants for openings, so Lynette asked me personally to take a look at your resume. I assumed you knew that."

"I didn't." A dull ache began to encroach on Brooke's heart.

As if sensing her sudden dismay, Jillian smiled. "Having a referral is very helpful in such a competitive environment, but you stood out from the applicant pool right away. Your resume had easily made it past the first rounds and was slated to hit my desk. I just specifically sought it out when Lynette asked me to."

"I appreciate that." Brooke shook her head. She didn't want to end her enjoyable interview on a dire note. "I'm sorry if I seem surprised."

Jillian waved her hand. "Lynette and I have been friends for several years, but she knows most of the key personnel in Folio Publishing. Her family has known the Atwoods for ages."

Brooke's reporter instinct kicked into high gear. She kept her voice casual as she said, "Oh, yes, the Atwoods. Their company owns *Clarity*."

"*Clarity* is their largest magazine holding." Jillian nodded. "They're mostly a book publisher, but they took over a few magazines when they acquired the Wilcox Media Group."

"Interesting." Brooke rose and extended her hand. "It was lovely having the opportunity to talk with you. Please let me know if there are any other questions I can answer."

"You do the same." Jillian shook her hand and walked with her to the door. "As I said, you can expect to hear from us soon."

Brooke thanked her again and left the office. Mandy looked up from her desk right outside the door.

"How did it go?" she asked in a stage whisper, her eyes bright with expectation.

"Very well, thanks." Brooke made a mental note to send the cheerful young woman a box of gourmet chocolates as a thank-you-for-being-so-nice gift. "Jillian said she'd get back to me soon."

"Word on the street is you're on the short list." Mandy winked.

Brooke smiled and said goodbye. She took the elevator to street level and stopped in the lobby to call Sam. Again, no answer. She started to text him the names *Lynette Hanover* and *Lincoln Atwood*, then stopped. She needed to talk with him face-to-face.

She stepped outside. The noise of snow-blowers and car engines filled the cold air. She hailed a cab to take her to the hotel. Later this afternoon, she'd get on a plane back to Bliss Cove.

But for the first time ever, she didn't know what would be waiting for her.

CHAPTER 26

*O*n his way home from the cabin on Friday afternoon, Sam turned into the same gas station where he and Brooke had stopped. He filled the tank of his truck and checked his phone.

He didn't use his phone often, so the lack of cell service at the cabin had never bothered him before. Now, he was frustrated to discover he'd missed several calls from Brooke.

He tried calling her, but got no response. Checking the clock, he calculated she was probably in the air.

His impatience intensified as he drove. He wanted to tell her about the book, though he didn't let himself think beyond that.

After getting back to the house, he tried her again. No response. He'd give her time to settle back in, then stop by her apartment.

He emailed his revised *Tripwire* manuscript to both his agent and his editor, then went out to pick up a bouquet of daisies and roses. By the time six-thirty rolled around, his impatience was at an all-time high. He drove to Brooke's duplex apartment and rang the front doorbell. Her apartment door opened, and she came down the stairs.

His heart thumped. She was wearing yoga pants and a T-shirt, and her hair was pulled back into a messy ponytail. Her eyes widened as she caught sight of him through the glass window.

She opened the door. He barely restrained himself from stepping forward and pulling her into his arms.

Something was wrong.

"Hi." He tightened his grip on the bouquet.

"Hi." She rubbed a hand over her arm.

"Are you okay?" Faint alarm flicked through him. She was unusually pale, with dark circles under her eyes. "I called a few times, but you didn't answer."

Her breath escaped. "My phone was off."

"Doesn't matter." He extended the flowers and raked his gaze over her. "What's wrong?"

She took the flowers. "Thank you for these, but we need to talk."

Though Sam wasn't a romance guy, he did know nothing good ever came after those four words.

He followed her into her apartment, experiencing the sudden, sick feeling that he'd missed the mark. Lost his chance.

"The last time we...I'm sorry I didn't get back to you." He closed the door behind him. He couldn't think of anything else to say. He was desperate to haul her into his arms and kiss her—a week away from her felt like an eternity—but there was a hard set to her shoulders, an invisible "keep away" wall in front of her.

"This isn't about not being in touch, Sam." She put the

flowers on the coffee table. "I think it was good for us to have some time apart. My trip went very well. I even had an unexpected interview with the senior editor of *Clarity*. I'd applied for a job there a few weeks ago, but coincidentally she had an opening this morning. In fact, she called me right before I got on the plane and offered me the job."

"That's fantastic." He exhaled in relief. "Congratulations. Not that I'm surprised."

"You shouldn't be, considering you were the one who set up the interview behind my back." She folded her arms, an accusatory glint hardening her eyes.

His blood chilled. "I didn't set up the interview. I asked my agent to mention you to the *Clarity* editor, that's all."

"You interfered because you couldn't leave me alone about Michael," Brooke snapped. "You hated that I was doing something you didn't agree with, so you tried to stop me another way."

"I didn't try to stop you from anything!" He paced away from her, his shoulders tightening. "I didn't even know the editor would interview you, much less offer you the job. All I did was try and get your resume in front of the right person."

"And it didn't occur to you to either tell me what you were doing or ask me if I even wanted your help?"

"Yes, it occurred to me, but I knew you'd say no."

"Of course I'd have said no!" she retorted. "And you know why. You're the only one who knows how hard it's been for me, the only one who knows why I didn't want to tell my family that I've been failing all over again. You're the only one who knows about Michael, and you didn't respect the fact that I told you all of that in confidence."

His blood burned at the sound of the other man's name. "I didn't tell anyone what you told me in confidence! I made one phone call on your behalf. Plenty of people get job offers and opportunities that way."

"You made a call that wasn't yours to make." Her mouth tightened. "I didn't want or need your help."

The sharp statement hit him right in the gut. "But you wanted and needed *his* help?"

"I was the one making the choice about *Empire*." Brooke pointed her thumb at her chest, her eyes flaring. "You, on the other hand, were making a choice for me. If I'd wanted to use someone else's personal connections, I could have asked my grandfather. In fact, he offered several times. But I've spent two full years depending on other people to keep me upright, and I wanted to finally do something on my own. You took that away from me."

"Oh, for God's sake." Frustration crawled up his spine. "You'd rather rely on your ex than let me make one fucking phone call for you? Your internal logic is totally flawed."

She stared at him. "My *internal logic*? What are you, a computer? Oh, right, I forgot. Sam Donovan doesn't do *feelings*."

"I'm *feeling* pissed off about this right now," he snapped. "Why is it okay for you to help me, but not for me to help you?"

She blinked. "What are you talking about?"

"What we've been doing for the past two weeks." He scraped a hand through his hair. "You offered to help me with my plot just because you wanted to, remember? You were ready to do it for nothing. Why can't I help you because I want to, because you deserve it, because the whole fucking world should know how good you are?"

Her features hardened. "That wasn't why I was offered the job."

"Yes, it was!" Sam strode toward her, wanting to grab her shoulders and force her to see the truth. "*Clarity* isn't going to hire a features writer as a *favor*. The editor never would have called you if she hadn't been impressed with your resume and writing. And she sure as hell wouldn't have offered you the job if you hadn't knocked the interview out of the park. This is why I hate that you thought that dirtbag was your only shot." He stepped away, his chest heaving. "You met with him in New York didn't you?"

She looked past him at the opposite wall. Her jaw tightened.

"I know bastards like him." Sam dug his fingers into his palms. "I grew up with one of them. What did he do, wine and dine you and tell you what an incredible writer you are before he made a pass at you?"

She paled, and his anger flared into a firestorm.

"What the fuck did he do, Brooke?"

She pressed her lips together. "None of your business. But I handled it without help from anyone."

"I told you assholes like him don't change." Shoving aside his own bitter memories, he paced to the fireplace and back again. "Look, I appreciate your plucky, can-do attitude, but you've spent way too long punishing yourself over a shitty relationship and a job that almost gave you a nervous breakdown. You still haven't realized walking away from that took courage. You've been too busy blaming yourself."

"And you can't admit that you were wrong!"

"You know what's wrong?" He stalked toward her. "Thinking there's only one way to get what you want. It's like the pen and the crossword."

Her eyebrows snapped together. "*Now* what are you talking about?"

"You told me that using a pen for a crossword means I think there's only one direction to take, one answer to every problem." He spread his arms out wide. His spine was stiff enough to break. "Which is total bullshit. There are a hundred directions, a thousand answers. But you only saw *one*. You didn't have faith in yourself."

"I know I'm a good writer." A flush of anger colored her face. "Which is why I've been working so hard to get a job that's a result of my talent and experience, not because my boyfriend-who's-not-really-my-boyfriend set it up for me. You didn't trust my judgement, and you didn't trust that I could do it on my own. You didn't trust *me*."

Disbelief flooded him. "Brooke, you're the *only* person I trust."

"Then why didn't you tell me about Lincoln?" she cried.

Shit.

Silence fell like a weight. The clock on the wall ticked.

Everything inside him locked down. "Lincoln has nothing to do with this."

"Considering he's your older brother, I beg to differ." A pulse beat heavily at the base of her throat.

"How…" Sam closed his eyes and pulled in a heavy breath. His chest knotted. "How did you find out?"

"I saw him in an elevator and thought he was you." Her voice was as tight as pulled wire. "Then a woman told me he was Lincoln Atwood, and when Jillian mentioned the

Atwoods and Folio Publishing at the interview…with a little research, it wasn't hard to put two and two together."

"I haven't talked to Lincoln in over five years." Sam hated the old inadequacy roiling in his chest. "I sure as hell didn't talk to him about you."

"But why…" She paused. "Why didn't you talk to *me* about *him*?"

"It doesn't matter." He strode to the window and stared down at the darkened street. *This* was fucking why—because Lincoln threw a shadow over everything Sam had ever done. "I told you I left New York ten years ago. I haven't seen much of my family since then. Last time I saw Lincoln was when our mother was dying."

"That doesn't answer my question."

He faced her. She stood with her arms tightly crossed, as if she were holding herself in.

"Were you *ever* planning to tell me?" she asked.

He'd already told her more than he'd ever told anyone. But no. He hadn't *planned* to tell her about his family.

He shook his head.

"It's one hell of a story, Sam." Her lips thinned. "An anonymous thriller writer whose older brother is an acclaimed Pulitzer-prize winning author. Family secrets, sibling rivalry, a publishing empire worth God knows how much money. Volatile, neglectful parents. The press would love it. That's the main reason you stayed off the grid, isn't it? You never wanted anyone to know the truth. Not even me. *Especially* not me."

"No." He shook his head, suddenly feeling as if they were standing on a thin, cracked sheet of ice. "I didn't tell you because my past has nothing to do with you. With *us*."

"*Everything* about you has to do with us." She rubbed her throat. "I love you, Sam. I think I started falling in love with you in the blanket fort when you admitted you tried to stay away from me because I'm a reporter. And I'll always be a reporter at heart. I'll always be curious and on the lookout for another story to tell. I'll always want to know more about people's lives."

Her *I love you* slammed up against the defenses of his heart. "Brooke, I didn't keep this from you because you're a reporter."

"Didn't you?"

"I *told* you about my parents. I told you about what happened to me."

"But you didn't tell me who you really are." Wariness suddenly darkened her eyes. "You didn't tell me about the Atwoods, or the truth about your parents and brother. You never *were* going to tell me."

"Because that all happened in another lifetime!" He fisted his hands and stalked back to the windows. "I didn't keep it from you because you're a reporter."

Did I?

The question appeared like black smoke in the back of his mind. He dug his fingers into his palms.

No fucking way.

Yeah, he'd spent the past year avoiding her because she worked for *The Gazette*, but that was before the snowstorm and the blanket fort. Before he'd discovered the taste of her skin and lost himself in her eyes. That was before he *felt* more for her than he knew what to do with.

A weight pressed down on him. He'd ignored the nagging sense that things with Brooke had been too easy, too fast, too perfect. Sooner or later, it would start crumbling right under his feet. Like an earthquake, and with him right on the fault line.

"I've told you more than I've told anyone, *ever*." His chest burned. He spread his hands out and turned to face her. "How the fuck is that not trusting you?"

"It's a great story, Sam." Bitterness cut through her voice. "Any reporter would love to break it."

"Except you." He flexed his hands. "I know you wouldn't do that, not to me or yourself. Do you know how I know? Because I trust you. I care about you. I—"

His voice broke off, snapping like a dead tree branch. Self-disgust smothered his anger.

Brooke stared at him for a long moment. The fire in her eyes began fading into ashes.

"So when you made the phone call to your agent," she said slowly, "did you consider that if I got the job, I'd be working for your family's company in New York? Did you think that wouldn't change everything? That I wouldn't find out about Folio and Lincoln? That we wouldn't have to deal with it at some point? Or did you think this was just the end of our hook-up and it no longer mattered?"

"All I thought about was you." He clenched his jaw. "And it was a hell of a lot more than a hook-up. You know that. You just told me…"

…*you love me.*

The words stuck inside him like a clogged drain pipe.

The air grew thick and hot.

"I. Love. You." She fisted her hands, her expression darkening. "Guess what, Sam? It takes courage to say those words. It takes honesty. It takes trust. But if you can't admit that, if you can't even say the word *love*, then maybe you need more than a Romance 101 course."

"Maybe I do," he snapped. "So let's both admit I'll never be what you need. We had fun, right? But we were never *actually together*. Since you don't want my help and would rather get it from your shithead ex, and since I apparently don't trust you, we might as well end it right now."

She stared at him. Her face drained of color and her eyes glittered.

He turned away. Shame and anger scorched him from the inside out.

He suddenly hated his warped view of love, every shitty secret, all his jagged mistrust. He hated that Brooke had helped him figure out how to make John Kane express his love, while Sam—the man who'd created the goddamned character—still didn't know what the hell it looked like in real life or how it could fix anything.

He hated the walls he'd built around himself, and he really fucking hated epic romances and Brooke's perfect man who "whispered sweet nothings" and declared his undying love for her every chance he got.

While Sam couldn't even say it *once*.

He'd known from the beginning that she deserved everything she'd ever wanted from love and relationships. Wanting to be with her forever wasn't enough. Feelings weren't actions. But there was one action he could take.

"Go to New York, Brooke." He turned to the door. "Start your new life. Find what you've been looking for with someone else because I sure as hell can't give it to you."

He walked back out into the dusk. For the first time ever, he felt his heart break.

CHAPTER 27

*F*lawed *internal logic.*

Hah.

Brooke stewed and steamed over Sam's accusation for the next two days—in-between crying and repeatedly picking up her phone and putting it back down again. If he was right about her "internal logic"—and maybe he sort of was, because in her brief moments of thinking straight she did recall saying she was using Michael as a contact—then *she* was definitely right about Sam's resistance to feelings.

Feelings of love and trust, at least.

She pulled herself together enough to think *logically* about the job offer with *Clarity*. She wasn't about to let her pride get in the way of a great career opportunity, even if this mess with Sam still simmered underneath it all.

She called Jillian Powers to discuss the contract details, and Jillian told her to take a few days to think it over and come to New York for another visit, if possible. Brooke decided that getting away again would be a good thing, so she booked another flight on her credit card.

Before the transaction cleared, she knew she'd accept the job. She'd be foolish not to. Still, she couldn't prevent a pang of unease over technically working for the Atwoods. Though Sam had kept a great deal from her, the things he had told her painted an unpleasant picture of his parents and his childhood. She might never know all the details, but her loyalty was still with him.

Even if he had flat-out rejected her love.

That was a sledgehammer to the heart. There was absolutely no bright side to discovering the man you'd let in all the way was not only leaving, but locking you out for good.

The sooner she left Bliss Cove, the easier it would be to start over. That was what she'd intended at the start of the new year, wasn't it? A clean slate. A new life path. A career boost.

She'd achieved her goals, even if she hadn't remotely expected the circumstances leading up to her success. She certainly wouldn't have chosen them.

Oh, yes, you would have.

Not even a sledgehammered heart could change the fact that she wouldn't have given up her time with Sam for anything. She'd always treasure the Eagle's Nest cabin, the blanket fort, their shared, whispered secrets, and their Romance 101 course. She'd remember him when she read a romance novel, when his next John Kane book came out, and whenever it snowed.

And she'd try very hard not to imagine what *might have been*, if he'd realized all the lessons about his fictional characters were actually real. If he'd learned love wasn't a lie. It was a great, glorious emotion that lifted your heart like a sunrise and made you see the world in bright, vivid colors.

Love was big, romantic gestures, yes, but mostly it was everyday things—making coffee with just the right amount of cream, stocking up on lemon-cayenne iced tea even though you didn't like it, holding hands.

It was forehead kisses, making cookies together, and getting safely home. Love was also complicated and sometimes prickly, but when you believed in it and trusted it, you held on together through all of life's storms and waves. You didn't give up. You didn't walk out.

Brooke would always secretly wish Sam had learned the truth about love. She would always hope, in some way, that he still would. He had too much to give to spend his life keeping the world at a distance.

Three days after their fight—she couldn't yet bring herself to call it a *break-up*—she went to the Meow and Then Cat Café for both best-friend commiseration and cat therapy.

While Aria made coffee and murmured consoling noises, Brooke confessed some of what had happened between her and Sam—namely, that she'd gone and fallen in love with him, and he hadn't returned the feeling.

"It all happened so fast." Brooke moved a pillow on the sofa in the Cat Lounge to make room for a large tabby named Velvet. "But in a good way, you know?"

"You two have always had a thing going on." Aria set a cup of coffee and a box of animal crackers on the table. "Even though you think it happened fast, it didn't really. You've been circling each other for the past year."

"Yeah, well, I should have known it would be impossible to break down the Great Wall of Bliss Cove." With a snort, Brooke reached for the coffee. She took a sip and forced a light note into her voice as she said, "Anyway, I've talked to Jillian, and we're getting all the details of the job figured out. I'm going back to New York the day after tomorrow to meet with her and get some paperwork signed."

"When does the job officially start?"

"March first, but I figure I might as well stay a couple of weeks in New York. I need to find a place to live and plan the move."

"Hunter knows a lot of people in New York." Aria sat down and sipped her green tea. "He can help you find something."

Absently petting Velvet, Brooke murmured a thank you and looked out the window at Mariposa Street. People sat at the tables outside the newly renovated Nico's, and Destiny stood in the doorway of Moonbeams, chatting up a young, good-looking college student. People wandered around the cobblestone street, looking into shop windows and sipping take-out drinks.

"Hey." Aria nudged her foot. "Why aren't you ecstatic over the job offer?"

"I am."

"You look like you're about to go to work sealing envelopes in an airless basement."

Brooke smiled. "It's an amazing job, and it'll be a huge career boost. I'm just going to miss Bliss Cove, that's all. But I need to pull on my big girl panties and make the move because that's what strong, brave adult women do."

"Strong, brave adult women also make no apologies about what's right for *them*," Aria pointed out. "Some new moms go back to work. Some stay at home. Some nurse their babies, others don't. Some women make a living selling crafts online. Others get promoted to CEO of an oil company. Some even take their kids to work."

Brooke narrowed her eyes. "What's with all the kids and baby talk? Are you trying to tell me something?"

"Not yet." Aria grinned. "My point is that women have different ideas about what they want to do. I own a cat café. Callie is a tenured professor. We'd both be miserable at the other person's job. We all have to make the choice that's right for us."

"The hard part is figuring out what's right." Brooke sighed and reached for the animal crackers. "I've already accepted the job, so I guess it's normal for me to be a little anxious. Especially after what happened the last time and getting comfortable back here…"

She paused and lifted a hand to Bee Delaney, the Bliss Cove librarian who'd just come into the café's front room. Bee waved back and hurried into the Cat Lounge, gently stopping a gray Persian from escaping.

"Hey, Bee." Aria rose to her feet. "What can I get for you?"

"Nothing, thanks." Her eyes bright with excitement, Bee perched on a chair and leaned toward them. "You're not going to believe this, so I had to tell you in person. Are you sitting down?"

Aria sat back down. "Yup."

Bee paused dramatically before announcing, "The Reading Project received an incredible donation for the bookmobile."

"Really?" Brooke smiled, thrilled for her friend. She knew how hard Bee had been working to be able to afford the truck that would serve as a mobile library for both Bliss Cove and neighboring towns. "That's fantastic."

"Actually, it's more than a donation. It's a lot more than a truck, even." Bee bent to run her fingers through the Persian's fur. "The donor bought us a gorgeous, new Airstream trailer, and a new four-by-four truck to haul it. *And* they included a budget for painting and outfitting the interior with shelves. We don't even need to use the Book Fair proceeds or our existing funds, which means we'll have a phenomenal budget for programs, events, and book purchases."

"Wow." Aria lifted her eyebrows. "That's super generous. Who's the donor?"

"Anonymous." Bee lifted her hands, faint regret filling her eyes. "I'm not into invading people's privacy, but I wish we knew who it was just so we could thank them personally. It's so much more than we could have imagined."

Lowering her eyes to hide her sudden bittersweet realization, Brooke took a few crackers from the box. "When are you picking it up?"

"It's going to be painted and outfitted next week." Bee took her phone out of her purse and swiped the screen. "That's why I wanted to talk to you, Brooke. I'm hoping we can debut it at the Bliss Cove Book Fair. Is there any room left on the square?"

"I think so, but I'll have to double-check with Gramps."

"Wonderful, thank you." Bee turned her phone screen to show them the sleek, silver trailer and truck. "I'm so excited. I could never have hoped for anything like this. People are going to be thrilled. Oh! Aria, I also wanted to ask if you'd be available to take a shift at the fair. Just an hour or so."

"Sign me up." Aria stood and picked up her tea mug. "I'm going to have a cat adoption booth there, but Hunter can run it if I'm at the bookmobile. Maybe we can even do a cat-themed book display."

"That would be awesome." Bee glanced at Brooke. "I know you'll be running around doing all the coordination, so I won't ask you. But we'd love to have you stop by."

Unease rustled through Brooke. "Uh, I'm not going to be at the Book Fair, unfortunately. I'll be in New York."

"Already?" Bee widened her eyes.

"The job doesn't officially start for six weeks, but I need to find a place to live and get settled." Brooke didn't bother explaining that the longer she stayed in Bliss Cove, the harder it would be to leave. "So I'm heading out on Thursday. I'll be back to pack up and arrange to have my things shipped over before making the final move."

"Can you come back for the Book Fair?" Bee asked. "That'll give you ten days in New York."

"Or maybe make it a working trip," Aria suggested. "You can pitch a story about how town book fairs are still going strong, despite all our reliance on technology."

"Or how Bliss Cove celebrates everything from artichokes to books to Valentine's Day." Bee smiled. "I'll bet there aren't that many towns who can do festivals like we do. Speaking of which, who's going to take over the Valentine's Day Festival?"

"I guess whoever wants to." Brooke ate a few of the crackers and sipped her coffee.

"You're the *founder* of the festival," Aria reminded her. "You should have a say in who will be the next coordinator."

"Are you okay?" Bee leaned forward, her forehead creasing. "For a woman with a great job opportunity, you seem kind of down."

Brooke gave her friend a reassuring smile. "It's just a big change, that's all. Especially when I weigh the options." She put her hands out and mimed a tilting balance. "Bliss Cove, where all my friends and family are but where I don't have a decent job, or a great job in New York, which gave me a breakdown the last time I lived there."

"Are those your only choices?" Bee asked.

"Of course."

Brooke suddenly recalled Sam's accusation that she saw only one path to take. Well, here she had two. She either took the job in New York or she turned it down and stayed in Bliss Cove, where she'd have to start from scratch again.

Either way, she was annoyed with herself for feeling anxious over her incredible new opportunity. Yes, she'd crashed and burned during her last attempt at a big-city, big-job life, but she couldn't just hide out in Bliss Cove forever.

She was an adult who had bills to pay and IRAs to start funding. She could still have a fondness for romance novels and memories of her One True Love, who had no idea he was even capable of being *anyone's* One True Love, but it was time for practical Brooke to take charge.

Aria studied her with a penetrating blue gaze. "Do you remember when Bee adopted Puffalump?"

Brooke blinked at the apparent non sequitur, but nodded. Last fall, Aria had been struggling to find a forever home for the older, overweight cat. Bee had offered to foster him, but Puffalump's excessive interest in her pet canary had made her nervous.

Instead of returning the cat to Meow and Then, Bee had

turned him into the Bliss Cove Library cat. Puffalump now lived happily at the library, where he enjoyed many patches of sunlight and much petting and attention from patrons.

"I always tell people the cats are looking for a forever home," Aria explained. "So the assumption is they need to go live with someone in an actual house or apartment. If the situation doesn't work, the cats end up back here at the café. But Bee found a different way to give Puffalump a home. A forever library."

"And Puff did turn out to be a rather scholarly cat." Bee nodded sagely.

Brooke scratched her head. "So the point is…"

"Sometimes there aren't only two things you need to weigh." Aria lifted her hands. "Sometimes there's a third option."

"Maybe for cats, but not for a thirty-year-old, almost broke reporter." Brooke put her coffee cup on the table and tucked the unfinished box of crackers into her purse. "I need this job. I love the magazine. I don't love that Sam did what he did, but I can appreciate why he did it. It's time for me to move on."

And hope I don't fail again.

She didn't think she could stand returning to Bliss Cove in shame and embarrassment again. She knew the whole town would rally around her a second time—even a third, fourth, and fifth, if needed—but God knew she didn't want them to have to.

"Whenever you need us, we'll be here," Aria promised.

Brooke hugged her friends and picked up her purse. As she left the café, she couldn't help wondering where Sam would be.

On her way back home, she detoured down Starfish Avenue and stopped at Title Wave. If things with him had to *end*, she didn't want them to end so horribly.

Somewhat to her surprise, the Open sign hung in the store window.

Taking a deep breath, she went inside. Sam was leaning against the front counter, his dark hair falling over his forehead and his features set with concentration as he studied a crossword puzzle. As the front bell rang, he glanced up.

Their eyes met. Brooke felt the contact clear down to her toes, but Sam's expression betrayed no emotion whatsoever. He was definitely back behind the wall, and the realization caused a stab of pain.

"Hi." Attempting to keep her voice casual, she approached the counter. "I wanted to...well, I'm sorry about how things ended."

He nodded shortly. "So am I."

"I also wanted to tell you I'm accepting the job." She pushed a lock of hair away from her forehead. "I still wish you hadn't made that call, but I know you meant well. And I wish..."

She let her voice trail off and shrugged. It was too late for wishes. Besides, Sam didn't believe in those either.

"I'm glad you're taking the job." He set the newspaper down. His voice was polite and devoid of emotion. "You deserve it. I'd also wanted to tell you I finished *Tripwire* when you were in New York. Revamped romance and all."

"Really?" For the first time in a while, pleasure rose in her. "That's wonderful. Congratulations."

"I couldn't have done it without you, so thank you."

"You're welcome." She wanted to ask him if she could

read it, but he was so remote that the question died in her throat.

She stepped back, hating the distance that was so firmly back in place between them. "Well, good luck with everything. I'm going back to New York to get things organized for the job, but I wanted to tell you goodbye."

"Goodbye, Brooke."

"Goodbye, Sam."

Could he hear her heart breaking all over again?

She started toward the door, then stopped. Unclasping the *Courage* bracelet from her wrist, she placed it on the counter in front of him.

"I don't need this anymore," she said. "But I think you do."

Not looking at him again, she turned and walked away.

CHAPTER 28

*S*am hit the speed ball faster than he ever had before. His arm muscles ached. Sweat ran down his temples. He wanted to get into the ring and spar, but his trainer had taken one look at him and told him to work it off alone first.

He hit the ball again and stepped back. His chest heaved. Three days after Brooke had come into Title Wave, *feelings* were still roiling through him, hot and chafing.

He was angry he'd fucked up. He hated that he'd lost the best thing that had ever happened to him. And he knew to his bones he'd never be the man Brooke needed or wanted.

He stalked to the heavy bag and threw cross punches, jabs, and hooks. He ran a couple of miles, shadow boxed, lifted weights, and jump-roped. By the time he hit the shower, he was physically exhausted, but his brain wouldn't stop working.

He pulled on jeans and a T-shirt and drove back to town. His rental house was the last place he wanted to be. Without Brooke's warm, cheerful presence, it was like a tomb.

He stopped at Title Wave, where Jake Ryan was working. The other man had opened the store for a morning shift, and he was busy stocking books and sorting inventory.

After a curt greeting, Sam went to the office to slog through paperwork. He opened a box of Barnum's animal crackers and finished them off in a couple of handfuls.

Maybe it was time to leave town. He'd never given his stay in Bliss Cove a deadline, but then he never planned to stay anywhere. He stopped where he wanted to and moved on whenever he was ready.

Taking over Title Wave had given him more reason to stay than anywhere else he'd lived, but someone else could run it. He'd turn the house back over to the rental company. Head down to Mexico and start figuring out the next John Kane book.

Without Brooke.

Shoving away from his desk, he stalked out to the front.

"Hey, a couple of the guys and I are shooting darts tonight, if you want to join us," Jake said.

"No, thanks." Sam eyed the carts. "What needs to be done?"

Jake lifted an eyebrow at his snappish tone and pointed at a cart. "I just loaded those up. You can shelve them."

Romance novels.

Great.

He rolled the cart to the Romance section and began putting the books into place. He suppressed the urge to set aside a few for Brooke, even though there were two new releases featuring pirate heroes. She had a weakness for pirates.

He pushed the empty cart back to the front as Jake disappeared in the storeroom. Sam picked up his crossword puzzle from beside the register. It was a mess of unfinished squares and scribbled-out words.

He never should have let himself step outside of his safety zone. There was a reason he'd chosen to keep his distance from people. His misery now was his own damned fault. He'd broken his own rule.

But for Brooke, he'd break it again, a thousand times over. He brushed his fingers over the *Courage* bracelet in his pocket. He'd told himself not to be a sentimental ass about a piece of jewelry, but he couldn't bring himself to throw it in a drawer and forget about it.

The bell over the door jingled. Charlie Castle entered, his gait steady but stilted due to his prosthetic leg.

Sam straightened. Unease tightened his chest. Charlie had come into the bookstore before, but usually went directly to the New Releases or the History section.

Now he was heading right for Sam.

"Afternoon, Charlie." Sam nodded in greeting.

The older man squinted. "My granddaughter tells me you're being a stubborn ass about the fair."

Sam sighed. "Considering this town has an average of six fairs and festivals a month, which one are we talking about?"

"The Book Fair." Charlie thumped his hand on the counter. "What kind of bookstore owner doesn't participate in the Book Fair?"

"This one."

Charlie frowned. "You disappointed my granddaughter."

Sam's heart hit his ribs. For an instant, he thought Charlie was talking about his and Brooke's *romance*.

"She's volunteered to help organize the Book Fair since she was in high school." Charlie's features settled into heavy creases of disapproval. "Aside from when she wasn't living here, this is the first time she's missing the fair."

Sam looked up sharply. "Why is she missing the fair?"

"She's in New York, getting stuff in place for her job." Charlie scratched his chin. "You didn't know?"

Sam shook his head. He hadn't known Brooke had left already, but he should have *felt* her absence from Bliss Cove.

"She's the best girl, my Brooke." Charlie frowned. "Smart, loyal as all hell, dedicated to her family. She talked about you a lot. How you wouldn't agree to an interview, but you kept the store so well-stocked. How you showed up at all the festivals and always had cash for donation jars. God knows why, but she seemed to like you. It was stupid of you to give her a hard time about the fair."

He deflected a stab of regret. The other man was playing him, and they both knew it.

But Sam no longer cared all that much about his privacy and secrets. He'd spent years holding on to them like a dragon hoarding gold.

Then a brown-eyed beauty had smiled her way right into his lair and shown him that unicorn pillow glitter was infinitely more valuable—and itchy—than gold. She'd proven blanket forts, Ferris wheels, and cotton candy could crumble stone walls, and that sometimes the greatest act of courage was a whisper in the dark.

What the hell did a few hours of working at a fair mean against all that? Nothing.

And likely he wouldn't be in town for much longer anyway, so—

"I'll ask Jake to staff a Title Wave booth," he finally said.

"Not talking about Jake." Charlie narrowed his eyes. "He's already doing a screenwriting workshop and about five or six read-aloud programs. And he's the MC for the elementary school plays."

Sam exhaled heavily. "I'll staff the booth, then."

"Don't do us any favors." Charlie's expression turned into a glare. "People around here aren't going to beg for you to be part of this community."

"You want me to do something for the fair or not?"

"Not if you're going to be a dick about it."

"Mr. Castle." Sam forced his voice to remain even. "It will be my *pleasure* to staff a booth at the Bliss Cove Book Fair."

Charlie shrugged. "If you want to."

If Sam had been holding a pencil, it would have snapped.

"Legion," Charlie said.

"What?"

"Fourteen down." Charlie punched his finger at the crossword puzzle. "*A great many on one leg.* Legion."

He turned and marched slowly back outside.

Only when the door shut behind him did Sam give a low laugh. He'd put money on that old guy in a sparring ring.

Jake carried a stack of books out of the storeroom. He was saying something about new releases and movies. Sam returned his attention to the crossword and wrote in the answer *LEGION*.

"Last I heard, the project still doesn't have any interest or funding." Jake set the books on the counter with a loud *thunk*.

"What project?"

"The movie adaptation of *Truth*." Jake shot him a narrow look. "Man, haven't you heard anything I've been saying?"

Old guilt nudged at Sam. He tossed the newspaper on the counter and went to straighten the new releases. Last summer, during a temporary stint back in Bliss Cove, Jake had gotten involved in the adaption of Lincoln Atwood's award-winning first book.

Sam had watched the progress of the casting negotiations from the distant sidelines—as always—but he hadn't told Jake that Lincoln was his brother. There had been no reason to. The movie had barely gotten to the casting stage before it was shelved. Jake had returned to Bliss Cove to both deal with the disastrous fallout and to focus on his own projects.

Sam had been disappointed on Jake's behalf, but the other man had taken the whole thing in stride. Movies were shelved all the time, and Jake been more invested in ensuring the former *Truth* director face justice for his predatory ways.

As far as Sam knew, Lincoln had had nothing to do with the film adaptation of *Truth*. Authors who optioned their books to producers usually gave up all rights, and Jake had never mentioned having contact with Lincoln. That might have changed if the movie had gone forward into the pre-production stage, but the whole thing had been shut down.

So what was Jake talking about now?

"The option expired a few weeks ago." Jake began sorting through the books. "A couple of directors were sniffing around, but they moved on to other projects when they found out *Truth* no longer has studio backing."

"So what does that mean?" Sam picked up several empty boxes and began breaking them down.

"It means the movie rights for the book are up for grabs

again." Jake checked a few books off the inventory sheet. "I don't know if there are any offers on the table yet. I'm thinking of looking into it."

Sam's spine stiffened. "You want to buy the rights to *Truth*?"

For a moment, Jake didn't answer. He checked off another book.

"I spent a lot of years playing Blaze Ripley," he finally said. "I got to know the character really well." His mouth twisted. "Excuse the actor crap, but I helped create him. Put a lot of myself into him. Even became him, in some ways.

"But the *Fatal Glory* movies were original screenplays, so the screenwriters, directors, and I all had a lot of freedom to develop Blaze's character. I've never played a role that was adapted from a book, where one author was responsible for creating the character first. I've never even had the opportunity to do a book-to-film role...and then I read *Truth*."

"It's a great book." Sam kept his voice carefully neutral.

He meant it. For all his trouble with Lincoln, his brother was an incredible writer. The protagonist of *Truth*, Tom Dillon, was a troubled Vietnam vet who embarked on a road trip of eventual self-discovery and healing.

Dillon had earned a place in literary history as a complex, multi-faceted character who was all the more fascinating for having been created by a twenty-four-year-old man. Sam could understand why any serious actor would be intrigued at the thought of portraying the character onscreen.

"Yeah." Jake tapped his pen on the paper and pulled his eyebrows together. "A lot of people thought I was an idiot for turning down another *Fatal Glory* role, but I could see myself playing Tom Dillon, you know? I felt like I knew him inside out. I saw myself in him. I saw my father…"

He shrugged, looking faintly embarrassed.

Sam folded another box. "Your father."

"He was a deadbeat, always out of work." Jake punched a few keys on the keyboard. His expression clouded. "A drunk who used his fists. He left us when I was thirteen. And that day…man, I was scared to death, but something clicked inside me. No fucking way was I going to be like him. I'd take care of my family and treat people right. I'd show up, and I wouldn't leave. I wouldn't fail."

Tension coiled around Sam's spine. Jake had succeeded beyond what he'd probably imagined.

"You did it," he said.

"Yeah." Jake let out his breath, his gaze on the computer. "I never saw my father again, but when I read *Truth*, I had this image of him on a similar journey. And when Dillon finally makes peace with himself and his past…I thought, man, that's *me*. I'd finally come to the same realization. And I knew I could bring Tom Dillon to life onscreen. It was one of those things. You just know."

"So what are you going to do?" Sam stacked the boxes in a pile.

"I'm thinking of contacting Lincoln Atwood's agent." Jake turned back to the inventory sheet. "I've never developed a project on my own from the ground up. That's why I started my production company. Now that the company structure and finances are in place, I'm ready to start looking. Can't help thinking there's a reason *Truth* is available again."

Sam picked up the broken-down boxes. "I'm going to take these out back."

He went outside and tossed them in the recycling bin.

I'd show up, and I wouldn't leave.

I wouldn't fail.

You just know.

When he returned to the front of the store, Jake was helping Mr. Hammersmith at the Reference section. Sam picked up his crossword and tried to focus.

Even though he hadn't spoken to Lincoln in five years, he'd known when his brother had sold the movie rights for *Truth* and when his next book was slated for publication. He knew about Lincoln's book tours and interviews because that kind of thing always appeared on book-related websites, press releases, and publisher newsletters.

Sam hadn't been able to avoid hearing about his brother, but he'd never had a reason to do anything with the information.

Jake and Mr. Hammersmith approached the counter, talking about a home repair book that Jake was holding. Sam stepped away to let him use the register. The two men were chatting about how best to fix a leaky faucet.

Unlike Sam, Jake had an easy way with people. Maybe because he was an actor, but more likely because he was a good guy. Since he'd moved back to Bliss Cove, he'd become increasingly less a "movie star" and more just a regular guy who occasionally used his fame for charities and fundraisers.

But mostly, when he wasn't working on his screenplay or his production company, Jake could be found spending time with his wife Callie, having a drink at the Mousehole, or getting involved in the Mariposa Street renovations.

He'd funded the restoration of the Vitaphone movie theater and was helping the Mortimers start a new film series. He guest-lectured at college and high-school film classes, paid regular visits to the Children's Hospital as his iconic character Blaze Ripley, and he was always available when Sam called him for help at Title Wave.

"Have a great day, Mr. Hammersmith." Jake put the receipt in a bag with the book. "Let me know how that sink repair turns out."

"Will do. Thanks, son." The older man took the bag and shuffled out of the store.

"You want me to take care of those returns?" Jake turned to Sam, pointing his thumb at the storeroom.

"Yeah, sure. Thanks." Sam set down his pen and straightened. "Also—"

Jake lifted his eyebrows in question.

"If you want to get in touch with Lincoln Atwood," Sam said, "I might be able to help you out."

CHAPTER 29

*a*fter a two-block slog from the subway station through the frozen, dirty slush, Brooke entered the lobby of the Granger Hotel with a sigh of relief. New York was in the middle of both a snowstorm and a sub-zero cold snap, which meant everything was covered in a layer of ice —including the air itself.

She stomped the slush off her boots and hurried toward the elevators. She'd spent the past few days meeting with Jillian Powers and various editors, going on tours of the *Clarity* offices, and learning the in-house computer system. She'd looked at apartments, met with property experts whom Hunter had recommended, and calculated her expenses.

She'd also been given her first *Clarity* story assignment, and she'd been anxious all day to talk to Gramps about it. After returning to her room, she took out her phone to call him.

"Castle." Her grandfather's voice elicited a pang of homesickness. Which was silly, since she'd only been gone for a week.

"Hi, Gramps, it's me." Brooke took a deep breath and told him about all she'd been doing.

Then she explained her *Lifelong Fling* proposal, which she'd pitched to Jillian with suggestions for how it could evolve into a series or a column. Jillian had loved the idea and planned to discuss its potential placement in upcoming issues with the rest of the staff.

"I want to feature the love story of you and Grandma Ruth first," Brooke told Charlie. "I think I'm so into romances and romance novels because I grew up with your story always in my mind. It has everything—love, devotion, sacrifice, compromise. Togetherness. I know you don't talk about it much, but would you let me write your story? Please?"

Charlie was silent for a second before he gruffly said, "Okay. For you."

She smiled. Her heart filled. "I love you."

"Yeah, yeah. You want to talk now or what? I got a few minutes before I need to get over to the boardwalk. Someone broke into the funnel cake booth and stole all the powdered sugar."

Brooke frowned. "Have you checked with Mrs. Gorlick at the elementary school? Her class is doing a life-sized snow scene for their winter weather unit. But she wouldn't *steal* the sugar."

"I'm guessing there'll be a trail somewhere." There was the sound of his keyboard clicking. "So what'd you want to ask me?"

"I'll be back for the Book Fair, so we can talk in detail then." She paused. "But how did you and Ruth get through being separated so much? You spent so much time traveling the world on assignment, and she stayed home. That can't have been easy on either one of you."

"No, but she was the one who held it all together, raising the kids, making a home. I couldn't have had the career I did without her."

"Did you ever think about quitting or starting a different career?" Brooke gazed at the floral patterned wallpaper on the other side of the room. "When it got especially tough?"

"Maybe, but Ruth wouldn't have let me. She knew I wanted to tell people's stories. To do what I could to tell the truth. Especially after 'Nam. She knew I was driven."

"She knew you were brave."

He huffed out a laugh. "Ruth was the brave one. Running toward the line of fire or going into a warzone...yeah, it takes guts...and recklessness...to head into the unknown. But Ruth...she waited. She was there. She built a life for us without always knowing if I was coming home. She had faith. It takes courage to leave, but it takes more courage to stay. You got more questions? I just got a text that the police found suspicious white fingerprints on the cotton-candy truck."

"Follow that tip, Gramps. I'll talk to you later."

She ended the call and went to take a shower and change into her pajamas.

Courage to stay.

Charlie had no doubt been brave during both the war and his overseas assignments, but he'd been the one to insist he and Ruth move back to Bliss Cove after she'd been diagnosed with cancer. He'd known she'd needed to be close to her family. He'd given up his reporter career, bought *The*

297

Gazette, and taken over the editor-in-chief position so both he and Ruth could stay.

Love in Bliss.

Maybe Brooke's two-year escape to her hometown hadn't been an act of cowardice and hiding after all. Maybe it had taken bravery to do what she needed for herself and her well-being.

And maybe *courage* was also knowing exactly where and what would make you happy…and finding a way to get them both.

"WHAT'S GOING TO HAPPEN TO IT?"

"It'll either go under or get taken over."

As Brooke waited for the elevator at the *Clarity* building the following day, she caught snippets of the conversation between an executive assistant and an editor who were standing behind her. She glanced over her shoulder to greet them both and let them know she wasn't pretending to be oblivious.

"Don't worry, we're not talking about *Clarity*." The assistant, Julie, smiled at her.

"Oh, I didn't think you were."

"It's that magazine, *Empire Monthly*." The editor nodded toward the open elevator.

Brooke managed to keep her voice casually curious as they entered the car. "*Empire*?"

"Rumor has it there was some big kerfuffle involving the investor." Balancing her coffee and a portfolio, Julie punched the button for the thirtieth floor. "So they're doing a big internal slash job, getting rid of some people and replacing them with fresh blood. But now they have money issues, so they might not last much longer."

She shrugged and sipped her coffee.

"Interesting." Brooke bit her lip. "What's going to happen to the editor-in-chief?"

"Oh, he's probably first on the chopping block." Julie rolled her eyes. "Good riddance, if you ask me. I met him at a party once. Total sleazebag."

For an instant, Brooke felt a cloud descending on her. Julie had discerned Michael's sleazebag-ness after one party. Brooke hadn't realized the full truth until…recently.

Nope. Lesson learned. And it's fine—in fact, it's worth it —to try and forgive someone one time. If they fail again, then game over.

She told the two women to have a good day and walked toward Jillian's office. Though she wished no ill on Michael —well, maybe just a tad—she didn't need Destiny Storm to tell her that karma was on the payroll and working hard.

"Morning, Brooke." Jillian waved her toward a chair. "I have *Lifelong Fling* on the agenda for Tuesday's meeting. Will you still be in town then?"

"I'm afraid not." Brooke opened her notebook. "I'm leaving Friday to head back home for a few days. We have a local Book Fair this weekend that I didn't want to miss."

"How charming." Jillian began making two cappuccinos. "Nice to know book fairs are still around. Sometimes I feel like technology is running the world. Though that's not to say it doesn't make life infinitely easier."

"I agree."

"Speaking of which…" Jillian placed the coffees on the

table and sat down. "I know your job hasn't officially started yet, but if you have an hour or so on Tuesday to video call in to the meeting, we'd love to have your input."

Brooke took a sip of the foamy coffee. "Does your staff often video call in to meetings?"

"All the time." Jillian waved a hand. "Of course, we prefer people to be here in person, but it saves both time and money when they video call. Will you be available Tuesday morning at ten Eastern?"

"Of course." Brooke set the coffee down and straightened her shoulders. "This also brings up another proposal I'd like to discuss with you."

"Certainly."

An hour and twenty minutes later, Brooke left Jillian's office with the sinking feeling that she might have just made a mistake. Maybe this was even worse than what had happened at *The New York Times*, and she'd have to leave her job before it even began.

She took the subway back to the Granger, again knocking the slush off her boots before starting toward the hotel elevators.

"Miss Castle?" The front desk receptionist waved her over. "There's a letter here for you."

Brooke approached to take the envelope, which was addressed to her in care of the hotel.

Though the envelope didn't have a return address, there was no mistaking the bold, spiky handwriting. She could see Sam standing in front of the whiteboard, his sleeves rolled up to the elbows as he scrawled notes and ideas about romance.

"Just arrived in today's mail," the receptionist informed her.

"Thank you." Slipping the envelope into her bag, she headed up to her room.

After changing into peach-colored sweatpants and a T-shirt, she sat on the bed to open the letter. Her hands shook as she unfolded the pages:

BROOKE,

ARIA TOLD ME YOU WERE STAYING AT THE GRANGER AGAIN, so I'm hoping this letter reaches you.

I'm writing for two reasons. The first is that my agent and editor both loved the revision of *Tripwire*. They said Kane and Patricia's romance was what they'd been hoping for. We're going to talk about revising the romance in the previous two books and issuing updated editions to keep it consistent. Everyone is happy.

So, thank you again. It's your book, too.

Second...it's tough to admit I'm a writer who's lousy with words. But I want to tell you some things I couldn't—or wouldn't—before. This is a feeble but honest way of telling you that I trust you. I always have, even when I was telling myself I had to avoid you. Took me a while to admit I was avoiding you not because you're a reporter, but because of all the things you could make me *feel*. See? I can even write that word now. :)

Lincoln is five years older than me. We were friends when we were kids...at least, that's how I remember it.

Tagging around after my older brother, playing video games, etc. He was good at everything, not just writing. Academics, sports, you name it. Seemed like he could do it all effortlessly.

I guess things got bad when I started school because our father set us up to compete. But I couldn't compete with my brother in anything…academics, writing, girls, whatever. That was just a fact.

Lincoln was great at all subjects, but teachers started noticing his talent for writing when he was in third grade. In fifth grade, he won a national youth writing award. I had a harder time with stuff…I liked writing, but I struggled with most other subjects. I hated team sports, and I didn't have a lot of friends.

It wasn't long before I figured out that if I caused trouble, people would stop noticing I wasn't as good as my brother in anything. If he was the golden boy, I'd be the troublemaker. You can imagine how that went over with my parents. There was a lot of fighting, threats, accusations, blame.

For a couple of months, I had an outlet in boxing. Then my father put Lincoln into training too, which pissed me off. I didn't want to compete with him again, but I refused to give it up. It was the only way I was better than him. I think he stopped boxing when he went to college, but he was a top-ranked student, full scholarship, the whole works.

I dropped out of high-school and took a few jobs in the city for a couple of years. One day, I was leafing through *New York* magazine and saw an article about the hundredth anniversary of Folio Publishing. There was an extensive profile of the Atwoods, including interviews with my parents and a whole piece about Lincoln, who was famous for his book deal by then.

There was no mention of me anywhere in the article, which was fine because I didn't care about magazine profiles anyway. And my parents had always tried to keep me in the background, so getting omitted from an article wasn't a surprise.

But the reporter had written about the Atwoods' *only son*, Lincoln. My parents talked about him as if he were their only child. My father even said they had one child. The profile on Lincoln didn't mention any siblings, much less a brother. It was like they'd obliterated me from existence.

I could have left it alone. Not cared. But I was hotheaded and angry...and I didn't leave it alone. You know that old saying, the pen is mightier than the sword? I knew the best way to get back at my illustrious literary family was to write about them.

So I did. I was living in this shithole apartment in Brooklyn, working construction. Every night, I'd go back home and write. It was fiction, but thinly veiled. After I finished the manuscript, I got an agent and eventually landed a contract.

When the book was published—under my given name, Sam Atwood—the press went crazy over all the salacious details, trying to figure out what was true and what was hyperbole. Most of it was true.

As I'd expected, my parents were furious that I'd divulge any secrets, even under the guise of fiction. My father threatened bookstores and publishers, telling them to bury the "piece of trash," as he called it. Critics either didn't bother with it or wrote scathing reviews.

But the book did some damage before it went out of print. That was as much as I'd wanted, I guess. To inflict some wounds before I left New York for good. But it was also a dividing line. Ever since, I've felt like I had a life before all that and then after.

The *after* has been writing as Sam Harris, traveling, and having minimal contact with my family. I went back to NY when my mother died, but mostly I've lived in the "after."

You're the first person who has ever made me want to put "happily ever" in front of that word.

THANKS FOR BEING SUNNY SIDE UP,
Sam

CHAPTER 30

*T*wo nights before the Bliss Cove Book Fair, Sam turned the Closed sign in the window and locked the door. He logged out of the computer and did his usual rounds of the store, straightening books and putting away misplaced items.

Rumor had it Brooke would be back from New York the day after tomorrow to attend the fair. No one had given him details on her arrival, but then he hadn't asked.

He also hadn't heard from her since he'd sent his letter a few days ago. Probably for the best. He'd already contacted a broker to find out about selling Title Wave, and he'd let his real-estate agent know he wouldn't be renewing the house lease.

Picking up a few stray mass-market paperbacks, he started toward the genre fiction shelves. He wasn't happy about the idea of leaving Bliss Cove, but he didn't want to stay here without Brooke. And since there was no way of staying here *with* her...

Shaking the dire thought out of his head, he began

shelving a few romance novels. Pirates, again. Billionaires. Firefighters. Navy SEALs. Lot of half-naked men. Lots of flowers. Lots of embracing couples in various states of undress.

He opened one of the books and skimmed the first sentence.

As it turned out, Cheetos dust incited Polly Lockhart's come-to-Jesus moment.

Curious, he sat on the floor and continued reading. Though he'd gotten Brooke's many points about a romance novel plot, this was the first one he'd actually read.

After he finished the story about a sweet, sexy bohemian heroine and the rigid CEO of a candy company, he picked up another book with a darker cover. The second romance was about a doctor who moves to a small town and butts heads with the local sheriff.

The heroine was a smart, headstrong neurologist, and the hero was a cop battling guilt after the suicide of his best friend. After finishing the book, Sam read a cute, funny story about a dog-walker's repeated encounters with the package delivery guy and their eventual path to love.

He finished the book and picked up a Regency romance about a duke and a commoner. He read it cover to cover and started another.

The evening light outside the windows began to darken. He moved to a chair with a stack of romances and read until midnight came and went. He kept reading. There were stories featuring heroines who were teachers, lawyers, shop owners, bakers, CEOs, FBI agents, and artists. They were intelligent, ambitious, creative, and sometimes klutzy.

The men were often stubborn and overprotective, but with an underlying vein of decency. Even when they fumbled and stumbled—which was often—they got their shit together in the end and frequently pulled off an impressive BRG.

There were romances about sports, espionage, body-guards, the mafia, vampires, and novels set in many historical eras. The sex was hot and erotic, sweet and easy, and everything in-between.

And the love…that was what Brooke had been talking about. No matter how different the couple was, how big the obstacles, how impossible it looked that they would ever find everlasting love together, they always did.

Always.

They made changes, accepted flaws, worked out compromises. The men weren't invincible superheroes who had it all figured out, but by the end they were determined to try.

Because a romance hero learns the truth about love. He finds a woman who fills a void he hadn't known existed. A woman who makes him want to be a better man. A woman he needs like air, whose smile increases the beat of his heart. A woman he wants to hold close every night and kiss every chance he gets. A woman who makes the stars whirl and the earth move under his feet.

As morning light broke through the gray clouds, Sam hauled himself up from his chair and reshelved the books he'd pored over all night. He went into his office and leafed through the notebook in which he'd scrawled notes about the romantic movies he and Brooke had watched together.

Scraping a hand through his hair, he opened the front door and stepped outside. Java Works across the street was already open, which meant it must be past six.

He turned and locked the door behind him.

"Morning, handsome." Destiny Storm walked past in a bright green caftan, a large takeout cup in her manicured hand. She ran her eye over him speculatively. "Rough night?"

"Just didn't get much sleep."

"The sexy, scruffy look works for you." She winked. "I'm pretty sure Brooke thinks so, too."

His heart bumped against his ribs. "Is she back?"

"She gets in on Saturday morning before the Book Fair starts." Destiny pursed her red lips. "You know, it's a shame about the cabin. Everyone was rooting for a snowbound romance between you two."

Sam's shoulders tensed. "Why's that?"

"Oh, your sexual and romantic energy has been off the charts for ages." Destiny waved her hand. "Not to mention, Brooke is a Pisces, which highly compatible with Aries."

"Uh." Sam had a pang of both guilt and embarrassment. "Actually, I'm a Scorpio."

"Ah hah!" With a musical little laugh, Destiny patted him on the chest. "I knew it, you scoundrel. Pisces and *Scorpio*, Sam. You have a deep emotional and physical connection. Am I right?"

He narrowed his eyes. "Maybe."

"Mmm hmm." She stroked his chest as if she were petting a dog, though her hand lingered on his abs. "You're mistrustful like a true Scorpio, aren't you? I would love to analyze you in more depth. Come over and see me at Moonbeams sometime. But for Lord's sake, stop scowling. A man like you should have a lot to look forward to in life. Radiate good energy, and you never know what could happen."

With another slow pat, she sauntered off toward Mariposa Street.

Sam started in the opposite direction. He'd probably always view the world with some level of mistrust, but to his core, he'd never trust anyone the way he trusted Brooke. He wouldn't have written that letter if he didn't.

And while he hoped she'd take his letter as he'd intended it—as proof of his love and trust—he didn't want her to feel obligated to reciprocate. She was off to a well-deserved opportunity clear across the country, and he wasn't about to screw it up for her by asking her to stay.

Unless...

He stopped. Turning, he headed toward Poppy Lane and *The Bliss Cove Gazette* offices. Halfway there, he saw Charlie Castle getting out of an old Buick parked at the curb. Sam hurried over to him.

The older man frowned. "What the hell happened to you, boy?"

Sam's heart started beating too fast. "Charlie, I need your help."

CHAPTER 31

*B*rooke reread Sam's letter countless times on her red-eye flight back to Bliss Cove. The undeniable warmth of his words, as well as the admission of trust, eased a bit of her lingering anxiety. She didn't read anything more into what he wrote, especially as Aria had texted her with "credible" rumors that Sam was planning to leave Bliss Cove soon.

Unfortunately, Brooke wasn't surprised. Now that *Tripwire* was finished, he'd move on to another town or even a whole new country.

While she loved his revelation that she helped him believe in "happily ever after," he'd said nothing about turning that into reality. And if her love couldn't fully break down his walls or convince him to stick around, then surely a letter, no matter how cathartic, wouldn't do it either.

Still, that didn't stop her from hoping she would see him again this weekend. As her flight landed at eight a.m., she only had time for a couple of hours' sleep at her parents' house before she grabbed her camera and headed out to the fair.

The California sun and ocean breeze was a welcome relief after the frigid winter of New York. Book-themed stalls and food booths lined Starfish Avenue, a ten-piece band belted out music in the gazebo, and people clustered around the sleek Airstream trailer that had been colorfully painted with books, flowers, and a skyline scene of fluffy white clouds and hot-air balloons.

After admiring the bookmobile, Brooke took numerous photos of the vehicle, the book displays, and the various programs going on around the square—games, read-aloud events, and "design your own book" craft tables.

She stopped to say hello to Charlie, who was supervising the letterpress printing demonstration, and spent a few minutes petting the cats prowling around Aria's Meow and Then enclosure. She greeted almost everyone she passed and took notes for her *Gazette* article about the fair, which she'd insisted on writing for free in exchange for Gramps' interview.

On the corner of Starfish and Dandelion Road, Callie and Rory Prescott were staffing a Sugar Joy Bakery booth. Platters held cookies and mini-cakes shaped and decorated like books.

"This one is chocolate and strawberry." Callie handed Brooke a plate bearing a *Pride and Prejudice* cake. "Oh, and don't forget to be over at the stage on the square right at eleven. That's when the elementary school play-writing winners are staging their productions."

"Okay."

"Eleven on the dot." Callie held up her forefingers and lifted her eyebrows. "Eleven *sharp*."

"Did you get that?" Rory smirked. "Not nine, not twelve, not ten-fifty-nine. Eleven."

"I'll be there." Accustomed to Callie's worship of punctuality, Brooke tapped her phone for emphasis. "I'll even set my alarm."

"Okay." Callie nodded in satisfaction. "And come back later to check out the comic book cookies. Mom's bringing them over after lunch."

"I will, thanks." Brooke took a bite of the delicious cake.

As she stepped aside to let other people approach the booth, she glanced over at Title Wave. The interior of the store was dark and the Closed sign hung on the door.

Aria had told her the residents, even Mayor Bowers, were unanimously disappointed to hear Sam might be moving away. Despite his reclusiveness, or perhaps because of it, he'd disarmed the whole town and become a steadfast fixture of Bliss Cove life.

Brooke smiled faintly. Over the past year, he'd become a fixture of her life, too. And over the past month, he'd become embedded in her heart. The thought of him no longer being there was a physical ache in the deepest part of her soul.

Polishing off the cake, she tossed the plate in the recycling bin and crossed the street. She knocked on the back door, in case he was in his office. No answer.

She'd make a quick trip to his house and see if he was there. She was leaving again in a few days, and he might not be here the next time she came back. If nothing else, she wanted to thank him for the letter and say goodbye again.

He wasn't at his house either, and his truck was gone.

Could he have already left?

No one had said anything about him having left for good, but she knew better than anyone that Sam wouldn't announce his departure. He'd just leave.

Checking her watch, she returned to the Book Fair. The fourth-grade winner of the play-writing contest had won for her classic Old West melodrama featuring a lasso-wielding heroine and a great deal of audience participation.

People sat on the grass, booing the villain, cheering for the hero and heroine, singing songs, and calling out advice—all prompted by two kids wearing cow costumes and holding up cue cards.

"I can't do it!" cried Cowgirl Kate.

"Believe in yourself!" shouted the audience.

Brooke took pictures of the production, actors, and crowd, pausing to add her own cheers and boos to the repertoire. As she moved around the square, a sudden *zinging* sensation pulsed through her. She paused and rubbed her arms.

She knew that zing. She'd felt it countless times over the past year whenever she was near—

Slowly, she turned. Next to the gazebo, a booth that had been empty earlier now bore a sign saying *Buy a Book for the Bookmobile*. Sam's truck was parked right behind the booth. Though Sam was nowhere in sight, Jake was unpacking books and setting them on the tables and shelves.

Title Wave was hosting a Book Fair booth. Brooke didn't know whether she was more astonished or delighted. A combination of both, it seemed, given the way her heart was rising on a bubble of happiness.

Then Sam stepped around from behind the truck and began unloading boxes. A touch of fear diluted her pleasure. Just the sight of him—messy dark hair, that ever-present stubble covering his jaw, the sleeves of his flannel shirt rolled up to reveal his muscular forearms—elicited a wave of love so strong it weighted her to the spot.

"I'll take that chance!" shouted Cowgirl Kate onstage.

"Yay!" the crowd roared.

Sam glanced toward the stage. His gaze stopped right on Brooke. A force charged through the air.

He lowered a box to the ground and straightened, still looking at her. Though they'd been apart for less than two weeks, the emotional and physical distance had stretched taut and thin. She'd missed him with every beat of her heart.

Gripping her camera in one hand, she made her way around blankets and lawn chairs toward him. Electricity crackled over her nerves, as if awakened by his gaze. She approached the booth slowly.

"Hey, Brooke." Jake, who was arranging a table of mystery novels, gave her his easy smile. "I heard you'd be back this weekend. How was New York?"

"Fine, thanks." She looked past him to where Sam still stood beside the truck.

Jake glanced from her to Sam and back again. "Uh, I'm going to run over to Sugar Joy and see if Callie needs anything."

Without waiting for a response, he headed off.

"You'll never learn, Mad Monroe!" called Cowboy Dan in the distance.

"Teach him a lesson, Cowboy Dan!" yelled the crowd.

Sam came closer, skimming his gaze over her as if he

hadn't seen her in months. As if he were drinking her in. Whatever fears Brooke might have had about any lingering anger quickly disappeared. He stopped on the other side of the table and pushed his hands into his pockets.

"Hi." She'd give up every last one of her pillow pets to feel his arms encircling her and pulling her close.

"Hi." A smile tugged at his mouth. "Good to see you."

"You, too." The area around her heart softened at the sight of his faint smile. She set her camera down and indicated the sign. "Did Charlie finally convince you to have a booth?"

"He might've had something to do with it." Sam rubbed the back of his neck. "It was a little last minute, so we had to rush the book orders and the set-up. That's why we're running late."

"I'm so glad you did this." Brooke ran her hand over a hardcover book of Greek myths. "The bookmobile is fantastic. Thank you for everything you've done. Even the things you don't want people to know about."

He shrugged, looking slightly embarrassed. "So you're starting the new job soon?"

"Look out!" shouted the audience.

"March first." Nervous at the mention of her job, Brooke traced her finger over the design on the book cover. "I'm doing a video call for a Tuesday meeting, then going back again to get everything finalized."

"That's great. Congratulations."

"Thanks. You too. For *Tripwire*, I mean. And thank you for the letter."

He nodded and glanced past her to the stage. "So, uh, I

want you to know it was great. You, I mean. With me. It was…you helped me out a lot. I appreciate it."

"You helped me a lot, too." She swallowed past a sudden constriction in her throat. "I heard you might be leaving Bliss Cove soon."

He returned his gaze to hers and nodded. "I'm hoping to."

"Boo!" yelled the crowd.

Brooke smiled faintly. "Sounds like they don't want you to go."

"I've been here a lot longer than I thought I would." He twisted his mouth. "I only planned to stay for a few weeks while I finished the first draft of *Tripwire*. Then I found out about the bookstore, and next thing I knew, I had another reason to stay."

Her heart bumped as she recalled his reason for stopping in Bliss Cove in the first place.

"Your wanderlust must be kicking into gear again." She tried to keep her tone light. "After all the places you've been and things you've done, I can see how our little town would start to get boring."

"It hasn't been boring at all. Just the opposite."

The audience burst into applause. Sam looked toward the stage again as the young actors took their bows to a standing ovation. A sudden tension radiated from him.

"Uh…" He stepped back and cleared his throat. "I should—"

"I didn't mean to—"

"Extra, extra, read all about it!" A boy, Tommy Perkins, wearing a cap and carrying a satchel full of newspapers, wove his way through the crowd. He held up a rolled paper.

"Breaking news! Get the latest headlines in this special edition of *The Bliss Cove Gazette*!"

Turning back to Sam, Brooke gave a small laugh. "I've never known Charlie to participate in the Book Fair performances."

"First time for everything, I guess." Though his tone was nonchalant, he shuffled his feet and shoved his hands deeper into his pockets.

"One dollar apiece, all proceeds going to The Reading Project!" Tommy paused to conduct transactions with several customers. "Get the special edition now, folks! Only available while supplies last."

He came closer to the Title Wave booth, still waving the rolled-up newspaper. "Read all about it!"

Read all about *what*?

"I'll take one, Tommy." Brooke dug into her bag for a five-dollar bill and held it out to the boy.

"Sure thing, Ms. Castle." Tommy hurried over, eyes bright with excitement. "I know you're into breaking news."

He stuffed the bill in his pocket. Waving away his attempt to give her change, Brooke thanked him and took the special edition.

She opened the paper. There, in 72-point Helvetica bold print, right underneath *The Bliss Cove Gazette* masthead, was the headline:

SAM LOVES BROOKE

She blinked and closed her eyes. A rollicking combination of disbelief, excitement, and outright joy swirled through her like ribbon candy. When she opened her eyes again, the words were still there. The *word* was there.

Loves.

The earth tilted a little under her feet. Around her, the crowd had gone oddly quiet, their chattering lessened to whispers and a few giggles.

Tightening her grip on the paper, Brooke lifted her head and looked at Sam. Her breath caught. He was watching her warily, his arms folded and his expression unreadable.

But she'd read his dark eyes a thousand times, and they contained a straightforward message of hope.

Lowering his arms, he walked around the table. Though her heart began pounding so hard it echoed in her head, she was distinctly aware of *the town* clustered around them as if they were the stars of the next stage play.

"Brooke..." Sam stopped in front of her, his gaze searching her face.

He wasn't going to...he wouldn't...not in front of all these people...

"I love you," he said.

Oh my god, he did.

She just stared at him. She couldn't move. It was as if she had to remain very still to absorb the power and beauty of his confession.

Taking a breath, Sam pressed a hand to his heart. "You were right when you said I've done a lot. I've been to almost every continent and lost myself in more cities than I can count. I've watched sunsets that look like fire and climbed mountains taller than the heavens. But it turns out the best damn thing that ever happened to me was walking into a cabin during a blizzard and finding you."

Oh, yes. She hadn't just landed on the outright love runway. She was getting off the plane, collecting her luggage, and heading straight home. She was totally, irrevocably *there*.

"I know…" He paused and swallowed. "I know I might've lost my chance, but I need to tell you this. You showed me that not only is love not a lie, it's the greatest truth in the universe. You showed me that having roots can make you stronger and that it's okay to let people in. You proved that life is so much better together than alone."

Her eyes filled with tears. "Those are some beautiful words, Sam Donovan."

"Yeah, well." A slight flush crested his cheekbones. "I practiced."

She smiled as a pure, radiant joy illuminated her entire being. "I love you, Sam. So very much."

A flurry of "Yays!" rose from the crowd. Sam grinned, his eyes lighting with happiness.

"You make clouds spin in my soul." He held out his arms to her. "When I'm with you, the earth moves and stars whirl. Everything inside me *lights up*."

"I *feel*…" With a laugh, Brooke leaped toward him, "exactly the same way."

He caught her up against him and lowered his head for a hard, passionate kiss that had the crowd breaking into applause.

When they finally parted, he glanced up with an abashed grin and a nod of acknowledgment. "Thanks, folks. I appreciate the help more than I can say."

The townspeople laughed and waved.

"Treat her right, or we're coming after you," Mr.

Hammersmith called, as the crowd began dispersing toward other activities.

"I can't believe it." Brooke rested her hand on his chest. "When did you arrange all this?"

"Not long after I heard you'd be back for the Book Fair." He pushed a lock of her hair behind her ear, his gaze warm and tender. "I figured it'd be a good setting for my BRG. I asked Charlie for help with the paper, and he recruited Tommy. Then I talked to the coordinator of the play, and we figured out the timing. Everyone was in on it. Callie was in charge of making sure you'd be near the stage when the play was over."

"Very good casting."

"I thought so." He brushed his knuckles against her cheek, as if he couldn't stop touching her. A crease appeared between his eyebrows. "By the way, you look tired."

"Red-eye flight. I just got in this morning."

"Hmm." He rested his hand on the side of her neck. "When we're alone again, I'll have to come over with some Indian food, a bottle of wine, and promises of a shoulder rub that will turn into a full-body massage."

Brooke laughed. "I can't wait. Did I happen to mention you got an A+ in Romance 101?"

"I was hoping for that." He stroked his thumb against the hollow of her throat, his expression sobering a bit. "I don't know if I can ever be the hero you want, Brooke. I like being alone, and I'm not one for talking a lot. I don't know the first thing about antiques or—"

She pulled him down for a kiss to stop his words. "You're the *man* I want, Sam. Fiction and books are all fine and good, but when it comes to *life*, I want you. I want us."

He smiled his heartbreakingly beautiful smile. "I want us, too."

"Oh." She pulled back, a touch of unease diluting her pleasure. "But you said you were planning to leave town."

"I am." He took hold of her hips and pulled her lower body against his. "I'm coming to New York with you. If you'll have me," he added quickly.

"Coming to..." Her voice trailed off as the truth struck her. "Oh, Sam."

"What?" His forehead furrowed. "I can live anywhere, write anywhere. And since you're going to live there, it makes sense for me to go with you."

"But you don't want to go back to New York."

"I'll go anywhere with you."

The romantic expansiveness of his words filled her heart. "I'll go anywhere with you, too, but I'd also love to stay right here."

He frowned, a puzzled look crossing his face.

"I had an idea about freelancing for the magazine when I was meeting with all the editors and staff," Brooke explained. "I did some research and found out that many of their writers and contributors work remotely. So I brought up the idea to Jillian, a contract where I can still work at least part-time from Bliss Cove.

"She was hesitant at first, but after we talked, she said we might be able to work something out. We're still negotiating, and likely we'll do a trial period, but it sounds promising. It would mean making trips to New York a few times a year, or somehow dividing my time, but it would be a way for me to both keep the job and not leave Bliss Cove entirely."

"That's amazing." He let out his breath and shook his head. "You would have the best of both worlds."

"I think so, too." She eased closer, slipping her arms around his waist. "Would you be okay with some long-distance time apart?"

"Brooke." He tilted her face to look up at him and brushed his thumb against her cheek. "When you need to go to New York, I'll go with you. And the rest of the time, I'd love to stay here with you. But honestly, wherever you want to go, wherever you want to stay, I'll be there. I just want to be with you. Bliss Cove is one of my favorite places in the world, but you're my home. You're my nest."

Happiness swept over her like a sunrise. "And you're my hero."

His eyes warm with love, Sam lowered his head. She stood on her tiptoes, and their lips met again.

As the kiss deepened, a nearby voice that sounded like Mayor Bowers remarked, "I *knew* those two weren't just whistling Dixie up in that cabin."

EPILOGUE

One month later

Snow capped the mountains and tree branches like frosting on a cake. Sunlight glittered off the expanse of white, and the air was crisp and cold. Winter would soon give way to spring.

Brooke breathed the fresh air in deeply as she followed in Sam's tracks to the front door of the Eagle's Nest. They'd stolen away for a weekend together before she flew to New York the following week for staff meetings and to discuss her continuing *Lifelong Fling* series.

"Hold on a sec." With a frown, Sam patted his pockets. "I can't find the key."

"Didn't Felix leave one by the door?" Brooke looked around for the fake rock that had held the front door key.

"No, because I picked it up from him at the hardware store yesterday." Sam scratched his head. "Last time I was here, he had a spare at the back door. I'll go around and check."

"I'll grab our bags."

He stomped through the snow around to the back of the cabin, while Brooke unloaded her travel bag and his duffle from the truck. She waited on the front porch, hoping they wouldn't have to drive back to the ranger's station to contact Felix.

After the four-hour drive, she was eager to start the weekend back at the place where her and Sam's epic romance had started. All week, he'd been checking multiple different weather forecasts, but there was no chance of another storm. They'd both been a tad disappointed about that.

She glanced at her watch. He must be having trouble finding another key.

She traipsed back to the car to bring over more of their stuff. As she was carrying a case of lemon-cayenne iced tea to the front porch, the door opened. Sam stood in the foyer with lights glowing behind him.

"Oh, good, you found it." Relieved, Brooke handed over the case of tea. "You got the generator going already, too?"

"I did, indeed." For some reason, he appeared inordinately proud of his efficiency. He set the tea on the bench in the foyer and picked up her travel bag and his duffle. "Let's get this stuff in. I'll unload the food later."

Brooke followed him inside and closed the door. The woodsmoke scent of a fire curled through the air.

"You already built a—" She stopped, her eyes widening.

A blanket fort made up of multiple colorful blankets and quilts filled a large part of the main room. Dozens of fairy lights decorated the top and sides, with more strings draped over the loft railing and around the windows. A fire burned cheerfully in the fireplace, filling the room with a warm, flickering glow.

"Oh, Sam." She brought her hand to her chest as tears blurred her eyes. "It's beautiful. When did you do this?"

He grinned. "I came up last weekend to get it set up so all I'd have to do was turn on the generator and light the fire."

After they'd taken off their boots and parkas, Sam turned off the overhead lights. He took her hand and led her around to the front of the fort.

The flaps were open to reveal the interior, where a fluffy mattress was piled high with animal-shaped pillows, pattered bedspreads and comforters, and huge, soft Indian-print cushions. More fairy lights twinkled around the border of the ceiling, and a tray held all the important supplies—popcorn, cookies, hot cocoa, animal crackers, board games, and romance novels.

"This is incredible." With a laugh, Brooke crawled inside and flopped back against the cloud-like pillows. "Thank you so much. I love it."

He came in after her and closed the flaps behind him. Then they were enclosed in their own private, softly lit world —which was still the way they both liked it the most.

Slowly, however, Sam had been easing out of his solitary lifestyle. After the Book Fair, he'd started helping out with The Reading Project, and he'd agreed to host several local author book signings at Title Wave.

He'd donated books to raffles for the Vitaphone's film series, and he'd told Brooke he planned to anonymously fund an expansion of the elementary school library. He didn't want to do things for attention or acclaim, and he'd never run for town council, but he had his own quiet way of showing he cared about the town they both called home.

Brooke had moved into his rental house as she worked out negotiations for her job's new structure, while also interviewing Bliss Cove residents for her *Lifelong Fling* series. Sam had started outlining the plot—and the romance—of the next John Kane book, while continuing to open Title Wave in-between writing and boxing.

They balanced intimate dinners at home with nights out at the Mousehole or a club. Sam had come with her to her father's birthday party, he'd taken to having the occasional beer with Charlie, and he'd joined Jake and Hunter for pool a couple of times.

Brooke had never been so happy. Their days were busy, their nights were hot and tender, and neither of them was in a hurry to figure out what happened next. They were both too busy enjoying *now*.

Sam settled back against the pillows beside her. Instinctively, she curled against his strong body and rested her head on his chest.

"As much as I love living in Bliss Cove, I think this cabin will always be my favorite place for *us*." She stroked her hand over his abdomen.

"Mine too." He pressed his lips to her forehead. "And that's a good thing, considering it's ours."

Brooke sat up. "What?"

He grinned, looking pleased with himself. "I bought it from Felix a couple of weeks ago. Not only the Eagle's Nest, but several acres of the surrounding land. I thought one day we might want to expand the cabin since it's not really big enough for a family."

She stared at him. *Zings* rocketed through her like fireworks.

Sam coughed. "Uh, I mean, if you want to…"

"I want to, Sam." She swooped down to kiss him hard. "One day."

"So do I." He put his hand on her nape and deepened the kiss. "I love you."

"I love you." She lifted her head, imagining a lifetime of looking into his dark eyes and finding herself there. Finding them *both* there. "So much."

Patting her rear, he eased away. "There's one more thing."

He took a boxy object from behind a cushion and set it up above their pillows. He flipped a switch. The sweet, gentle music of *When You Wish Upon A Star* drifted through the fort.

Her throat constricted. "Is that—"

Sam pointed upward. Bright, glowing stars and a smiling moon rotated slowly across the patterned ceiling. Her heart overflowing with joy and love, Brooke nestled back beside him.

He took her hand and rested it on his chest. His heartbeat thumped against her palm.

Together, they watched the musical universe rolling over them. The constellations were so big they looked as if they might tumble out of the sky and sprinkle them with glitter and stardust. Maybe they already had.

"Make a wish," she whispered.

He tightened his hand around hers. "It already came true."

♥

Ready for more Bliss Cove?

High school lit teacher Grace Berry knows nothing about real-life romance…until Lincoln, Sam Atwood's mysterious author brother, shows her what the fuss is all about.

Turn the page
for an excerpt from the next book in the series:

BOOK OF LOVE
(GRACE & LINCOLN'S STORY)

∾

SNEAK PEEK

BOOK OF LOVE (BLISS COVE #6)

"*Y*ou were hired to teach Shakespeare, Miss Berry. Do your job."

"I teach Shakespeare all the time!" Grace countered, her jaw aching from the effort of controlling her temper. "We're doing a vocabulary lesson right now. But it's equally important to talk about his work in relation to writers whom history has often excluded."

"History has *excluded* writers like that Behn woman for obvious reasons." Principal Spruce strode to the door. "Stick to the traditional curriculum, Miss Berry. I guarantee you don't want to be forced to defend yourself to the school board against the charge of corrupting a student. Not only will you lose your job, you'll never teach anywhere again."

He slammed out of the room. Grace sank down at her desk and put her head in her hands.

What a crappy way to end the week.

Taking a breath, Grace gathered up her belongings. She hurried through the rain to the parking lot. After coaxing her ancient car to life, she drove to her tiny, one-bedroom cottage located in a modest neighborhood near the harbor.

She'd known when she bought the place four years ago that an old house would have occasional problems, but she hadn't expected multiple problems at the same time.

In the past few months, the house had developed water pipe issues, a leaky roof, and mildew around the windows. She could only hope her extra income from summer school would cover the repair costs.

Though she'd have liked to crash right into bed, she picked up the stack of coupons on the kitchen counter and headed back outside. She stopped at the grocery store, the library, and the drugstore before driving to her father's apartment building.

She'd spent weeks searching for the right apartment for him, one that was within walking distance of downtown and a short drive to both the beach and the state parks. Six months after moving to Bliss Cove from rural Tulare County, her father had yet to take advantage of the convenience or... anything else, really.

"What are you doing here?" He answered her knock with a frown.

"Great to see you too, Dad." Pasting a smile on her face, she carted the grocery bags into the kitchen. "How was your day?"

He grunted. A tall man with a thicket of silvery-gray hair and a weather-lined face, Ray Berry had been the dominant presence in Grace's life. Growing up on Berry Farms, she'd thought her big, strong father was invincible. Up at four in the morning to milk and feed the cows, he'd worked nonstop throughout the day to keep the operation running smoothly.

Until not even hard work had been enough to save Berry Farms.

"You get any steak?" He eyed the grocery bags that she set on the counter.

Grace swallowed the instinct to remind him that he was supposed to cut back on his red-meat intake. Not to mention, steak was expensive.

"It didn't look very good." She began putting away the groceries, noticing the salmon filet she'd brought over last night that was still in the fridge. "Why didn't you eat the fish?"

"Fish belong in the sea, not on a plate."

"Dad, fish is one of the healthiest things you can eat." Grace set a carton of milk in the fridge. "Did you get outside for a walk today?"

"Why don't you put a tracker on my phone so you don't have to ask?"

Grace supposed it would be a bad idea at that moment to ask if he'd visited the senior center yet.

She continued unpacking. Ray looked at a container of yogurt with distaste.

Sighing, Grace washed the dirty dishes in the sink and tided up the apartment, tossing his clothes in the wash and checking his medication refills. "What would you like for dinner?" she asked. "I can make turkey burgers or maybe a spinach and tomato omelet?"

"Grace, stop fussing." Ray groused and dragged a hand down his face. "I'm not a damned invalid. I can fix my own food, and I'll eat when I'm hungry. Don't you have some work to do?"

That was his semi-tactful way of telling her he didn't want her there.

"Yes, I...I guess I do have papers to grade." She didn't, actually. "I'll see you tomorrow. Call if you need anything."

She pressed a kiss to his cheek and went back outside, making a mental note to call the landlord about fixing the loose railing on the front steps. After her father's heart-failure diagnosis two years ago, she'd spent a lot of time and energy trying to convince him to sell the family's dairy farm and move to town.

He'd stubbornly refused.

But when soaring grain prices had pushed Berry Farms to the edge of bankruptcy, Ray had unwillingly signed the papers surrendering the property he'd owned for over thirty years.

Though Grace's heart had broken at having to let the farm go, she'd known it was both inevitable and necessary. Her father could no longer safely or successfully run the business, and it was better for both of them if he lived in Bliss Cove close to both medical care and his daughter.

Of course, Ray didn't see it that way. And even now, Grace sometimes wondered if she'd done the right thing.

He'd lost weight since his heart attack and diagnosis, and his plaid shirt hung loosely on his frame. His skin, once so tanned, was now pale and waxy.

Worst of all, his twinkling blue eyes had dulled to the color of metal. Close to sixty years old, he'd always seemed twenty years younger...until now.

She got into her car. Almost eight, according to the dash-board clock. Though she was wiped out, she suddenly didn't want to go back to her empty house with the stupid leaking roof.

Maybe she'd take a risk and just drive…somewhere. Anywhere but here.

She headed toward the interstate.

AND *THIS* WAS THE REASON GRACE LIKED TO PLAN THINGS IN advance.

After five minutes on the interstate, her gas tank indicator light turned on, mocking her with further evidence of her disordered frame of mind.

The rain came down harder as she continued to the next off-ramp, where there was a gas station beside a truck stop.

A blinking neon sign read *Lou's Diner*. After filling her tank, she found herself parked in front of the diner.

Pies Baked Fresh Every Day! proclaimed another sign in the window.

When was the last time she'd had pie?

Heartened, she picked up her book bag and hurried through the rain to the diner. The smells of coffee, fried food, and charred beef filled the air. Truckers and several couples occupied the plastic booths, and a few men sat at the counter.

"Help yourself to a booth, hon." A busty waitress with an orange-colored beehive hairdo waved her toward the main dining room. "I'll be right over."

Grace wiped the rain off her sweater and hair while grabbing the nearest booth.

The waitress, whose nametag read Nancy, strolled over with a coffee-pot and a mug. "Regular or decaf?"

"Regular, please."

"You okay, hon?" Nancy placed the mug on the table and peered at her through eyes fringed with thickly mascaraed lashes. "You look a little down."

Grace smiled faintly. "I thought the psychic diner waitress archetype was a myth."

Nancy chuckled and poured the coffee. "Nah, you just talk to and see enough folks passing through, you learn to read them pretty well."

"It's been a rough day." Grace reached for a sugar packet. "Hope you don't mind if I sit here awhile."

"Be my guest." Nancy set a laminated menu down in front of her. "Meatloaf special tonight. Dessert menu is by the salt and pepper shakers. I'll be back in a couple of minutes."

Grace studied the meal offerings, then picked up the dessert menu. Even though she hadn't had dinner, she was hungry for only one thing. She perused the dessert selection, skipping past the creamy silk and fluffy meringue pies to the last item on the list.

"Find something you want?" Nancy came back to the table, digging into her apron pocket for an order pad.

"Yes, but I think I'm just going to stick with dessert tonight."

"My kind of girl." Nancy grinned, displaying a large gap between her front teeth. "Chocolate brownie? Ice cream sundae?"

"Rhubarb pie." Grace tapped her finger on the menu item. "I haven't had rhubarb pie since...I don't even know when."

"Well, you're in luck." Nancy pointed her pencil toward

the kitchen. "The gal who does our baking said she got some nice, fresh rhubarb yesterday. She brought one of her special double-crust rhubarb pies over this morning. You want a scoop of vanilla ice cream to go with it?"

"Nope, just a big slice of pie. There aren't any strawberries or other fruit in it, are there?"

"Not a speck. Plain rhubarb."

"Great. And a glass of whole milk, please. Nice and cold."

"You got it, hon." Nancy tore the sheet of paper off and dropped the pad into her pocket. "Back in a jiff."

Grace dug into her book bag for her lesson planner. Her fingers touched her well-worn copy of *Shakespeare's Sonnets and Quotations*. She thumbed through the pages, all of which contained penciled notes and underlined phrases.

The book had been a graduation gift from her favorite college literature teacher, Georgia Sands, whose love for both teaching and poetry had inspired Grace's career path. Professor Sands had encouraged, admired, and challenged Grace's writing and her thinking. In the process, Grace had discovered that she could make a difference doing what she loved.

She skimmed the pages and paused at several quotes she'd underlined twice.

Our doubts are traitors, and make us lose the good we oft might win, by fearing to attempt.

This above all: To thine ownself be true.

Hadn't she always tried to be true to herself, especially back when she was a bright-eyed college student? She'd wanted to be a high-school teacher, and she knew she was good at it. She'd shaped her students' lives, introduced them to the beauty of words, listened to their problems, tried to help however she could.

Her students then went off to make their mark on the world and pursue their dreams. Many of them still kept in touch, whether they were studying at Princeton, earning their electrician certificate, or working at the family business. She was proud of them and proud of whatever influence she'd had on their lives.

But some days it was really hard to hold on to the *good*.

"Bad news, hon." Nancy bustled back and set a tall glass of milk on the table. She tilted her head toward a man seated at the counter. "Handsome devil over there got the last piece of rhubarb pie."

Grace swallowed. "Excuse me?"

"He ordered, like, a minute before you did, and Sue served him the last piece." Nancy twisted her mouth in regret. "Sorry about that. How about a nice piece of apple or blueberry instead? Or we have an amazing peach cobbler that might change your life."

"No, I..." A ridiculous tightness filled her throat. She reached for the dessert menu again. "Could you give me a minute, please?"

"Sure." Nancy's forehead furrowed with pity. "There's plenty of other options, hon."

Grace nodded, ducking her head to hide the tears filling her eyes.

"Take your time." The waitress hesitated a second before going back to the counter.

Grace tried to focus on the dessert menu, but the words blurred in her vision. Her lip trembled.

Really, Grace? A lost piece of rhubarb pie is your breaking point?

Apparently so.

A fat tear plopped onto the photo of a brownie sundae. Trying to suppress a hiccup, she grabbed the paper napkin and wiped her eyes.

Okay, come on. You like pecan pie. Cherry pie. Or what about a chocolate meri—

A sob burst out of her constricted throat. She couldn't blink fast enough to stop the tears from rolling down her cheeks in a sudden deluge. Her eyes burned.

She had to get out of here. Gulping back another sob, she fumbled for her bag and started to scoot out of the booth.

A massive shadow fell over the table then. Grace looked up sharply. She couldn't see much through her watery vision, but she registered a tall, dark-haired man whose wide shoulders and chest blocked the view of the counter. Of the whole restaurant, actually.

"Um…" She hiccupped again.

He set a plate on the table in front of her. "I haven't taken a bite. I was just about to, but then I noticed…well, I'd rather you eat it."

Grace dragged her gaze from him to the plate, which bore a large piece of rhubarb pie. "But…"

"I overheard your waitress," he explained. "Given how upset you seem by that fact that there isn't any more rhubarb pie left, there's no way I could eat the last piece."

"Oh." Grace scrubbed her eyes with the wadded-up napkin, feeling more than a bit ridiculous. "Really, you don't have to do this. I'm just having a bad day."

"So maybe the pie will help." He nudged the plate

toward her. "I insist. Here." He took a roll of clean silverware from a nearby table and set it beside the plate. "Enjoy."

She caught the flash of a smile—beautiful, white teeth and eyes that creased at the corners—before he started toward the cash register. She stared at the pie, which had a golden-brown lattice crust and a mouth-wateringly juicy, ruby-red filling.

Grace looked at the man again. He stopped at the counter and dug into his pocket for his wallet.

"Wait." Her voice came out thick and tear-choked. "Sir?"

He turned back.

His rumpled, black hair was threaded with both gold and silver strands that shone in the overhead lights. He had strong, classic features—straight nose, well-shaped mouth, and a square jaw mitigated by dark eyebrows and ridiculously thick eyelashes.

But his eyes were the most arresting part of his face. A deep, golden-brown like buckwheat honey, his eyes gleamed with sharp intelligence and a sense of mystery.

Though Grace usually avoided talking to men she didn't know, she found herself gesturing to the seat across from her.

"Uh, what if we…split the slice?"

— End of Excerpt —

Find out what happens next for Grace & Lincoln in:

BOOK OF LOVE
(Bliss Cove, Book 6)
Available Now

a tidy life. And that, thank you, is exactly how she wants it…until action hero Jake Ryan arrives in town and wants some close-up action with the brilliant, beautiful professor.

LOVE ME TENDER

Rory Prescott and tavern owner Grant Taylor make a deal — she'll be his date to his brother's wedding if he'll let her stay short-term in his cottage. But what happens when this fake relationship becomes passionately real?

WORDS OF LOVE

When chirpy reporter Brooke Castle gets trapped in a snowstorm with grumpy bookstore owner Sam Donovan, the fire isn't the only thing heating up the cabin.

BOOK OF LOVE

High school literature teacher Grace Berry has no time for romance. But when sexy, award-winning author Lincoln Atwood comes into her classroom, Grace is eager for his lessons in love.

Looking for even **more** steam & emotions in your romances?

If so, check out my **NINA LANE** books here!

CHECK OUT MY **NINA LANE** BOOKS!

In the mood for even **more** swoon and steam? With all the feels and a roller coaster of emotions? My **NINA LANE** books reportedly make some readers cry their eyes out… between fanning the sizzling heat coming off their ereaders. If that sounds like your cup of tea, go check 'em out HERE.

Born and raised in California, NEW YORK TIMES & USA TODAY bestselling author Nina Lane now lives in Wisconsin where the winters are freezing and the cheese is exceptional. Mom to two teens and a neurotic dog, half her life consists of laundry, Girl Scouts, horses, and football, while the other half is filled with hot, swoony alpha heroes and the women who bring them to their knees. Nina's a fan of popcorn, print magazines, working out, and checking the weather daily with her meteorologist husband. She holds a PhD in Art History and an MA in Library and Information Studies, but considers writing epic, emotional romances her one true calling in life. Thus, she is grateful and ecstatic to be able to bring the stories in her head to life for all her amazing fans. ♥

Learn more at: www.ninalane.com

AND CLICK HERE TO JOIN THE BOOK NINJAS!

ABOUT THE AUTHOR

Nina Lindsey writes romances filled with heart, heat, and happy endings. She is delighted to introduce readers to Bliss Cove, California, a coastal town with an abundance of warm cookies, ocean breezes, and the ever-present possibility of love.

Nina loves all things spicy and sweet, with chili chocolates being at the top of the list. She is also a fan of glossy magazines, pop culture, Gilmore Girls, energy bites, Orangetheory, and the sound of silence.

She lives in Wisconsin with her meteorologist husband (yes, she asks him daily, "What's the weather forecast?"), their two children, an overly energetic dog, and a snail named Pipsqueak.

www.ninalindsey.com

facebook.com/ninalindseyauthor
instagram.com/ninalindsey.author
goodreads.com/ninalindsey